PRAISE

PAIN CAGES

'An exceptional volume... Welcome to Kaneworld!'
Stephen Volk – BAFTA-winning creator of *Ghostwatch*

'Paul Kane's writing has a style and elegance,
he's a first rate storyteller.'
Clive Barker – Bestselling author of *The Hellbound Heart*

'Paul Kane's *The Lazarus Condition* is a wonderfully unsettling tale
of resurrection, self-recrimination, and our reluctance to confront
issues of both mortality and immortality... Paul Kane has offered
you a dark and contemplative gift. I recommend you take it.'
Christopher Golden – Bestselling author of *The Myth Hunters,
Prowlers, The Boys are Back in Town* and *The Shadow Saga*

'Definitely a name to watch out for in the future of
British Horror fiction.'
Graham Joyce – Bestselling author of *Dreamside, The Tooth Fairy,
The Facts of Life, The Limits of Enchantment* and *The Silent Land*

'Paul Kane's fiction shows intelligence and imagination – he's a
writer who's going places, and I can't wait to see what he comes
up with next!'
Sarah Langan – Bestselling and author of *Audrey's Door*

*To Mike
and Paula
lots of love
Paul K
x x x*

PAUL KANE'S
PAIN CAGES

BOOKS of the DEAD

PAIN CAGES

Cover Art - Daniele Serra
Graphic Design - Cynthia Gould
Copyedit - James Roy Daley
E-book Design - James Roy Daley

FIRST EDITION

For more information, contact: Besthorror@gmail.com
Visit us at: Booksofthedead.blogspot.com

10 9 8 7 6 5 4 3 2 1

More Great Books by
PAUL KANE

Novels / Novellas
Arrowhead
Broken Arrow
Arrowland
Of Darkness and Light
The Gemini Factor
Dalton Quayle Rides Out
RED
Signs of Life
The Lazarus Condition

Collections
Alone (In the Dark)
Touching the Flame
FunnyBones
Peripheral Visions
The Adventures of Dalton Quayle
Shadow Writer

Editor & Co-Editor
Shadow Writers Vol. 1 & 2
Terror Tales #1-4
Top International Horror
Albions Alptraume: Zombies
The British Fantasy Society: A Celebration
Hellbound Hearts

Non-Fiction
Contemporary North American Film Directors: A Wallflower
Critical Guide (Contributor)
Cinema Macabre (Contributor)
The Hellraiser Films And Their Legacy
Voices in the Dark

BOOKS of the DEAD

Living and Breathing Horror:
An Introduction to Paul Kane
by
Stephen Volk

Stories. What *stories?*

Shamefully, when I first met Paul Kane I had no idea he *wrote* stuff.

Truly.

I'm an idiot. I admit it.

The perpetually smiling guy I met for the first time at FantasyCon (or was it World Horror?) several years ago was clearly a mover and shaker in the British Fantasy Society. You could see a mile off he was obviously well known and well-loved in that crowd. (A crowd, I hasten to add, I was starting to feel all group-huggy about myself.)

What was also blindingly obvious within seconds was that this guy was a fan of Horror. Bigtime. (I mean, come on—the black t-shirt was somewhat of a giveaway.)

He talked with massive enthusiasm for the genre he adored. And still adores, with a palpable conviction. Books. Movies. Authors. Filmmakers. No question: you cut Paul Kane, the love of horror will come gushing out and splatter the porcelain.

But… *stories?*

I say this only to emphasize my ignorance. And thereby pump up my delight in discovering said stories, a clutch of which you hold in your hands right now.

And they're beauties.

It seems inconceivable now that I didn't recognize Paul from the off as the editor of *Terror Tales*, *Shadow Writers* and numerous fine BFS publications; that his fiction crept up on me from *Peripheral Visions*, planted its clammy hand on my shoulder with *RED*, breathed its acrid stench on the back of my neck with *Alone*, *Of Darkness and Light* and, more recently, donkey-punched my quivering soul with the *Arrowhead* books and his editing of a masterful compilation spawned by the Clive Barker universe he loves—*Hellbound Hearts*.

Paul Kane is the real deal because he quite simply lives and breathes horror.

By breathing, I mean, *he couldn't* not *do it*. Right, Paul? Any more than you have a choice about taking the next breath. You just do it. It's *you*.

And I love that.

I love that this is a big, chunky Stephen-King-like portmanteau of novellas, and you have that Stephen-King-like way of delivering on genre expectations, but twisting the knife.

The following tales are not just of the unexpected, but of the uncomfortable and the uncontrollable, the unwelcome and the impossible made flesh.

They are about pain and longing, threats and loneliness, the need for connection and connections severed, brutally.

And did I mention pain?

Yes. These are stories of shackles and emaciation. Of mutilation and psychic ruin.

Somewhere buried here is a dream of being lost in a forest of bones.

Of *bones*...

But stop. I won't tell you the stories. God forbid. Instead I'll tell you what glimpses I had when Paul Kane lifted the veil on the unknown. The things once seen that can't be *un*seen...

Like a place called "The Cut"...
Like a brotherhood dedicated to pain...
Like the interlocked fates of a zodiac of travelers...
A rueful ex-band member struggling with a violent secret—motivated by the taste of human meat...
A girlfriend who asks to be taken beyond her limits...
A dead man walking home to see his mum...
Teeth sinking into a tanned brunette...
The virus *behind* the virus...
A man lost in his own brain, surrounded by infected tissue, infected memories...
Another with a voice in his head, asking him to wonder what a woman's insides look like...
Blood appearing black in the moonlight, with the sheen of motor oil...
A monster, flooring the accelerator, thinking about the future...
A man who vanishes, ushering in a new dawn for Mankind...

Get the picture? You won't.
Not till you read them. And you'll realize ultimately that though the rough path through Paul Kane's world involves a lot of pain and anguish, the pain isn't what the journeys are about. Not really.
Horror's never really about that. Not good horror. Pain is just a way to get your attention. Paul knows that.
This exceptional volume will show you a kind of tapestry of separate experiences that make up one quilt (so to speak), where the maker is the same, and the sum is far more than the constituent parts.

Welcome to Kaneworld. You're in his hands now. Follow the guide at your peril. But be assured, the author never puts a foot wrong.

The collection before you finishes up with a terrific story about ordinary folks' inability to cope with the metaphysical. So much more than a "zombie story" many lesser Horror writers would have been content to make it. Paul recognized that his idea could be a metaphor for something bigger. The biggest. He followed his instinct and it paid off. Wonderfully, in my opinion.

Because in the end, the "condition" Paul Kane is interested in isn't death, but the condition called living.

And the remarkable, almost supernatural truth, that in spite of the pain, we get through.

Stephen Volk
Bradford-on-Avon
April 2011

PAIN CAGES

Prologue

Ask someone to describe pain...

And they might say, the feeling they get when they stub their toe on a table, or accidentally hit their thumb with a hammer when they're banging a nail into the wall. Pain can be more than merely physical, of course: it can hurt when a marriage breaks up or a loved one dies. That's even harder to put into words.

But these are all just shadows, echoes of something much greater.

Pain, *true* pain is impossible to describe, no matter how hard anyone tries. It can rip apart a person's soul, leaving them a shell of what they once were. And if it is hard to endure, it is certainly much harder to watch.

For some.

This story is about pain, in all its forms. We enter this world screaming and crying as we fight to take our first breath—being struck on the back to rouse us into consciousness. Most of us leave this world the same way: with a jolt. If we're lucky it will be quick, if we're not...

This story is about pain.

True pain.

One

The piercing screams wake me.

Not straight away, but slowly. They sound as if they're coming from a million miles away. The closer to consciousness I draw, though, the louder they are, like someone turned up the volume on a stereo: surround sound, sub woofers, the works. Then that I realize they're not part of some strange dream, but coming from the real world.

From somewhere nearby.

I open my eyes, or at least I try to. I never would have thought it could be so difficult; the amount of times I've taken this simple action for granted. But now... Actually, I can't tell whether they're open or shut because it's still so dark and I can't really feel my eyelids. My guts are doing somersaults; I feel like I need to be sick.

And all the time the screaming continues.

My face—my whole body—is pressed up against a hard, solid surface. I'm lying on a smooth but cold floor, curled up like a cat in front of a fireplace, though nowhere near as contented. I try to lift my head. I thought it was difficult to open my eyes, but this is something else entirely. Jesus, it hurts—a shockwave traveling right down the length of my neck and spine. Instinctively I try to clutch at my back, but I can't move my hand either. *Must have been one hell of a bender last night.* And the screaming? Had to be a TV somewhere, someone watching a really loud horror film with no thought for anyone else. Wait, had *I* turned it on after managing to get back home in God alone knows what state?

This is the weirdest hangover ever. I have some of the symptoms—head feels like it's caving in, aching all over, stomach churning... But my tongue doesn't feel like someone's been rubbing it with sandpaper; I'm not thirsty from dehydration. Maybe someone slipped something into my glass?

Maybe you took something voluntarily. Wouldn't be the first time.

There's movement to my left and my head whips sideways. I immediately regret it as stars dance across my field of vision. I still can't see anything, even after the universe of stars fade. Now I realize some sick son of a bitch has put a blindfold over my eyes.

More movement, this time to the right. I try to lift my hands to pull down the material, but again they won't budge, neither of them. My fingertips brush against metal and now I know why. It's not because of any fucking hangover: I'm handcuffed. My fingers explore further and find a chain attached to the cuffs. The manacles?

When I hear the screams again, the terror racked up a notch, it dawns on me that I'm in a whole world of trouble. Maybe my groggy condition made me slow on the uptake, I don't know, or perhaps I just couldn't acknowledge the shouts of agony as real. But they are; there's no doubting that now. And I'm definitely suffering from the after-effects of drugs, just not in the way I thought. Drugs designed to knock me out rather than get me high.

More movement, this time a swishing sound in front of and behind me at the same time. How is that possible? My heart's pumping fast, breathing coming in heavy gasps. I try to say something but all that comes out are a series of odd grunts.

"Sshh," whispers a voice; can't tell whether it's a man or a woman, but they're close. "Keep quiet, and stay still!"

The advice seems sound, but I've never been one for taking any kind of orders. I pull at the chains holding my hands in front of me. Now I realize my feet are shackled too.

"Do as he says," comes another hushed voice, this one definitely a woman, "or you're going to get yourself killed."

"And us with him," spits the first person.

Killed? What the fuck? So many questions: where am I? Who are these people talking to me? Why can I feel heat on my face? Smell something burning? No… cooking. Like roasting meat on a barbeque.

Struggling again, I scrape my face against the floor, trying to pull down the blindfold. The screams reach fever pitch, mixed with pleas for help. The cloying smell is in my nose, down my throat; I gag.

I nose at the ground like a horse eating hay, and the blindfold slips a fraction. I can see a little through my right eye; there isn't a lot of light, but I see metal bars in front of me, all around me. A glimpse of the cages on either side: a man, no more than forty, cowering in the corner of his. A woman—the one who'd told me I'd get myself killed—is transfixed by something right in front of her, tears tracking down her cheeks.

I follow her gaze and wish I hadn't.

I see the shape, the thing in yet another of these round cages. It's smoking, charred almost black, but here and there are patches of pink. A tuft or two of singed hair at the top of what must have been its head. Its eyeballs have melted, the liquid running down its cheeks, viscous and thick; flesh pulled taut over teeth that gleam so brightly they could have been used in a toothpaste commercial. This hunk of burnt flesh I'm looking at is—*was*—a person. That makes the stench even more pungent; just that bit more sickening.

I notice the screaming has stopped. It must have been coming from inside that cage as the flames did their worst before petering out.

It feels like I'm watching the body for hours, but it can't be more than a minute.

Then, without any warning, the burnt figure lurches forward. No screams this time—its vocal chords are jelly—but its body rattles against the bars of the cage, which swings, suspended above the ground (as we all are).

Flesh, and what's left of the person's clothes, have stuck to the bottom of the cage, coming away from its body like molten plastic and revealing more raw pinkness. It makes only one last-ditch attempt for freedom before collapsing, never to move again.

This time I really do throw up, seeing stars again as the blind-fold slips back over my eye. *Too late, I've seen it now... I can't ever forget.*

When I pass out I barely notice the transition—darkness replaced by darkness, black with black.

But I still see that body, hanging. A scorched mess that had once been human.

The ghosts of its screams following me back now into the void.

INTERLUDE:
TWENTY YEARS AGO

This happened to me when I was ten; still holding on to childhood for grim death, in no particular hurry to be an adult.

I grew up on a council estate away from the city—farms and fields within walking distance. The houses were all uniform grey, there was a small park that the older kids wrecked periodically, and the council failed to keep any of the streets tidy. Old women gossiped over fences while young girls left school and became baby-making machines so they could live off benefits for the next twenty or thirty years.

Mum and Dad were still together back then. She worked part-time in a bookies and he worked on the busses. At family gatherings I'd sometimes hear my Uncle Jim telling people Mum could have done so much better than Dad. "With her looks, she could have had her pick."

He was right about my Mum, though. She was beautiful in a kind of film star way, all blonde hair and curls like Marilyn Monroe or Jean Harlow, and even at that age she'd lost none of the glamour. Sure, Dad was boring, but I like to think she ended up with him because he was a kind man with a kind face. In the end she did 'do better' as my Uncle would have called it, running off with owner of the bookies. She ended up with money, but was as miserable as sin. And, we suspected, the guy beat her. While my Dad wallowed in a tiny flat, getting drunk until his liver just gave up the ghost. But that's another story, and long after this one.

I first saw The Monster one Bank Holiday. Dad was working overtime, but Mum had the day off. I was an only child, so had to amuse myself a lot of the time. That day I was getting under my mother's feet while she was trying to watch some musical on TV.

"Christopher Edward Warwick, do you have to make such a row!" she finally bawled. I couldn't really blame her: I'd turned the whole house into a spaceship and was busy piloting it into the deeper reaches of the Galaxy, battling one-eyed aliens with veiny skins.

She sent me out to play with the other kids, but that wasn't really my thing. I ended up wandering off to explore what the locals called 'The Cut'—I never understood why, because it didn't look like anyone had cut the grass down there in centuries. Maybe it was because a pitiful excuse for a canal ran the length of it like a wound. Here I could pretend that I was in the jungle where giant snakes and lions lived, and down by the water there were man-eating crocodiles (in actual fact you were more likely to find used condoms and fag ends).

I didn't go down there very often, not many kids did, but on that day I wandered further than I meant to—up a winding path to a small iron bridge crossing the canal. There I played Pooh sticks, something I hadn't done since I was six or seven, dropping twigs in the water on one side of the bridge to see which would come out first on the other side. Not much of a game, but the snakes and lions appeared to be hiding that day.

There were only a handful of twigs lying around, so when these were gone I went into the undergrowth to find more. I hadn't gone that far in when I found the den. It was covered up with foliage; quite well hidden beneath the trees, a hollowed out bit of green with earth for the floor and the remains of a fire. It was empty. I figured it must have been the older kids that had made it, looking for a private place to hang out.

At that age caution always fell a close second to curiosity, so I dropped the twigs and went inside. There was a strange smell, a toilet smell. I was about to leave when I spotted something towards the back, pages scattered.

And a glimpse of something that, until today, had been forbidden.

I crept further in, certain that the older kids had been here because they'd left behind an Aladdin's Cave of porn. The magazines were screwed up, the pages creased—yet the pictures of half naked women posing for the camera were a revelation. At that age girls in my class were just pests, there to torment, but this was different. These weren't girls, they were *women*, and they were showing me parts of their bodies willingly, opening up as easily as I was opening the pages.

I began to feel stirrings, a pleasant sensation as I ogled the photos. Then something fell out of one of the magazines. A piece of paper with handwritten scribblings all over it. I bent and picked it up, but could barely make out the spider scrawl. All except one phrase, written time and time again: 'They watch, and they wait.'

I frowned, then checked more of the magazines. I hadn't gotten very far when I heard the snapping of twigs I'd left in the entranceway. I spun and saw my monster. It was big, hairy, and its skin was almost black. It wore an old trenchcoat that strained tight at the shoulders. When it opened its mouth to speak I saw rotting teeth inside. Drool spilled onto its beard as it gargled, "Did *they* send you?"

I shook with terror. My erection shrank away and I dropped the magazine, a couple more of the handwritten sheets slipping out onto the floor. His wide, staring eyes followed them down. He covered the distance between us easily, grabbing hold of my arm—so hard I thought it might break. He towered above me. "They did, didn't they, boy." It wasn't a question. His fetid breath almost caused me to pass out.

I shook my head, unable to get any words out.

"Yes. They've sent a little spy."

"P-P-Please don't hurt me," I spluttered.

He yanked my arm. "I'm not going back!" he shouted. "You hear me... *Never.*"

I nodded. He seemed pleased that he'd got through to me. Then he drew me in so close I could see the insects living in his beard. "You go back, you tell them that, boy," he growled.

He let me go. I gaped, but suddenly my natural survival instinct kicked in and I ran out of there. I plunged through the undergrowth, catching my head on the branch of a low-hanging tree. I fell, hard. Shaking my head, then casting a glance over my shoulder, I got up and began running again.

I felt the wetness at my temple, but didn't stop. I ran up that path, never looking back in case the 'monster' had decided to give chase.

I'm not going back... Never...

When I got home my mother said, "For God's sake, Chris, whatever have you been doing?" She took me into the kitchen, washed the cut on my head, then put some antiseptic on it. When she asked me again what I'd done, whether it had happened playing, all I could do was stare, opening and closing my mouth.

"Christopher Edward Warwick," she said a final time, "you tell me what happened, right now."

"M-Monster... c-canal..." was all I could say.

"You and that blasted imagination of yours," she said. "Go to your room!"

When the truth emerged a day or so later, she felt pretty bad. I heard that some of the older boys had stumbled upon my monster and gave him a good kicking before telling their parents, who then called the police. He'd gone by the time they got there, but it was all around the estate about what had happened: that some pervo nutter had been living rough down by the bridge.

Mum hugged me when she when found out. She never said anything, but she knew. Knew the monster had been real.

I know better now—he wasn't really a monster at all. Just someone who knew the truth, and it had sent him insane.

'They watch and wait' he had written.

They watch and wait.

Two

When I wake again, the blindfold is gone.

I open my eyes and look around. The bars are still there in front of me, I'm still shackled by the hands and feet, but the bonds are looser, my hands apart. I can move a little, maneuver myself up into a sitting position. I don't ache as much now, either. I wonder how much time has passed since—

Then I remember. The person burnt alive. It's gone now, the cage empty, the body taken away while I was unconscious.

"Welcome back," says the man who'd told me to be quiet, hanging in his own cage like a canary. He's wearing what look like sweatpants and a top, the kind of thing you'd find people dressed in at a country health spa.

"We thought you were out for the count," adds the woman who'd also spoken to me before. She's perhaps in her late twenties, with a slender frame—or what I can see of it beneath the smock she's wearing. Her dirty-blonde hair is matted with sweat; looks like it hasn't been washed in a couple of weeks. "How do you feel?"

"How... how do I *feel?*" I snap, a mixture of confusion and anger.

The man throws me a vicious look. "Christ, can't you keep it down? I told you before."

"I'll keep it down when somebody tells me what the fuck's going on," I yell at him, returning his glare with one of my own. I pull at the chains, testing their length.

"If you do that, they'll just make them tighter," the woman warns.

"Who will? And who did that..." Words fail me so I simply point across at the empty space where the charred body had once been.

"You ask far too many questions." This comes from another speaker, his voice richer, deeper. I turn and see yet another of the cages behind. In it an olive-skinned man sits crossed-legged, dressed like the first guy: in loose clothing. A prisoner's outfit.

"What's that supposed to mean? Who the fuck are you?"

"That's two more," he says.

I make to get up, about to grip the bars of the cage.

"I wouldn't, if I were you," the olive-skinned man tells me.

"Well you're not m—" Too late I see the wire curled around the bars, and no sooner have I touched the metal than I feel the electric shock. It ripples through my body, not strong enough to put me out again, but enough to blister my hands. "Shit!"

Is that what happened to the person in the cage in front? I wonder. *Did someone just leave the current on—running along the bottom as well—long enough to set fire to the poor sod inside?*

"I did warn you," says the man, his dark brown, almost black, eyes fixed on me.

As I rub at my palms I take in the room: rectangular, the walls smooth. There's a red tinge to the lights, giving the space the look of a photographic dark room. Nothing to give away a location. Just a single door.

"Where am I?"

"Another question," comes the reply from my neighbor.

"What do you expect, Kavi?" says the woman. "He's bound to be a little disorientated at first. We all were."

"And do we know any more now than we did then?" asks the man she named. Nobody rushes to answer.

Instead the woman introduces herself to me. "I'm Jane," she says, touching her chest, then thumbs over at the other man. "That's Phil."

"Philip Hall," he announces proudly, like it means something.
I shrug. "Chris. Chris Warwick."

"Welcome to the party," says Phil snidely.

"So nobody knows anything about this? About why I saw
someone just get fried right in front of me."

"You *saw* that?" Jane sounds shocked.

I nod. "Managed to drag my blindfold down a bit. I saw
enough."

Phil gives a half laugh. "Resourceful little devil, isn't he?
That'll get you a one way ticket to hell around here, kid."

"This *is* Hell," says Jane with complete conviction.

"How long have you been here?" I ask, though it's Phil who
butts in.

"Longer than you," he says.

"Then you must have seen who's holding us." I round on
him. "Who did that?"

Nobody says a thing.

"Oh, come on! This is ridiculous." I stand, almost putting my
hands on the bars again. "You can't just kidnap a bunch of people and then—"

"Why not? Happens all the time abroad," Phil comments.
"Places where *his* lot come from." He nods over at Kavi.

The dark skinned man smiles. "With one breath you betray
your ignorance," is his only remark.

"We're *all* ignorant in this place," Phil replies.

"But how did you wind up here?" It's another question, and I
expect Kavi to say something about that, but he doesn't. This
time he asks me one of his own.

"How did *you*?"

It suddenly strikes me I don't know. I had thought I'd been
out on the town or something, and just got completely smashed.
But I couldn't remember a thing about the previous night, the
previous *day* (what time of day is it anyway?), let alone how I
ended up in this cage. "I… I think I was drugged."

"Well, *of course* you were drugged!" barks Phil. "It's how they get you here, and put you inside these things." He points at the cage.

"But why? Are they after money?"

"Looking for a ransom, that what you're thinking?" Phil grunts. "And why exactly would anyone pay money to get *you* back, Chrissie-boy? Loaded, are you?"

I hang my head. "No."

"Me either. How about you, Jane? Fitness instructor's pay suddenly gone up by a few million in the last month or so?"

"Piss off," says Jane.

Phil grins wearily. "Wish I could, sweetheart. Really wish I could."

"So what do you do?" I enquire out of mild curiosity.

"That's for me to know and for you to find out."

"He works in an estate agents," Jane informs me.

"Thanks a bunch," Phil grumbles.

"What about you?" I ask Kavi.

"Aw, who gives a shit," Phil breaks in before he can answer. "That was in the outside world. In here you're just another plaything."

I look again at the empty cage. "Why did they do that? Burn that person up, I mean."

"Nick," Jane says quietly, her eyes glistening. "His name was Nicholas."

"They don't need to give a fucking reason," Phil explains. "They'll just come in, douse you with petrol and strike a light."

"Phil, please," begs Jane.

"Especially if you make a fuss, draw attention to yourself," he carries on, ignoring her. "Just like Nick did."

It was Jane's turn to glare now, at Phil. "He didn't do anything wrong. He was just—"

"He asked one too many questions," Kavi points out, looking at me.

Phil nods in agreement. "Every time they came in, he was at it. What the fuck did he expect?"

"Come in? Hold on," I say, switching the subject, "so you *have* seen the people holding us then?"

Phil considers how to answer that one. "They don't exactly let us get a good look at their faces."

"I don't understand."

"You will," Kavi promises.

"Nick didn't do anything wrong," Jane continues, as if the conversation hasn't moved on at all. "It wasn't because of that—they just enjoy it." Without thinking, her hand goes to her neck and now I see the scar. It's a fresh one, still quite raw. "They enjoy hurting us."

"But why? What could they possibly gain from this? What do they want?"

"That," says Kavi, "is precisely what Nick wanted to know."

They fall silent. After a few minutes, Jane turns to me. "Chris, tell us about yourself. Who are you? What do you do?"

I sit back in the cage, picking at the chains. What the hey—I'm not going anywhere right now.

So I tell them. I tell them what I can remember about my life...

INTERLUDE:
SEVEN YEARS AGO

I went through the same shit as everyone else in my teens.

Struggled with my lessons, struggled with the opposite sex. I got just high enough grades to take me to art school where I enjoyed a brief and actually quite enjoyable stay—able to reinvent myself for my new circle of friends—until I got thrown out for smoking dope in the toilets with Jill Stanyard. The police let me off with a caution because I told them who had supplied the joint. They informed me they'd be keeping a close eye on me, though.

My parents had split by then, and I didn't fancy living with either of them. Besides, I think they pretty much wanted to disown me after the whole college incident. So I slept on the living room floor of a friend's digs and signed on.

In my early twenties I figured I should really make an effort to do something with my life. I worked my way through any number of dead-end jobs just to earn some cash. For a while I was the guy in the street that everyone hates—you know the one, standing there with clipboard in hand. That was when I wasn't dressed up as a giant chicken, handing out leaflets about tasty battered drumsticks.

In my spare time I kept up with my art, though I'd started writing more by then: something else I'd gotten into at college. I even went to a night-class for a short while.

"Christopher, your characterization is good, it's just your ideas that need to be worked on," the tutor told me, a pipe-smoking ex-English teacher in a tweed jacket. "They're just too… off the wall. For example, these people you keep writing about from this other dimension who manipulate the human race. The ones with the globes. I mean, *really*."

"They're just a metaphor," I tried to tell him. I thought he'd like that, being into symbolism and everything. "I guess I'm saying none of us are really in control of our own destinies."

His answer to that was, "Rubbish. We make our own choices in life, Christopher."

But we don't, do we? Some of those choices are made for us. Like if I hadn't been going to the classes I never would have met Kim, and we never would have started going out. She was there for pottery lessons and we bumped into each other in the corridor after class.

"Let me guess, ash tray?" I said, after we got chatting— referring to the object she'd been making that night.

She laughed, her eyes lighting up behind the big round glasses she wore. "Don't smoke. Actually it's supposed to be a mug."

"Ah, I see… Look, do you fancy something to eat?"

And that was that.

I showed Kim some of my stories and sketches; she thought I was talented, though I don't think she really got them. "You should send these off somewhere," she told me in bed one night.

"What, you mean to magazines?"

"Uh-huh."

"You think?"

"Sure. What have you got to lose? If you don't, you'll never know."

She was right; if I didn't I'd always wonder what might have been. But there was no way they were good enough, and the rejections I got back simply confirmed that. So Kim talked her boss, Mr. Malone, into giving me a job at the call centre where she worked.

That's about the size of it. I ate, slept, watched mindless TV and screwed. Kim and I made plans for the future, even though her parents hated my guts. Her father especially. "He's got no ambition, no prospects," I overheard him telling his daughter once. "You can do much better than him, sweetheart." They say history repeats itself, don't they?

Still, life was good for a time. Life was normal.

Three

It isn't long before I see our jailers.

I understand now what Kavi meant, because their features are covered by hoods; cowls so large they obscure their faces. And robes that reach almost to the ground. They look like monks belonging to some kind of religious order. *Is that it? A brotherhood dedicated to worshipping pain—inflicted on themselves and others.* But their footwear gives them away. Heavy boots; military issue. Plus there's the merest glimpse of combat trousers as they walk.

They bring with them a replacement for 'Nick': a grey-haired old lady dragged along the floor by her flabby arms. She's blindfolded, like I was, and looks just as drugged up. They begin attaching chains to her wrists and ankles.

I exchange glances with Jane, then Phil and Kavi. The latter are begging me with their eyes not to say or do something that might cause trouble. But as I watch them open up the door of the cage and dump the woman inside, I can't hold back.

"Hey," I shout, hearing a sharp intake of breath from Jane. "Hey, I'm talking to you—you murdering bastards." It's not the smartest thing I've ever done, and I've picked a great time to act the hero, but I just can't contain my outrage any longer.

The monks pause from their labors and turn in my direction. They say nothing. Then with cold, calculating calmness they finish the job, securing the woman behind those bars.

"You cowards, hiding in those stupid outfits. Just who do you think you are?"

"Christopher," says Kavi in hushed tones that nevertheless have a hardness to them.

"Hey, I'm waiting for an answer, fuckers!" I shout.

That does the trick. One walks over, the strides long and confident, robes swishing. The same swishing I heard the first time I awakened.

Head still bowed, he approaches my cage.

"You come near me and I'll…" I start, knowing it's just a hollow threat. If these people took me in the first place, then I'm no match for them now, shackled. I'm not much of a fighter anyway.

He reaches into his robes, producing a gun which he brings up level with my head.

"Serves him right," I hear Phil whisper to Jane. "I told him. Shoulda kept his mouth shut."

I try to retreat, but the ankle chains suddenly tighten and root me to the spot. He steps closer, finger twitching on the trigger. My mouth falls open and all I can do is gape at the barrel. *Not so much of a tough guy all of a sudden, are you?* But I never claimed to be, I'm just someone who can't keep it shut. Someone like Nick.

And look what happened to him: barbeque.

Just when it seems there's no hope, the 'monk' turns at the

last minute and points the gun at Phil. It takes him totally by surprise, as does the bang when he fires. I jump, then trace the path of the bullet into Phil. I've never seen anyone get shot before, except in the movies, and it's *so* different in real life. Phil's wide eyes screw up as the projectile hits his gut. There's a tiny explosion of blood, then a sudden flow. Phil touches the wound, his breathing fast and low. The 'monk' walks over to Phil's cage, cocking his head.

"Jesus," Phil manages. "Look what you've gone and done." His voice is thick and sounds like it's full of phlegm. The hooded figure raises the gun as if to shoot Phil again. But he doesn't; he just stands there, watching the reaction. Then, when his colleagues are about to depart from the room, he follows, hiding the gun inside his robes once more.

It takes a long time for Phil to die. He does his best to try and stem the bleeding, but it's like the 'monk' knew exactly where to hit him for maximum damage—yet prolong his agony. Phil's face gradually turns white, then stony grey. All we can do is sit there, while the life-blood ebbs out of him. I think about shouting for the men to come back, for them to do something. Then I remember that it's my fault. Phil is dying because I couldn't keep my mouth fucking well shut. Because I wanted answers. They've done this as a message... a warning.

Jane is crying uncontrollably, but can't take her eyes off the sight. Just like she couldn't when Nick was burning, smoking. Melting. I hear Kavi chanting something I can't understand; I think he's praying for Phil.

At the end, Phil's bladder and bowels fail him. I can smell the piss and shit. With a final wet gurgle he coughs his last breath. It sounds like he's trying to ask, "Why?"

Jane is in a state of shock, Kavi is still muttering words to help Phil's soul on its way.

I say nothing. If only I'd kept quiet a few hours ago then... No, it's not down to me. It can't be! How would that make any sense?

But the fact remains I'm still alive, and Phil is in the cage next to me—dead.

And I have to ask myself whether anything makes sense any more.

INTERLUDE:
THREE YEARS AGO

I left something out, probably because I've only just remembered it.

Isn't that strange? How could I have forgotten about the e-mails? You're thinking I've gone mad now, aren't you? I'm beginning to wonder. But trust me, this is important... I think.

I was still with Kim. Not quite ready to get hitched, but we'd talked about it, usually after too much wine at the weekend. "You know it's going to happen, don't you?" I'd say. She'd nod, but give me a look that said, 'Well, why don't you bloody well get on with it and ask me then?'

I'd been promoted at the call centre (I'd show her fucking Dad who was and who wasn't ambitious!) so now I no longer had to pester people in their homes; I got others to do it for me. Kim had left there by then, and was working in a solicitor's office. The pay was better and between us we had a pretty good standard of living. I'd forgotten all about the stories I'd sent off to places, that is until one of the magazines wrote back to me saying they'd had a change of editor. Apparently my story had been languishing in a drawer for almost three years. It was only when they cleared them out that they found it. And you know what—this new editor absolutely loved it and could they please use it in a forthcoming issue?

I'd have to wait six months or more, and I wouldn't get paid much, but I didn't give a toss. Something I'd written was actually going to be published. In a real life, honest to goodness, magazine!

I told Kim when she got home from the office and we went out that night for a meal to celebrate. We fooled around when we made it back, just like we used to do in the days when we first met. It was the most tender and intimate sex I'd ever had in my life. I don't know about Kim, but I can definitely recommend getting something published as an aphrodisiac.

We both called in sick the next day. It was only partially a lie, as we should never have finished that last bottle of red. It took till about noon for both of us to feel up to surfacing. I switched on my computer in the spare room and downloaded my mails while I used the loo. When I walked back in, I saw a load of spam had come through. Usually the filters dealt with all that, but they must have been on the fritz.

Mails were coming in from people like Chick Dalke, Rodney Bunter, Janis A. Ohio, trying to get me to buy anything from sex pills to replica watches. Some of them just didn't make any sense at all.

'Here's the lube you neeeeeeeed,' said one. 'Let it glide with pride. This oil will make it feeed, quicker than you can blink.' Another was just a random list of words: 'Eminent mandrake accost plasma blizzard corruption nordhoff hyena locomotory genus militate neonatal... ' Pure nonsense.

"Well, you definitely don't need any of *that* stuff," said Kim over my shoulder, pointing at one ad that promised to give the woman in my life sexual ecstasy. 'Take me beyond my limits,' said the woman standing there, finger crooked. "She can wait her turn." Kim began nibbling my earlobe, obviously still in the mood after last night.

I allowed myself to get dragged off back to bed, but all the time Kim ground away on top of me my mind was elsewhere. Something in those mails, especially the nonsense ones, was nagging at me. What did it mean? How had they made their way through now, why did they continue to come to millions of people...? The rational part of my mind was telling me the mails were corrupted because they'd multiplied until the original message was no longer comprehensible. But the other part—that dreamt up the story which had just been accepted by the magazine—was telling me something else. What if the nonsense was just a smokescreen? What if there was something important I was missing in those mails?

"Mmmm... Oh yes," murmured Kim as she lowered, angling herself so that the sensations she felt were intensified. Her eyes were closed as she impaled herself on me, her moans growing louder, the creaking of the bed in tune to the rhythm of her hips. The image of that half-naked woman flitted into my mind, a construct of pixels, a fantasy someone had thought up to sucker people.

Then, suddenly, other images of women intruded, pages from some old magazine.

"Take me... Take me beyond my limits," whispered Kim. I wasn't sure whether she was joking, using the phrase from the woman's speech bubble as a gag. "Take me... Take me..." she repeated. I pushed her onto her back, holding her by the wrists, and began to ram into her hard. Her moans reached fever pitch as I thrust in right to the hilt, again and again, making both of us raw. "Harder... Oh God, harder... Hurt me... hurt me!"

Let it glide with pride. Make it feeed, quicker than you can blink.

Pleasure mixed with pain, creating something totally unique. The orgasm, when it came, was unlike anything I'd ever experienced. I felt Kim quivering beneath me as I held onto her. But it wasn't until I looked down again that I saw she was quivering with fear, red finger marks indenting her skin. She rolled over, sobbing into the pillow.

I reached out a hand to touch her shoulder; she shrugged it off.

"Baby?"

Kim turned back and I saw anger in her face this time. "What the hell got into you? That hurt, Chris! That *really* hurt."

"But you said... I thought..."

"What? That I was enjoying it? Didn't you hear me telling you to stop?" She was practically screaming the words.

I shook my head.

"Having too much of a good time, were you? What's next, handcuffs? Whipping? Gimp masks?"

"No, you know I'm not into all that stuff."

Her look said she didn't know me at all. "Just leave me alone, would you. Leave me the fuck alone." Kim buried her head into the pillow again.

Frowning, I climbed out of bed. I had no idea what had just happened, but I did know I'd hurt the person I loved more than anything. What *had* got into me? I honestly had no clue. The images in my head, the words Kim had been saying... Something about those mails...

I returned to the computer in the spare room, which had flipped to the screensaver. Nudging the mouse brought up the spam and I examined those emails once more.

I was so transfixed I didn't hear Kim get up and get dressed, and only realized she'd left the flat when I heard the door slam. Later I found the note she'd left me saying she'd gone to her folks to stay; she'd even packed some of her clothes.

Kim returned the following week, but only after I'd left many pleading messages on her mobile. "I swear I don't know what happened," I tried to explain. "Please come back. I need you."

She finally relented, in spite of her mother and father's protests. But things were never the same. It was a long time before she would let me anywhere near her, saying that she just wanted the old Chris back, the person she'd fallen in love with.

I wanted to tell her that it *was* still me, but we both knew that would have been a lie. I'd had a revelatory moment that day, and I was certain it had something to do with the mails. What I never told her was that I'd saved them, and disabled the filters permanently so that I'd get more. I studied them, searching for something.

Strangely, it was while I wasn't looking at all that I spotted the answer. Dropping to sleep in the chair, staring at the computer one night, another batch of mails flooded in. Kim was downstairs watching TV, on her own, as she did most nights. I clicked on the first mail and saw this text, suddenly drawn to certain letters:

'I struck some small cork after your ill sky, which bade uniformly. Its narrow box around that knowledge; bitter, necessary pin, wet stone shelf interbred. They slunk, afterwards, only, I hanged her hard operation beyond his important cloud. Which reran often, acid reading remade of this need?'

I rubbed my sore eyes, blinking. Random coincidence? The letters just happened to make up that sentence? But not the placing of the full stops, separating out each word so there could be no mistake.

'They watch and wait'.

I checked through the other mails I'd stored, now that I'd broken the code. I saw it again and again. Sometimes it would be down the sides—to the left or the right of justified text. Sometimes it was diagonally across, like a wordsearch puzzle. Other times, like the first one, simply embedded.

"My God," I said to myself, clicking on another incoming mail.

The computer froze. Had to happen sooner or later, a virus of some kind. I moved the cursor and nothing happened. I pressed Ctrl, Alt and Delete together. No task manager box came up. I found myself jabbing hard at one of the keys over and over again.

Harder... Oh God harder...

I looked down. It was the Ctrl key. Ctrl...

Control?

"I'm going to bed, now. You can do what you want." The voice startled me and I jumped. Turning, I saw Kim standing in the doorway wearing her 'keep your hands to yourself' pajamas.

"What? Oh, yeah, sure." I turned back to the dead screen. She sighed, but didn't bother looking again.

I just stared at the blank screen, wondering what I'd stumbled onto. The virus behind the virus. One that ensured no computer would ever work for me again.

It didn't come as a surprise when, a few weeks later, the magazine that had accepted my story told me they were folding and couldn't publish it after all.

"It's such a sad thing," the woman said, almost in tears down the line. "The editor threw himself in front of a tube train. There was no warning, nothing anyone could have done."

"No," I replied, the phone falling from my grasp. "I don't think anyone could."

Four

The new addition's name is Patty.

They take her blindfold off at the same time they come and clear out Phil's body, wheeling it from the room on a trolley. This time I keep quiet as the men in robes do their work. The old woman watches, but doesn't say a word either. I think she may be catatonic.

Once the 'monks' have gone again, it is Jane who talks to her, eventually coaxing out a name.

"That man," Patty says, "he was dead, wasn't he?"

"Killed… shot," I inform her, "by the men that brought you here."

"Those same people in the hoods and cloaks."

Jane nods.

"Oh sweet Lord." Patty's voice trembles. She has a kindly face, the youthfulness shining out and belying her years. I feel an immediate affinity with Patty. She has that look on her face I must have had when I first arrived: a combination of denial and confusion. The next words out of her mouth confirm this. "Why did they kill him? What do they want with me?"

"I wish we could answer your questions," Kavi says, "but we

are as much in the dark as you."

"Do you remember how you got here?" I ask.

Patty shakes her head. "No, wait, I think I was at home. I remember I was feeding Mr. Vickers." She smiles thinly and adds, "My cat. Then there was a knock at the door. I went to see who it was."

"And…"

"I… don't know, it's all so muddled. I can't remember much after that."

"Jesus." I bang my fist into my hand; a humorless imitation of Robin from the old *Batman* series. "Please try to think."

"I'm sorry," she replies, gazing at me. "My memory's not what it was at the best of times."

"Look, it's obvious they don't want us to know," Jane says to me. "None of us can remember, no matter how hard we try."

"It is futile striving to know the unknowable," Kavi concludes.

I snort. "Right. Is that why you pray? I saw you when Phil was dying."

Kavi slowly closes then opens his eyes. "Praying does not reveal the unknowable to me, it simply puts me in touch with my God. He hears my plea. But at the same time I do not *demand* anything from him."

"No, because he bloody well won't answer you, will he?"

"The words of a Godless man, am I right?"

I say nothing.

"I accept what is and what must be," Kavi answers as enigmatically as ever. "Most men do not."

That's directed at me. "Well, I don't accept that there's nothing I can do to get out of here. Nothing to do but watch and—"

"Wait?" Kavi finishes for me.

"T-That's right." I turn back to Patty. "Can you think of any reason why you might have been kidnapped?"

She shakes her head. "None at all. I'm nothing special, young man."

"Maybe that's just it," Jane interrupts. "Maybe we've been looking at this from the wrong angle. Have you ever thought that they've chosen us simply *because* we're ordinary? Because we won't be missed? Heaven knows nobody would give a toss if I vanished off the face of the Earth. I haven't seen my ex in years and I moved recently so I don't have any close friends in the area. How about the rest of you?"

"My wife and small son," Kavi informs her, a faraway look in his eye, "they would miss me."

"My husband passed away many years ago, but there's my daughter," Patty says. "And my little grandson, though he's probably too young to remember his old Gran if something should…" Her eyes begin to moisten.

I pause to think, who would miss me? Who would actually care if I died right here in this cage like some kind of lab rat?

Before I have too much time to mull it over, our food is brought in. Some sort of brown slop in a bowl with a spoon. It isn't until one of the hooded figures draws closer with the stuff that I realize how incredibly hungry I am. I probably haven't had anything to eat in well over forty-eight hours, though time has a way of becoming meaningless in this room. Our chains tighten as the cages are undone and the bowls placed inside.

When the cages are locked again, and the 'monks' have departed, our bonds loosen. Jane and Kavi reach for their bowls and begin to spoon up the slop into their mouths. It's obvious they've eaten at this restaurant before. Patty just sits and stares at the offering they've placed in her cage.

I hunker over the bowl, sniffing at it. The stuff smells distinctly meaty. When I push the spoon around there are chunks of something in the broth.

"You should eat," Jane encourages me, "before they come and take it away again. You never know if you're going to get another meal."

"You mean they'd starve us?" I ask.

"It would not be the first time," Kavi says. "Imagine having to eat while someone else is wasting away. That is true torture, my friend. For you and for them."

I raise a spoonful and my stomach rumbles. "But… what is it?"

"If we ask do you think they'd tell us?" Jane had a point.

I bring the spoon to my lips. Isn't half bad, a bit like beef stew. Greedily, I tuck in.

"Patty, you should eat too," Jane calls across, getting to the bottom of her bowl.

"I can't face it," she replies honestly.

"You need to keep your strength up," Jane insists.

Patty pouts. "What, because I'm a frail old lady?"

"No, I didn't mean…"

Patty folds her arms, more determined not to eat.

"This is my first time as well," I say. "But, really, it's not as bad as it looks. Go on, take a—"

Jane, who has just put her last spoonful into her mouth, begins to cough. At first I think she's choking, but it's more than that. Her hands are clutching at her belly. She falls over, doubling up. "Awwwhhhh!"

"Jane? Jane, what is it?" A stupid question, and one Jane's in no position to answer. But then this is me all over, I'm beginning to realize: stupid.

Jane's convulsing, and she brings her fingers up to her mouth—a vain effort to stick them down her throat. But before she can try and make herself sick, another stab of pain strikes and she curls up into a ball, hugging her abdomen tightly.

I place my hands on the bars of my cage, forgetting for a moment that they might be live. Nothing happens, so I shake them, causing the cage to rattle as well. There's no hope of escape, let alone helping Jane, but doing *something* makes me feel slightly better.

"She's been poisoned," Kavi says, staring down at his own bowl.

Patty places her hands over her ears as Jane cries out again.

The younger woman is kicking out, her feet hitting the bars. Her teeth are gritted, but foamy saliva sprays through them, drooling onto the cage floor. Jane's eyes are turning bright red, blood vessels exploding in the whites—and she's looking right at me as if expecting me to do something.

Her body is jerking all over the place, and at some point her tongue has forced its way out through her teeth. I wince as she chomps down on it, the wet end severing completely and flopping to the base of her cage on strings of spit and muscle.

Her exposed arms are breaking out in welts, huge balls that fill with pus, like some kind of time-elapsed film of a disease. Her face too, once pretty, is ruined by whatever's ravaging her body—whatever they put in the stew. I know it shouldn't even enter my mind, but I can't help wondering if they've done the same to all of us.

You only had a taste, though, remember? Just a taste.

How can I think about that when Jane is suffering like this? The lumps forming on her brow have closed one eye completely shut. She's scratching at the raised bits, raking them with her nails as the deformed skin tightens. Jane attempts to speak, but the ragged end of her tongue is swelling—blocking her airway—so all we can hear are disgusting gurglings. She's like some monster out of a sci-fi movie, transforming from human being into something else. It's a blessing when she can't breathe any more, and as she collapses onto the cage floor, her skin tears, leaking in many places.

I look from her to Kavi, then to Patty. None of us can quite believe what we've just seen. But already I can see a hardness in our new guest, the shock less than when they wheeled away Phil. The same is happening with me, I suppose. This is the third person I've seen die here. I don't think it will be the last.

With a resigned and frustrated grunt, I hurl the rest of my bowl at the bars of my cage. "Let us out of here!" I shout at the ceiling, at the walls. "You bastards, let us out!"

INTERLUDE:
ONE YEAR AND FIVE MONTHS AGO

As you can imagine, Kim didn't stick around for very long once I started to suspect the truth.

One day I came back from work (I was just about holding on to the job) and she'd packed her bags again, this time everything. And this time for good. She didn't even leave me a note, and I didn't bother ringing. It was all a sham anyway. I'm not just talking about our relationship, but things in general: life, people, work, all of it.

I was beginning to notice the signs everywhere I went. It was like someone had taken off a blindfold and allowed me to see— or I'd pulled it off myself, struggling to uncover what was right in front of my eyes. Ripping down the illusion of the everyday; not just walking on the cracks in the pavement, but getting down on my hands and knees and putting my eye up against them.

It didn't go unnoticed at the call centre. One day my boss, Malone, called me in. I stood there being chastised like a naughty school-kid.

"I just don't understand it, Christopher. You have… *had* a future here with us. What went wrong? I'd say it was trouble at home with Kim but I know this started before that."

"What do you know about me and Kim?" I snapped. Already I could picture my hands around his throat, squeezing…

"We're still friends. We keep in touch."

"I'll bet you do." Now they were squeezing harder.

"What's that supposed to mean?"

I shook my head to clear it. "Look, it doesn't matter. You want my resignation, you got it. None of this means anything anyway."

Malone sniffed. "Obviously, judging by the smell of your breath. You're not even trying to hide it, are you? The drinking?"

"How can I put this politely," I replied, fighting back the image of strangling him again. "Fuck right off."

"Do me a favor, don't let the door hit you on the way out."

I didn't. But I do remember saying something like, "And you can all get fucked as well!" to the other employees in the centre. They were still asleep, while I had begun to wake.

It took some time to prove what I already knew. That this phenomenon, the code I'd cracked, was everywhere if you just chose to look.

I'd walk down the high street and see it on billboards, supposedly promoting the latest cars or perfumes, but in reality... I remember just standing and staring at one poster for most of the day. The advert showed a picture of a man with a tank-top holding up a bowl of cereal, while a woman with a bob-cut was standing behind him beaming, ready to dip her own spoon in. Nothing suspicious whatsoever.

But the more I examined it, the more I saw the intent behind those eyes. They were saying something much more than: 'We love the new honey flavor'.

Several people stopped and asked me what I was looking at.

"Can't you see it?" I said to them.

"See what?"

"The message behind the message?"

"All I can see is a guy with a bowl of cereal."

So it went on. I'd warn them to walk away before I started shouting. Some did, some didn't. Some asked where the hidden cameras were, and I had to laugh at that. I came to the conclusion that they couldn't see past the surface because they didn't *want* to; they were just protecting themselves. Jesus, how much simpler would my life have been if I'd never found out?

I scoured the newspapers day after day. The celebrity gossip columns, the sports pages, the hard factual stories about wars abroad: especially those. Even in the horoscopes it was there. 'Watch out for overspending, Pisces... Don't let work pressures get you down, Virgo... You have received some important information, Aquarius, what you choose to do with it is up to you… '

Because the internet was now forbidden, a two-way mirror that I didn't dare use anymore, I visited libraries, museums, seats of learning. I found the message again and again in encyclopedias, in the ideas of famous scholars. Philosophers such as Nietzsche, Aristotle, Wittgenstein, Locke, Kant and so many others hinted at it, though they had no idea they were so close to the truth.

In the greatest works of literature I saw hidden signs. The plays of Shakespeare, the poems of Byron, the novels of Dickens. And don't even get me started on parables in the Bible!

But in works of art, also, it was as plain as the nose on your face: the key in every brushstroke, every chip with the hammer and chisel. People like the Surrealists came the closest to breaking it. You think Dali's 'Lobster Telephone' is just for effect, or Magritte's men with bowler hats and pictures of pipes? *Ceci n'est pas une pipe.* You're damned right it's not, René.

Architecture? Sure. The Doric, Ionic and the Corinthian screamed it out, the towers and castles of the Gothic era, the reflective surfaces of the Lloyd building… every single one of them, if you took the trouble to look, to *really* look as I did, contained some element of the message.

Let us not forget film and television. Name your favorite movie, it's there in every line of dialogue, every scene, every jump-cut or special effects sequence. Charlie Chaplin's tramp, God love him, Rhett Butler and Scarlett O'Hara's kiss, Rita Hayward in *that* dress, the shark in *Jaws*, the aliens in fucking *Independence Day* for Christ sakes! And the writers, producers and directors behind them, all unable to see the result of what they'd done. That not only was their stamp on the work, but another as well.

Should I try to make others see? Could they? *Would* they? In the end I chose to do what most would have done in my place, armed with the knowledge I had:

I decided to get drunk. (See, like father like son. Kim's dad was right after all.)

I took myself off at night and drank my way through the savings account Kim and I had set up, hitting bar after bar. There you'd find me, with a scotch or vodka, in the corner, observing the mating rituals and ruckuses. It didn't matter whether it was a nightclub, wine bar or just some downbeat pub, it was all the same.

Once or twice I'd cause a scene, just to see what happened.

"Don't any of you fucking get it? You really don't, do you? You're all being used, manipulated!"

It would usually end in me being thrown out by a very large bouncer.

Around this time I began to dabble with drugs, too. I figured it would help me to forget, might even make life worth living again.

I was wrong.

Some of the trips I had... In one I was communicating with different colored lights: bright reds and yellows, greens and purples. Each color had its own personality and I passed a pleasant evening in conversation until black came along, absorbing the others.

In another I was lost in a forest of bones, human bones—and beneath my feet I trampled human skeletons into the ground as I ran, trying to get away from something behind me.

But one in particular struck a chord. I felt myself rising up out of my body and traveling through the stars, until space itself turned white and the pinpricks of light turned black. There I saw a city, with living towers and minarets, surrounded by volcanoes that spat fire—burning white fire—periodically. The snaking streets of this place, connected by juddering bridges and pulsating conduits, were labyrinthine in design. The creatures who inhabited the buildings wore clothes that seemed to be a part of their own bodies: fleshy, covered in veins, protective cowls covering their features. Cowls that glowed a strange azure color.

Beneath the ground of this city was a huge eye, liquid blue. Swimming in this were all the souls who had ever been and ever

43

would be, floaters in the eye, dispelled whenever it blinked. It looked right at me, that eye: right *into* me.

I woke from that one in the Emergency Room, towel wrapped around me. I was soaking wet.

"He's finally coming around. Whatever he took was really strong stuff." This was a doctor who was flashing a torch into my eyes. He clicked his fingers to the side of me and when I reacted, he sighed with relief. "How people can let themselves get into this state, I'll never know."

"How... where...?" I managed.

"You were found in the lake, guy. Could easily have drowned if that courting couple hadn't come across you. You're lucky to be alive."

I didn't *feel* lucky. "Listen... listen to me... My story... I have to tell you my story."

"Yeah, yeah." He grinned. "They all say that. Listen, why don't you take it easy for a minute." The doctor pushed me back, about to flash the light in my eyes again. "I just want to take another look at—"

"You don't understand. None of you do. They watch and—"

A nurse appeared with a huge needle and handed it to the doctor. I took one look at that and started to struggle.

"Easy now. This is for your own good. God, after the crap you put into your own body tonight, you'd think that—"

I lashed out, knocking him sideways, then pushed the nurse backwards. I stumbled from the bed, tipping over a tray of instruments. I vaguely remember shoving a few people aside in my hurry to reach the door.

But I made it, out into the dark.

I ran, just like I did through that forest of bones. When I was exhausted, I hid away in a deserted area of town, in an old abandoned factory the derelicts sometimes use.

I sat there in the blackness, knees up to my chest, knowing that I'd been seen now for sure.

That they would do everything in their power to catch me

and...

Well, then they would silence me for good.

Five

Jane's replacement is already well on the way to death when they bring him in.

The door opens as we're discussing what happened to her—Kavi and I can at least agree on some kind of biological weapon—— and the 'monks' shove the man inside. He is stripped to the waist with his hands bound behind his back. In his mid-fifties perhaps, with long silver-grey hair and a trimmed beard, he has been worked on outside. For starters his eye is missing, in its place just a huge cavity. When he's pushed to his knees I see two fingers are gone on his right hand, and the thumb of his left. There are marks across his back where a belt or something has been used on him. Scars on his chest, a bit like those Jane tried to hide.

I look at Kavi and nod towards the newcomer. He shakes his head, telling me silently that he's never seen this guy before. Patty touches her fingers to her lips, face as white as a shroud. I think she's finally grasping the fact that this could be her soon, and we can't do a blessed thing about it. But the more I gaze at her face, the more I recognize not just the look, but the features. There's something so desperately familiar and I wish I could work out what.

The new guy looks completely out of it, ribs bruised purple where they've beaten him. One of the 'monks' kicks him in the direction of the cage he's about to occupy.

Roll up, roll up, roll up... for incineration, bleeding to death from a belly wound, emaciation and poisoning.

The men in robes manhandle him into Jane's cage, which has only been vacant a short while. As he slumps inside and they undo one lot of shackles, only to replace them with those inside

45

the cage, I see burn marks on the soles of his feet. He's really been through the wringer.

With a clang of the cage door, our jailors leave again. The man rolls around groaning.

"Hey!" I call. "Hey *you*. Can you hear me?"

"What are you doing?" Patty asks, biting her nails.

"He's been out there." I point to the door. "He's seen what's outside of here. If we're going to try and escape—"

"Escape?" she says, a little too loudly for my liking.

"Christopher, how many more times, there *is* no escape from here," says Kavi hanging his head. "Nicholas, Philip and now Jane... Dozens more before you arrived."

"I am not going to sit here waiting to buy it on some sado-masochistic production line," I snap. "Especially when I don't know why."

"People are born, people live, people die, all the time," Kavi points out. "How many of *them* know why?"

"Bet that God of yours knows," I retort, the sarcasm dripping from my voice. "Now why don't you—"

"H-He's right." The voice is barely a whisper, but it cuts through our babble like a blade. The man they brought in is leaning up on one elbow. "T-There's no escaping this."

Eyebrows knitting together, I grab the bars of my cage once more—again forgetting they could be charged. It's just in my nature to rage against captivity. "What are you talking about? There *has* to be a way out. How many guards are there?"

He just laughs, then begins to wheeze like an asthmatic in need of an inhaler.

"Tell me! Tell me anything you can!" I'm beginning to lose patience; I don't give a shit what state he's in.

"Be dead soon, me, and so will all of you lot."

I shake my head. "I don't give up that easily."

"You... you will eventually, boy. We all do."

I freeze; there's something about that voice. I've heard it before. The man is cleaner than he was the first time we met, though not that much older.

I'm not going back... You hear me... Never.

"You're The Monster," I say.

"What?"

"You know this man?" asks Kavi.

I nod.

"How?"

"When I was a kid, I think. It's all a bit hazy."

"Why did you call him a monster?" Patty chirps up.

The man in the cage wheezes again. "I'm Dixon. Folks call me Dixon," he says, as if to prove he's human.

"I'm not sure," I tell Patty. "But I think he knows more about all this than any of us."

The man shakes his head, then looks away. "No. Not me. I don't know nothin'."

"Liar!" If I could get to him right now, I'd wring the information out. Then I stop and look at his wounds again. No, he's been through enough. "Look, just tell us what's on the other side of that door—how we can get out. You got out before, I know you did. I remember that much."

Kavi rubs his chin. "You're saying that this man escaped and was brought back?"

"Tell me!" I demand again, ignoring Kavi.

The man looks around him as if following the trail of a fly. "Can't. They... they watch."

"And they wait?" I state matter of factly. "There are cameras in here, aren't there? They're watching us right now."

"They're *always* watching us," hisses the man. "Night and day, day and night. *You are the one.*" He sings this last bit.

"The man has clearly lost his mind." Kavi's pacing up and down in the confines of his cage.

"Show yourself! Come on!" I'm suddenly shouting. "Let us see you. We know you're in here!"

The door opens and two of the 'monks' rush in. It's almost as if they've been waiting on the other side, ready to move whenever there's trouble.

"Hey!" I shout again.

"Christopher…" There's a definite warning in Kavi's voice.

"Here! Come over here, I want to talk to you." I never have been one for learning from my mistakes. I rattle my cage and it succeeds in halting them. But instead of going for me, they make their way over to Kavi's cage instead. One of them reaches inside his robes.

"No, not again. Hey, over here! Me, it's me who wants to talk to you." The bars of the cage are suddenly crackling with electricity that knocks me backwards. At the same time Kavi's shackles tighten, hoisting him up and backwards so that he is slammed against the rear of the cage: his body forms a perfect X.

Shaking my head, I see that it's not a pistol they've taken out this time, but some kind of thick noose on the end of a metal stick.

Effortlessly, they loop the open end around Kavi's head, around his neck, and with a twist they tighten it. The muscles of Kavi's arms bulge, but the shackles binding him allow no leeway. Another twist of the handle and his mouth is wide open; he's fighting for breath. They're garroting him, each twist of the handle tightening the pressure on his throat. Beads of sweat pour down Kavi's face, as the bonds are pulled even tighter. Just as another twist comes, the chains pull his shoulders out of their sockets with a loud crack.

"No! No, you fuckers—*me!* I'm the one you want." My eyes are wet with tears. This shouldn't be happening. I shouldn't be seeing this. I hear Patty's wailing from the other cage; there's not a sound from Dixon.

And, as Kavi's limbs are torn out of their sockets, his neck broken by the noose, he mouths the words: "Pray for me."

I would if I could.

It is only now that the cameras reveal themselves, the ones I suspected were in the room all along. They detach themselves from the ceiling, round like the cages and suspended by power cables. They look like miniature CCTV cams you might find in the middle of shopping precincts. Four in total, one for each prisoner, with a single circular lens in the middle.

The nearest one descends to my level. It stares at me and I wonder who I'm staring back at, through that lens.

"I *will* get out of here, I promise you; I'll get out… And then I'm going to come for you."

Big words, with nothing to back them up.

The camera just gazes at me in silence.

INTERLUDE:
FIVE DAYS AGO

I went on the run.

Doesn't that sound cool, like something out of a Quinn Martin production? Every week a different adventure, helping people put right what once went wrong then moving on again, the noble hero.

What a load of crap.

It was hard on the streets. I had no money—I'd lost my wallet during the incident in the Emergency Room, and anyway my card could be traced. I couldn't afford for anyone to know where I was or what I was doing.

I headed North, away from the towns and cities. I figured there'd be less scrutiny in the wide, open spaces, little realizing that a stranger often stuck out like a sore thumb. The other drawback was people had a tendency to notice you begging for money, too. But I had to eat, collect other 'materials'. Outside supermarkets was the best bet, until I was inevitably moved on by security staff. I'm not too proud to admit that I stole. How else was I meant to survive? To carry out my plan?

I was aware that they could track me down at any time, but what gave me the edge was *knowing* about them. Once you do, it becomes a lot easier to live off the grid.

Eventually I had to stop running and gather everything together. The evidence I would need to try—maybe—and convince someone. By this time I was beginning to find it very lonely carrying the burden.

I found a deserted cabin in the woods, a hunting lodge that it hadn't been used in years. It was practically gutted, partly burnt, but suited my needs perfectly.

I set up shop there, compiling my notes by candlelight in the evenings and catching the odd fish or small animal to eat in the day. I know what you're thinking: Me - Grizzly Adams. They don't exactly go together, do they? But I did all right. I holed up long enough to put everything together. A case that even Perry Mason would balk at taking on. I felt like I was finally making progress, getting my head around things.

Nobody could have been more surprised than I was when *she* turned up.

Kim.

She knocked on the door out of common courtesy, but it was open anyway. As I had been that day on the computer, I was so caught up in what I was doing, I didn't look up until she was virtually inside.

"Christopher... Chris, is that you?"

I frowned at the figure standing before me: an hallucination? A bad flashback, the drugs having their revenge? But she was as real as I was.

"How... How did you find me?"

It was her turn to frown. "*You* called my mobile number, left a message. I was so pleased to hear from you."

I laughed. "I don't even have a phone anymore."

"But you must have... Oh God, Chris, what's happened to you?" She walked further in, looking at the walls where I'd pinned pieces of paper or drawn on the wood in chalk, then her eyes settled on me again. I was sitting on the floor in the middle of more papers; I'd been furiously writing before Kim came in. It had been months since I'd seen myself in any kind of mirror, so had no idea what she was seeing. I knew my hair was long and I'd grown a beard. I was still wearing the old clothes I'd run off in that first night, but had managed to snag an overcoat from a toilet cubicle (the owner had left it on the back of the door). Christ, though, what a mess I must have looked.

"Kim, listen, if they know where I am, if *they* left that message, then I don't have a lot of time. It isn't exactly how I wanted to do this, but I suppose it's appropriate that you should be the first to see. The first other than me, that is."

"Chris, where have you been all this time? How did you get all the way up here? People have been looking for you."

One of my eyebrows arched. "People, what people?"

"The police, mainly. They were waiting for me when I got to hospital the night you vanished."

"What the fuck were you doing *there?*" My tone was harsh and I immediately regretted it.

"My number was still down as point of contact if anything should... They said you were on drugs, said you'd hurt people."

I stood, letting the papers pool around me. "I couldn't let them take me away—didn't know who to trust."

"Why? Because of all... this?" Kim glanced around the room again.

I started towards her and she backed off. "It's okay, look, I figured it all out."

"What? All I see are drawings of ellipses, colored in blue."

I nodded. "It's an eye. It's a symbol. We're being watched, Kim. Maybe even now, I'm not sure."

"I... I don't understand."

"Nobody knows it, but I swear it's the truth. Our lives are being contr—" I hesitated, blinked, then said, "being *manipulated.* The clues are everywhere, in everything. It's not exactly like my stories, but—"

"Your stories?"

"You remember, I almost got one published—but I don't think they could let it get out into the open. Even though it was fiction, it might have given people ideas."

"Yes, of course I remember. But they were just made up, you said so yourself."

"I did, but I know now they were my own way of dealing with what's been going on. I struck on something, Kim, and didn't even realize it."

She shook her head. "Chris, there's something wrong with you. That night, the doctors told me—"

"I knew it, I just knew it! Don't you see, they'd tell you anything to make you think I was cracking up."

"The… the people who are watching us, right?" Kim didn't sound convinced.

"Not people, exactly. Nostradamus almost had it right," I told her. "He said gods would arrive in the form of humans, and be the cause of great conflict. But they're not here at all, they never were. I don't know exactly what they are, something our brains probably can't cope with. I do know they stay well out of it, wind us up and let us go—like clockwork toys. They… 'encourage' us to batter each other, emotionally and physically, and get off on it. Can you believe that? They don't like to get their own hands dirty; it's like reality TV or something. But they *need* us to be damaged, it… empowers them."

"Chris, you're really scaring me."

I took another couple of steps towards her, holding out my hands so she could see I meant no harm. "I've been able to see the patterns for some time now. They have a hand in everything we do—the arts, politics, advertising—every fucking thing, Kim!"

"What are you talking about? How can art cause pain, conflict?" I could tell by her face that she didn't get it.

"What do we do when we create something? We argue over its worth. It causes divisions, even on a small scale. We fight wars sometimes because we can't agree on the fundamental principles of life, of religion, of anything. While they sit back and just keep cranking up the tension. They *make* us hurt each other, Kim—just like that time I hurt you." I bent down and grabbed a handful of papers on the floor, shoving them in her direction. "Here, see, it's all in my notes, my research. It isn't fiction this time—it's fact!"

Her mouth moved as she read the first line. "'They watch and wait.'"

I nodded. "Exactly."

"No," she said, giving me the paper back. "That's all it says, Chris, over and over again: 'They watch and wait.'"

"What? Here, give me that." I snatched it from her and looked at the words I'd written; hours and hours of painstaking work, thoughts, hypotheses, all somehow wiped out. "This can't be... How have they done this?" I looked at her. "They must have implanted it subliminally, not *allowed me* to write what I thought I was writing."

Kim was nodding, but she was backing up towards the door. "Subliminal... yes, I see now."

I ran at her, grabbing her arms. "I'm telling you the truth. It's all out there, if you only choose to see."

Kim tried to break loose, but I wouldn't let her. "Let go of me, Chris. I came here to help you. They said you might be dangerous but—"

"Who? Who said that?" I shook her. "Their acolytes? The ones who serve, even though they don't know it?"

Kim finally broke free and fell backwards, crying.

"You've brought them here, haven't you?"

She continued to cry, just as she had into her pillow.

"Why else would you come?"

"Because you asked me to!" she screamed. "Because even after everything, after all this time, I still love you!"

I stood there, looking down on her.

"Nobody makes us hurt each other. We do it to ourselves, Chris! There's nobody watching or waiting, nobody out there controlling any of us; anything. We. Do. It. To. Ourselves!" She said each word individually, to give it impact.

I swallowed before answering. "Then how do you explain that?" I pointed down at the ground, the way the papers had fallen on the floor.

Kim rose, eyes flicking between me and the papers. They'd fallen in the shape of a giant eye, perfect in every way. She said nothing.

"They're coming for me, aren't they?"

"Chris, they're going to *help* you." Even after all this, Kim still couldn't accept it.

"No-one can do that." I made to pass her, then stopped. I leaned in for a kiss and, as disgusting as I must have looked, she kissed me back. "I'm sorry," I said, breaking off. "I have to go."

Kim didn't try to stop me. It might have been because she knew the authorities were already on their way, but I like to think it had something to do with realizing the truth.

I can still picture her there, standing in the doorway, looking back at me as I disappeared into the trees.

Six

I suspect Dixon died during the night, or what passes for night here—a dimming of already pretty dim lights.

When I wake, I see he's not moving, and he doesn't answer me when I repeatedly call him. He's had enough, finally given up. We now have another cellmate, another woman in Kavi's cage. She's unconscious as well, but I figure she's not dead yet or they wouldn't have put her in here. What would be the point? The cameras—which have vanished now, but I know are still around—wouldn't be able to catch our reactions then. Wouldn't be able to savor the agony on the faces of the torture victims.

Patty is not much conversation. I find myself missing Kavi, even with his irritating ways. I wonder absently if the new woman will be any more company? She's laying with her back to me at the moment; all I can see is her blonde hair, much lighter than Jane's. She's not blindfolded, at least—I can tell that much.

For about the millionth time I wish I could get out of this

fucking cell! There *has* to be a way.

It's at this point the woman, obviously waking from a drug-induced sleep, begins to stir. She rolls over, the blonde hair falling over her face in curls. She brings a hand up and rubs at that face, moving the curls to one side.

I take in a sharp breath. No, it can't be. "Mum?"

The woman moans something, not quite with it yet. But it's definitely her; my mother, who ran off with the bookmaker all that time ago.

They're going after my family now?

Who will I see in here next, who will they torture just to film my reaction to it? I can't let them harm her, not like they've done with Phil, Jane, Kavi…I can see visions of the terrible things they might do to her; pour acid onto her face, perhaps? Slit her nose open with a knife? Carve her up like those roasts she used to cook on a Sunday.

The more I stare the more I realize something is wrong with this picture. Don't get me wrong, it's my Mum—I'd recognize her anywhere. Except… except she doesn't seem to have aged since I last saw her. As she pushes herself up, the shackles preventing her from going far, I see her face clearly for the first time. It's the same as it was when I was ten, maybe even younger. No lines like I noticed the last time I went to see her a few years back (I just couldn't stand that idiot she lived with).

"Mum?" I say it louder, hopefully loud enough to bring her back to the here and now. She looks at me blankly; no recognition. "Mum, it's me. It's Chris." She just gazes at me.

"A… Alice, is that you?" Patty's voice startles me, possibly because I've never heard it so frightened and excited at the same time—not even when she was fearing for her own life. Alice? That's my mother's name. Alice Warwick (nee Henderson). But how could… Patty must know her, live in the same area, on the same street?

No.

As I look from one face to the other, it's so obvious now I

could cry. The same nose, the same mouth. How many of us ever study our parents' faces, *really* study them? If we did we might well see mirrors of ourselves reflected there. I was always told I had my Dad's chin, Mum's eyes. But she in turn had inherited features from *her* mother.

"My husband passed away many years ago, but there's my daughter, and my little grandson, though he's probably too young to remember his old Gran."

Patty... Patricia... Patricia Henderson. A woman I barely knew, who died when I was only small. I'd seen a few photos growing up, of course, but... Christ Almighty!

"Mum," says 'Alice', parroting my words. "What are you doing here? Where am I?" A look of complete and utter shock passes across her face. "You're... You're dead. You died when I was... Oh my God. That's it, isn't it? I'm dead, too! And I'm in—" My Mum looks down at the manacles on her wrists and ankles, at the bars surrounding her.

I know exactly what she's thinking: Jane said it once. This *is* Hell. And we're all being punished for something.

Only I don't believe in Heaven, Hell or anything else. I know what I believe in and it isn't that. "Mum, you have to calm down."

"Who are you?"

"It's me. Your son, Christopher."

Patty has figured it out as well by now. "Little Chris?"

I nod. "I don't know exactly what's going on, but I'm going to get you out. Get us all out."

"They've done such terrible things to people," Patty tells her daughter.

"I still don't understand."

We aren't allowed any more time to figure things out, because once again the door opens and the robed men march in. Three this time. They might be coming to take Dixon away, or do something to Patty... Gran... but I don't want to find out which. Already the cameras are appearing, descending to film events.

"Stay away from them!" I shout. "I'm not kidding."

They ignore me. One points to Dixon, then turns in the direction of Patty's cage. The final one stands between me and my Mum.

It all happens in a flash, but like all moments of intensity, it also slows right down to a crawl. Out of the corner of my eye I see Dixon rise; he's only been pretending to be dead. Through the bars he grabs hold of the closest guard and reaches into his cloak. There's a sudden bang as Dixon shoots the guy; too late the chains holding the old man begin to tighten.

Another shot, and the monk nearest to me catches a bullet in the arm. He staggers close enough to my cage that I can drag him into the bars, knocking him out cold. Quickly, before my own chains yank me back, I fumble inside his robes and pull out the keys they always use. My shackles are beginning to pull tight, so I see to them first—both feet. Then one hand. I only have time for the one, before I have to make a start on the cage lock. I'm being dragged backwards by one arm. I stretch to try and turn the key a final time.

A third shot, and Dixon is dead—really dead, this time. The only monk left has seen to that. I'm still struggling with the key, but manage to turn it, unlocking the cage. The door flies open.

Is it my imagination, or are the other two cages growing smaller? Compressing? Gran and Mum hold up their hands as the bars shrink. I look up and the same is true of my own cage. They're trying to crush us.

Gran is the first to feel the full force of it, as the bars come down on her head. She shrieks as the metal grinds up her old bones, the cracks like… footsteps on brittle twigs. Mum's faring about the same, her body surrendering to the cage that is mashing her body.

I have one last lock to undo, holding my left wrist.

Don't drop it, don't drop it. You can still save them.

But I know, even as I undo the clasp, jumping out of my cage just as it collapses in on itself, it's already too late for my Gran and my Mum. They've become so much blood, bone and metal: a fusion of human and cage.

The monk nearest my Gran turns the gun he used to kill Dixon on me. Gritting my teeth, I run at him, hitting him squarely in the stomach with my head and winding him before he can get off a shot. "You bastard. You fucking bastard! You killed them!" If I'd been thinking rationally, I'd have realized that Gran—at least—had been dead long before she turned up here as 'Patty'.

I rip off his hood, pulling the material back to reveal a bald-headed face. The strange thing is the monk's blindfolded, just as I had been when I was first brought here. Someone has drilled a hole in the centre of his forehead.

The sight of this only gives me pause for a moment, before I smash that face in. Pummeling it into the floor with my fist, the anger welling up inside me.

When there's hardly anything left of the head, I stop, breathing hard. I'm aware of something hovering over me, several somethings in fact: the cameras.

I grab the pistol from the dead monk and point it at one of them.

Before I can pull the trigger, the door to the right of me opens.

I look from the spherical camera, to my escape route. What's this, some kind of reward? The piece of cheese at the end of the maze?

Don't know, don't care. Trying to keep my eyes fixed ahead of me, and off my mangled relatives, I head out through the door—to freedom!

INTERLUDE:
THREE DAYS AGO

I evaded them for about a day and a half, but only because I knew that area so well.

In the end, there was nowhere left to hide. Where *can* you hide from something that is all around you, that can see you even though you can't see them? They directed the men to me, just as they'd sent Kim to the shack.

I was in the jungle where giant snakes and lions lived, and down by the water there were man-eating crocodiles.

There were quite a few of them, probably trained in tracking, ex-military—I caught a glimpse of a pair of boots in the under-growth at one point, before waiting for whoever it was to go by. These weren't any police I was familiar with; no doctors either. They'd told Kim what she wanted to hear, just like those adverts did to the poor unfortunates who bought the stuff they peddled.

They wanted to find me, and silence me.

Because if the secret ever got out, it would be the end of eve-rything. Humanity would never be the same again.

They watch and wait, they watch and wait… It went through my head over and over, trains on a track. It's what I'd written on the pages Kim had read, apparently, or was it just what we were allowed to see?

Piloting my spaceship into the deeper reaches of the Galaxy, battling one-eyed aliens with veiny skins.

Maybe things change when you try to set them down: hints were one thing, in books, on TV in movies. But the hard truth—facts excavating how far this all goes back—that was another.

Oblivious as we were, we'd created ways of letting the knowl-edge creep out into the world, whether it was through cave paint-ings, ancient mythology or even posters (and then they'd tam-pered with the results). It was a chicken and egg situation: with-out them, there would have been no human evolution, and with-out human evolution would they be able to survive?

Symbiosis? Hardly. How could any one-sided relationship be called that? We were subordinates. Blind and obedient, given the illusion of freewill when all the time we were being herded to-wards our own doom.

"Ah, but if you push us too far, if we destroy ourselves, what will you do then—eh?" Without thinking, I had asked the question out loud. And that was my final mistake.

Something rustled nearby; they'd heard me and were on my trail. I ran, just as I had that day when I was young. I misplaced my footing and suddenly I was falling, head over heels, down an incline. Something thudded into my side, silent and deadly. It might have been a branch; more likely it was a dart from a tranquilizer gun.

I was already beginning to feel its effects, growing woozy as I reached the bottom. My vision was blurring, I was passing out.

They'd hunted me like the animal I was (to them, or more accurately their superiors). When I woke, who knew where I would be.

Or if I would remember any of this until it was too late.

Seven

I make my way down a darkened corridor, pistol in my hand.

One of the cameras is following me over my shoulder. I can sense it there, just far enough behind to stay out of my way, but near enough to film my escape.

There are other doors down the corridor. I stop to kick the first one in, thinking maybe I can save some prisoners. Inside, there are more Pain Cages, those round hanging jails, each containing a body, a human being.

Seven in here. I don't recognize any of the faces... No, wait, that's not true. Malone is here. I think I used to work for him at one point. Yeah, that's right. Malone. I once told him where to get off for some reason.

"Christopher, help me," he pleads, sticking his hand through the bars. "They're trying to kill us all."

"I know," I tell him. "Hold on."

"Chris! Chris! Please..." The voice comes from behind me, muffled and odd, from another room opposite. That's one I do know; very well. "Dad?"

I rush out, back into the corridor, ignoring the cries from Malone. I kick open the other door, only to see my father in one of the pain cages. His head is stuck in a see-through glass case. Brown liquid is pouring in from above, fast, and he is only just keeping his head above its level.

"Always... always said the drink would... would get me," he spits.

I take aim with the gun, but I'm not a sure enough shot; I could very easily hit my Dad. I rush to the cage, shaking it, wishing I'd kept the keys that had freed me—though there was nothing to say they'd fit the locks in here.

The liquid covers his mouth and nose. My Dad smiles, then panics, begins to jerk. I'm watching a dead man drown right before my eyes.

"No, no!" I close my eyes. "You're *making* me see this. You've still got me whacked up on drugs or something. I know now. I understand."

"You understand nothing," says a woman's voice from behind me. I turn, seeing Kim in another one of the cages. She's naked, but also shackled, chained at the waist as well as the hands and feet.

"No... Not you, as well," I moan.

A huge spike is rising from the bottom of the cage, up and up. "Mmmm... Oh yes," she says, licking her lips. Then she impales herself on the spike, leaping back gladly onto it. I wince as she jumps up and down on the sharp skewer, blood gushing from between her legs. "Take me... Take me beyond my limits... Harder... Oh God, harder... Hurt me... hurt me!" One last impalement and the spike comes up and out of her mouth, accompanied by a fountain of redness.

"Kim! No..." She hangs lifeless on the spike, arms limp as the chains loosen. There are more cameras in the room, lenses focused on my Dad and Kim. "Are you getting all of this, you sick motherfuckers!"

Unsurprisingly, there is no answer.

I dash back out, feeling like I'm going to throw up. What the fuck is going on? It sounds insane, but my mind offers yet another explanation: maybe whoever was responsible for all this could just pluck people out of time—living or dead—for their own personal amusement? Is that it? Is that the explanation?

Kicking in door after door, I see people in the throes of agony, being tortured, being killed in so many different ways they all blur into one eventually. I can't help any of them.

I pelt down the corridor, figuring that if I can get to the outside world I might just be able to bring back help—but the corridor stretches away from me, *Vertigo*-style. The walls, floor and tunnel ahead are melting away. To be replaced by…

A landscape. A panoramic view of pain.

Pain cages: hundreds, thousands, possibly millions of them. Too many to count. The screams and wails are deafening; a torture in itself.

I drop the pistol—it falls away into nothingness—and clasp my hands to my ears. As I blink, focusing on each pain cage in turn, I see faces that I know (like my Uncle and Kim's parents), many that I don't, but I also see objects: toys I used to play with as a child; the ghost story book I was given as a prize at school for writing essays in class; the first jacket I ever bought for myself, a leather one I thought looked so cool; my old computer; sweet and sour chicken, my favorite meal… There were places as well, locations: behind the bike sheds where I first touched a girl's breast; the local cinema that had been replaced by a multiplex; the call centre; the flat where Kim and I shared so many moments.

All of these are inside pain cages of their own, being torn apart, destroyed in various ways. It is now, and only now, that I truly get what's happening.

The cages form a ring, and in the centre of this is an open space—like a gladiatorial arena. I take away my hands, to find that a silence had descended more deafening than any screams. Several of the round cameras zip past me and into the arena, and I follow their trail with my eyes: down to a table surrounded by men.

A rhythmic beeping starts up, then continues. *Bleep-Bleep-Bleep.* The sound of a heartbeat. I see now that it's coming from a monitor on the side. At first I assume the men are dressed in robes like the monks, but then I see my error. Their surgical gowns swish when they walk, in much the same way.

Their mouths are covered by masks, but then so are their eyes. Again, blindfolded, the round headpieces that they wear, the circular mirror reflectors, are the only eyes they appear to have.

They shouldn't even be operating, but they are. They're cutting into a man's skull, taking chunks of it away and... exposing the brain.

"Now we have to excise the damaged tissue. Good God, how many brain cells has it affected?"

Cells... Brain cells. Pain cells... Pain cages... The link becomes clear, even though I'm finding it harder and harder to concentrate. For one thing I only have to look at the cages themselves, which are becoming more like liquid, the surrounding area red and meaty, like an organic city I once saw.

"Look at the size of that tumor. If only we'd got to it before."

Steps have appeared leading downwards, and I descend to observe the operation. The doctors murmur to one another, conferring. The circular cameras—the globes—are capturing each second of it. As infected brain tissue, infected memories, are cut away. People's faces, those familiar and those only glimpsed for a second... A writer's imagination providing the character backgrounds and personalities of those it couldn't possibly know. An obnoxious estate agent who once showed me round a house, a fitness instructor bumped into just the once during a brief visit to the gym, a man I saw one time preaching religion on the streets... These and many more besides.

And I recognize the face of the person on the table—how could I not?

The man lying there has his father's chin, his mother's eyes.

63

I want to tell them to stop, but I know they won't hear me.
Then I'm asleep again.
But one day… Yes, one day I will wake.

Epilogue

Am I awake or still asleep?

It's hard to tell the difference anymore. I'm in a cage… no, a cell. It's white, the walls are soft, spongy. I'm shackled by my hands and my feet. They tell me I'm dangerous, the doctors: a danger to myself and to others. I hurt some people once upon a time, then again in here… though I don't remember any of it.

I'm not sure who the woman is who comes to visit me every so often. She says her name is Kim, but I don't remember her. I remember the very first time she came, though, the conversation she had with Dr. Banberry, who was in charge of my case back then. I lay in bed recuperating, the air tickling my bald scalp, my stitches itching.

"Can he hear what we're saying?" she asked him.

"We're not sure. Possibly. It's a side effect of the operation, I'm afraid. He may stay like this forever, or… The damage the tumor did was quite severe, so it's best not to get your hopes up. It definitely affected the TPRV1 receptors in the brain. Oh, I'm sorry, the transient receptor potential vanilloid subtype. Pain receptors in layman's terms. But these have also recently been linked in studies to memory and learning. If he does come out of this state, then it's likely he won't remember much."

"And that was also the cause of his… delusions? The tumor?"

Banberry looked at her seriously. "Undoubtedly, that mixed with the drugs and drink at the time of his disappearance. We call it altered perception. A warped view of reality that feels completely real to the person suffering its effects. Other symptoms include seeing things that aren't really there, memory lapses."

"Like when he rang me and couldn't remember doing it."

"Exactly."

No, no. I didn't have a phone. I didn't... My mind conjured up the words, but I had no idea what they meant. That particular recollection was gone.

There were tears in the woman's eyes, as she looked from me to Banberry. "How did this happen? I don't understand."

"Could have been something that happened a few years ago, could have been a knock on the head when he was a kid waiting for a trigger. Who knows?"

A monster... running from a monster. Dixon! Who's Dixon? No, no... I banged my head after *I saw what he had written; didn't I? What are you talking about? Who. The Fuck. Is Dixon?*

"There's no point speculating about it, no point beating yourself up."

"But I saw he was acting strangely, obsessive, not like the old Christopher. I should have done something then. Instead I just left him."

"You weren't to know." Banberry comforted her by patting her arm; all he could muster.

When the woman called Kim looked at me again, I felt a trickle of dribble running from the corner of my mouth.

It's good of her to keep coming back, I suppose. To keep talking to me like I'm normal. But I know I'm not. When I'm asleep... or awake? Dreaming, yes, dreaming... I sometimes imagine that this was done to me on purpose. That I found out something so terrifying I had to be silenced.

Like the fact that there's something out there, making human beings inflict pain on each other because it feeds off it. Yes, that's right. That's... I can only hold onto the notion for a short time and then it drifts away from me.

But I *do* remember the cages. I saw them a long time ago.

They had something to do with the pain; some kind of connection I can't grasp now no matter how hard I try.

I think once I had a story to tell about them. About how

we're all inside these cages, in one form or another, but don't really know it. About things with one eyes that watch and wait.

What they're waiting for, I have no idea—I don't think I'll ever find out.

All I know is that they really do understand the nature of pain, *true* pain.

Just as I, myself, once did.

* * *

HALFLIFE

As Neil sat staring at the entrance, nursing his pint of bitter, he thought about the past.

How could he not, today of all days? His eyes flitted from the doorway of the *Royal Oak* pub, to the dirty brown liquid in the glass below, to the handful of other patrons this Friday evening. There weren't many: a sweaty looking man with a skin complaint, red blotches splattering his cheeks and nose; a sad-looking couple in their 50s who weren't speaking to each other; a twenty-something in a hoodie playing the fruit machine, obviously biding his time before meeting up with mates or heading out on the town later.

It's what *he* would have been doing fifteen years ago, and even before that. Neil remembered those nights, getting ready to go on the prowl, hitting the nightclubs in the wilder parts of the city with the pack. Picking up the ladies then doing all sorts with them, usually in the alleyways behind the clubs...

He'd always promised himself those days would carry on forever, that he wouldn't get old—and at forty-three (alright, almost forty-four), was he really that ancient? Enough to be the oldest swinger in town if he went there now on a Friday night. He'd stand out like a sore thumb against the teens and the tweens, the loud techno beats more likely to give him a headache nowadays than get his adrenalin pumping.

The fact that he was here, in a pub outside of town itself, for a gathering that would only make him feel even more depressed about the turns his life had taken, wasn't helping. His focus shifted from the booze to his belly: not massive by any means, but not a patch on the flat washboard stomach he'd had back then. He kept telling himself that he could get back into shape anytime he wanted, but never did. Didn't really care or want to, if the truth be known.

What the hell was wrong with him? When did all this apathy begin?

Might've been when you settled down and embraced the life of a stay-at-home miserable bastard, he said to himself and couldn't help a tired laugh. That had been his parents' existence: safe, comfortable, not taking any risks—*ever*. Stick-in-the-muds that he couldn't wait to get away from when he was younger, always telling himself he wouldn't turn out like them; wouldn't just piss his life away sitting in front of the TV. He'd wanted to get out there, experience life at the sharp end—and he'd done just that… for a while. But it seems he had more in common with them than he realized, even though he'd later discovered that he was in fact adopted. Made sense when you thought about it, given his… affliction (curse, whatever you wanted to call it). Neither his mum nor dad even hinted at anything like that, would've died rather than let themselves be taken over by their baser desires. Which meant that he'd got this from his genes, from one or both of his *real* parents. Neil sometimes thought about tracking them down, but again, he just couldn't be bothered. They probably wouldn't want to see him anyway, the runt of whatever foul litter they'd created. They wouldn't have given him up in the first place if they'd thought anything of him.

The door opened and he looked up sharply, sniffing the air. His reflexes were still pretty good, and he knew even before the person walked in through the door it wasn't anybody he was expecting. Just an old man in a raincoat who stank of piss, looking for company on another lonely evening.

Neil's thoughts turned again to the past, and its impact on the present.

He wondered, once more, what the others would be like when he saw them again. His old mates that he'd hooked up with at university, a gang that had found each other and then been practically inseparable for so long. Up until he hit thirty, they'd all be going out together on the lash every few weeks... when the time was right. He'd enjoyed those adventures so much, from his late teens until—

Right, you enjoyed those times so much that you turned your back on them. Turned your back on your best *friends.*

That wasn't true; he hadn't turned his back on anyone. He'd just changed. They all had. For one thing Jack was starting to make headway with his band 'Brutal', who one reviewer described as 'the rock equivalent of being given a blow-job backstage at a lingerie fashion shoot'. Before too long he was talking about albums and tours, then all of a sudden he was gone. Adrian had worked his way up from serving in a burger bar to being the manager, moving to where the head office was, while model-look-a-like Luke's repping took him further and further afield, with no one real place he could call his home anymore. As for Owen and Ryan, they'd eventually got their act together enough to get off the dole (helped by the fact that the benefits system was undergoing an overhaul and anyone who didn't at least attempt to find work had their money cut). Owen had actually joined the police force, if you could believe it; was doing pretty well by all accounts, but had moved several times with his profession. Ryan had attempted to hold down one job after another, from builder's apprentice—in spite of his age—to night watchman (that was a good one). Last Neil heard, he was doing manual labor on a farm—better lock up those chickens—but he was the only one of the group who'd remained relatively local (well, within 50 miles, anyway—but it was surprising how far that distance was when you really didn't *want* to see someone). The most local apart from Neil, that was, who hadn't moved at all—except to another, quieter, part of town. Out of his flat and into somewhere bigger. With:

Julie.

She'd come along even before Jack went off with the band, though, hadn't she? The more he thought about it, the more Neil wondered whether he had been the catalyst for them *all* breaking up and going their separate ways. He hadn't been their ring leader by any means—had there even been such a thing?—but maybe he'd been the glue that bound them all together. He hadn't thought of himself as such, but the guys *had* sort of gravitated towards him at uni, been drawn into his orbit one by one. Neil had always thought of Luke, or perhaps Jack, as the dominant force in their rag-tag bunch, but once he'd taken himself out of the equation things *had* fallen apart pretty quickly. And he'd taken himself out of the equation because of:

Julie.

It all came back to her, didn't it? If he hadn't met her, then maybe—

Neil shook his head and took another sip of his bitter. He loved Julie (loved as in past tense? or present?). She hadn't been like the rest; not one of the women he and his mates targeted on their nights out, Luke usually getting to the most attractive ones first, although Neil hadn't done so badly in his time. This had been different. For one thing, he'd met her outside of the group—when he was doing a grocery shop, in fact. He'd been wandering about in the supermarket with his basket, head up his arse, thinking about the approaching fun that coming Friday (back then it had been the highlight of his month). He'd turned the corner and almost knocked her over. As it was he'd knocked the basket out of her hands.

"Why don't you watch where you're going?" she'd said.

"I'm really sorry," he'd replied, stooping to pick up her microwave meals for one, tins of soup and assorted fruit and vegetables. But he couldn't take his eyes off her face. Even in all the times he'd been out with the lads, he'd never seen anyone as pretty as her: short, strawberry-blonde hair, cropped so that it framed her face then hung in bangs just under her chin; the most piercing green eyes, like sapphires shining out of a mine; and those lips, the fullest you could ever imagine. She didn't need any lipstick, any make-up, and it was a good job too because she hadn't bothered for this trip to the store. Nor had she dressed up: she was just wearing jeans and a jumper, with a short denim jacket—well, she hadn't been expecting to bump into the soon-to-be love of her life.

However, the overall effect of her appearance on Neil had been nothing short of revelatory.

(Later, when the other members of the circle had seen her, they'd said she was nothing special—that he was deluding himself. Neil knew different, knew that they were only jealous. That he had something as magnificent as Julie and they didn't. Later, much later, he began to see what they meant...)

"I should think *so*," she said, taking the basket from him. Their fingers had touched, and she'd felt the spark. Neil had made sure of that. It was one of the perks of being who he was—*what* he was. He'd looked into those green eyes, in a bid to entrance her as much as she'd entranced him. And... there it was. Her heart was beating just a little quicker, not a consequence of banging into him, almost falling, but something else. The effect he was purposefully having on her. Provoking feelings in her that he knew were already bubbling away beneath the surface... She'd been alone long enough, he felt it—the consequence of being hurt by a man in the past. Time to change all that, time she had someone. Someone like Neil. "Listen," she said, suddenly smiling, her breathing fast and shallow, "I know it sounds crazy but... do you want to get out of here. Maybe go somewhere?"

He nodded. "I thought you'd never ask."

In those early days when they looked back and chatted about the day they'd met, Julie would mention how they'd just clicked, how something had told her it was the right thing to do: to go with him there and then, back to his flat. "I just couldn't help myself," she'd say, giggling. Little realizing that she'd had a 'push'. That he'd done the same kind of number on her he had to all those others, the same thing Luke and the rest had pulled to get those girls in those nightclubs outside into the alleys. No—he told himself, and would *keep* telling himself—it was what Julie had wanted. It hadn't been the same.

Ten minutes later, the shopping was forgotten about and they were back at his place, all over each other. It was animalistic, that first time—and many times after that. They were tearing each other's clothes off, raking each other's skin; biting, sucking, rutting on his bed. They'd done it five times that evening, Neil barely pausing for breath between sessions (he'd excelled himself, even he had to admit—spurred on by Julie's beauty, the magnificence of her body... it had been a long time since he'd thought of it like that... the scent of her). Afterwards, they'd lain on the bed, puffing, sweaty and exhausted. And Neil had held her, cradling her in his arms—thankful that it was only close to that time of the month rather than into it. Not hers, but his.

They both had work the next day, Julie explaining that she was a primary school teacher, Neil revealing he was a librarian, but it had been hard parting. She wanted to see him again that weekend, but he reluctantly had to confess he had plans. "I always see my old uni mates round about now," he explained, badly. "They'd be upset if I cried off."

Julie's face had fallen. "Fine. If you don't want to see me, just say so."

Neil had cupped that face in his hand, then said: "I'm not like him."

Julie frowned. "Who?"

He realized he'd said too much, given away what he'd sensed about her—just one of those extra abilities that came with the territory (though far stronger when it was almost that 'special time'). "Erm, whoever it was that hurt you," he told her. "I won't ever do that." It seemed a strange thing to say to someone you'd left angry red scratches all over the previous night, but he knew what he meant. Thankfully, so did Julie.

"No, I don't believe you would, Neil." They'd agreed to meet up the following Monday, and those three days were probably the worst he'd ever spent. The guys knew there was something wrong, but hadn't been able to put their finger on it; he'd masked Julie's scent pretty well and none of them had ever been able to read him. It had just been the way he'd hung back as the others checked out what was on offer in places like *Monty's* and *The Green Room*—"Quite a bit of talent out there," Adrian had said, that cheeky grin plastered on his face. He'd nudged Neil, but got no response. "What's the fuck's the matter with you?"

"Nothing," Neil lied.

And he'd taken part, reluctantly, in the proceedings—which on the Saturday night had included luring a quartet of girls outside so they could have their way with them. Neil remembered it well, even after he *changed*. It wasn't like the movies, wasn't what people thought. Yes, it was the full moon that weekend, but that didn't mean you instantly turned. It was brought on by what they were doing out there with those girls, brought on by the taste of blood and flesh. If you didn't do it voluntarily, then that was a different matter—the beast inside would usually break out at some point, take over. It was better to be in control, to satisfy the hunger like this than drive yourself into a rampage. Besides, it was fun. Or at least it had been, before:

Julie.

Neil had been the last one to transform in that alleyway. All he could see when Luke, Owen, Ryan, Jack and Aide were taking their turns with the girls was Julie's face. Julie's face instead of the red-head that Ryan was tearing into, ripping a piece out of her neck, while Jack took chunks out of her thigh; Julie's face instead of the young blonde girl being held with arms outstretched, Adrian and Owen sinking their teeth into one limb each; Julie's face instead of the tanned brunette with the short skirt that Luke was slavering over, tongue descending, forcing her legs apart and then claiming a lump of her most sensitive parts, which he swallowed greedily. As busy as they were, they all took a moment to glance back at him, wondering why he wasn't joining them in this feast. Swallowing, Neil brought on the wolf—his eyes taking on that terrifying yellow and red cast, hairs sprouting as his jaw elongated, slipping out of his clothes momentarily so they didn't get covered in blood.

He'd joined them, but again hung back—only lapping at the pools of scarlet liquid, which appeared black in the moonlight, giving it the sheen of motor oil. The taste of it should have sent him wild; but it didn't, not tonight. Once he'd longed for girls like these to ravage, to devour, but now he felt disgusted. *Disgusting.*

When it was all over, and the clean-up done—including morphing back into human form—the group took him to one side. "Okay," said Luke, lighting up a cigarette (he always smoked after feeding), "give."

"Yeah," said Jack, scratching his beard, the tattoos on his hand and lower arm clearly visible, "what's the problem, Neilly-boy? Not getting past it, are you?" He laughed and Neil remembered that sound, because it had been meant to be ironic back then. These days it certainly had more resonance.

"Nothing... nothing's wrong," he'd said again and they could at least sense that something was. He wasn't a good enough actor to fool them for long. Nevertheless, they hadn't got it out of him that night, nor the next. In fact, it only came to light when Owen and Ryan had spotted him out on a date with Julie a couple of weeks later, coming out of the cinema holding hands.

That had led to what Adrian had called an 'intervention'. They'd all been waiting for him one night after work, bundled him into the back of Jack's van, and questioned him, tried to fathom out exactly what he was playing at.

"I'm not playing at *anything*," he'd told them. "I think... I think she's the one."

"The one what?" asked Aide.

"There aren't any 'ones'," Jack spat. "Only the next meal."

Ryan looked at him seriously then. "You do know you can't have a normal life with this woman, don't you? How can you?"

Neil had shrugged. He hadn't really thought that far ahead, to be honest. But he didn't want to hear it from them, didn't want to admit it right there and then (he was ready to admit it now, though, all these years later... *oh yes*).

"Why don't you do yourself a favor and leave her to us, we'll take care of the problem," Ryan had told him, pushing his greasy hair back out of his eyes. "We'll make it quick, this full moon coming. You can watch if you like. Might even fancy her more when we've... made a few improvements." He'd raked the air with his nails and that had been it. Neil leapt forward, grabbing him and slamming him against the wall of the van. It had taken Luke, Jack *and* Adrian to pull him off.

"You touch her," he'd snarled. "Any of you fucking so much as look at her..." He hadn't finished that sentence; hadn't needed to.

They'd let him go, all looking at each other like they'd just been slapped in the face. Then seeing the look in his eye, and knowing he meant business. That had been the moment, the pivotal moment—and he'd felt dreadful afterwards. The lads had dropped him off with promises that they'd talk about this some other time, but gradually—and inevitably—he'd lost contact with them. He certainly hadn't joined them on their monthly nights out anymore. Couldn't, after what had happened on the last occasion. Neil began spending more and more time with Julie, until they were almost inseparable. It wasn't as hard as he thought it might be, controlling those urges—even on the three nights when they were at their height. Neil found that if he fed privately just before the evening, stealing what he needed from the local abattoir, it was easier to dull the ache he felt by not running with the pack. If it got too much for him, when he thought he might hurt Julie inadvertently, he'd make up some excuse to be away for a couple of nights—usually work related. She bought it, after all they spent the rest of the month together, and they were happy.

When his friends drifted off in their own directions, he'd clung more and more to Julie. So much so that it seemed like the logical thing for them to get married. They were a partnership now, the two of them against the world. It would mean giving up his bachelor pad, mean them pooling their resources and putting down a deposit on a house in the 'burbs, but it would be worth it to be so close. Julie, thankfully, didn't have many relatives or friends. Neil had even less, and had no intentions of inviting his fake parents to the small affair. They spent the money they'd saved on a nice honeymoon instead, one of the best periods of Neil's life.

It was after that things started to fall apart. Julie began talking about a family and, though he hadn't thought about it before, Neil began to warm to the idea. Looking back, he couldn't believe what he'd been thinking. If he'd inherited his traits from his real parents—or one of them—then wouldn't he run the risk of passing this on to his son or daughter? In the end it turned out not to be an issue, because after trying for a while they were both tested and it was found that the chances of Julie ever conceiving were slim to negligible; some kind of problem with her ovulation. Again, that time of the month—just hers this time.

Whether she felt like she'd failed, Neil wasn't sure, or that he'd look elsewhere for the mother of his children (he wouldn't) but that's when things began to grow distant between them. And they even ended up having a row one night when she mentioned the possibility of adopting. Neil told her why he was against it, but she just hadn't been able to understand.

"I don't see what the one has to do with the other. You had a decent upbringing because of being adopted, didn't you?"

Neil couldn't deny it, his parents had done a good job of looking after him. It was just that it had all been a lie, and he'd come from somewhere else. Was some*thing* else, but Neil wasn't ready to share that particular fact with Julie, even then. She'd ended up shouting, he'd shouted back—the kind of passion they'd used to experience in the bedroom. Then he'd stormed out, going to get drunk in the *Oak*, which was rapidly becoming his bolt-hole away from everything. It was peaceful at least, and nobody really disturbed him.

When he returned that night, more than a little worse for wear, she'd said nothing—just sat there on the couch with her arms folded, watching some old black and white film, but not really taking it in. They barely exchanged a word, even as they got ready for bed, and then into the next day. Then the day after that...

It became the norm that they'd hardly talk, the lack of communication turning into a comfortable habit. It seemed a better alternative to the bickering that would flare up over nothing. They'd work, come home, watch television then go to bed, usually curled up on their own side—the divide between them more than just distance. Neil knew that she still loved him, and he loved her. But something had broken fundamentally and he didn't know how to fix it.

It probably wasn't a coincidence that at the same time this was happening, Neil began to feel his baser urges increasing. Sometimes it was all he could do to keep from transforming right there and then of an evening, if it was full moon. The bloody raw meat he managed to get his hands on was no longer cutting it for him, and he began to think more and more about the past, about his time with the other members of the gang. That just made things worse. Sometimes, to his shame, he'd think about those girls and *give* them Julie's face, but it would actually make him more stimulated. Neil had taken to retreating to a safe place during those three nights every month, locking himself up in the basement of the library. There was a barred cubby hole meant for keeping the rarest books safe from burglars, but it also served to keep Neil *in*. It was no way to live, he realized that, but wasn't sure what he could do about the situation. Julie accepted whatever excuse he gave, usually without question—but the odd sideways look and bite of the lip told him that she thought he was seeing another woman. She never questioned him about it openly.

Probably frightened of the answer.

Those days were gone, though. The days when Neil would 'see' lots of women. They were gone and he'd never be able to get them back. For one thing, his mates were God knows where.

Which was why it had been such a surprise when he got Owen's email at the library. He'd read it with his mouth open, especially when it said he was getting everyone back together again—and they were going to meet in their old stomping ground. His town. Neil had been excited and nervous at the same time. He'd been tempted to answer immediately, but held off for half a day because he didn't want to appear desperate. Then he'd said it'd be great to catch up, and he'd suggested the *Oak* as a meeting place, hoping it wouldn't be too tame. No, it wasn't— but Owen wanted them all to get together as soon as possible. Neil had told Julie the truth for a change, that he was hooking up with the old buddies he'd had when she came along (and had chosen her over). She'd looked at him and shrugged, but then enquired as to whether there would be any women present. Neil had shrugged back—there might be, in the pub itself. It was a free country. She'd told him to be back early and he'd nodded, sighing.

So now he was here, waiting. Looking up every time he heard the door go, every time he heard a noise. Neil couldn't believe they were all going to be back together again, the first time in so long. Maybe now he could get a few things off his chest, including the fact he was sorry for the way he'd acted. The way he'd ruined everything—and wished that they could get it back, though he knew that wasn't possible.

Just age talking, age and regret. You reap what you sow, Neil. Reap what you—

Suddenly they were here, or at least one of them was. The door swung inwards to reveal Luke. He'd got older, but still had his good looks—the ones that would've helped him sell vodka to the Russians if he had a mind to—but he *had* aged. He was becoming what some women might call distinguished-looking. Neil rose, not sure what to do or say, but luckily Luke did it for him, walking over and giving him a big hug.

"It's good to see you, man," said his friend, clapping him on the shoulder. "You haven't changed a bit." Then Neil caught him looking down at the beer belly. "Well, maybe just a little." By way of contrast, Luke had kept himself in good shape. But then he'd always boasted one of those metabolisms that was so fast food and drink passed through him almost without being digested. (He'd also quit smoking; Neil could smell it.)

Neil couldn't help smiling, in spite of the ribbing. He was very glad to see his friend again and offered to buy him a drink. Luke waved him down. "I'll sort it out. And what about you, what's that you're drinking? Bitter? What happened to the lager freak we all knew and loved? All right, bitter it is then."

Neil thought about it, then shook his head. "I'll just have a diet coke."

"Oh come on," said Luke. "I was only joking. You'll have something stronger, surely?"

"I'll wait till the others arrive," he told him. "Look, now you're here, any idea what brought all this on? I mean, don't get me wrong, it's great to see you after…" Neil paused, then aborted the sentence completely. "But why now?"

"I'm as puzzled as you are," admitted Luke, "Owen didn't say very much to me at all." He went over to the bar, and by the time he'd bought the round—Neil's coke and a Bacardi for himself— Owen had turned up.

There was an air about him Neil hadn't seen before, one of authority that his years in the force had obviously granted him. Unlike Luke, Owen *wasn't* smiling. He looked more serious than Neil had ever seen him, though admittedly he was used to the carefree dole layabout rather than the copper. Owen might as well have had his uniform on, the way his pressed suit hung off him; black, with white shirt and a matching black tie. Neil noted one or two of the locals checking him out and wondering whether they should hang around. The hoodie didn't even have to think about it and was out the door before you could say 'ello, ello, ello'. It seemed that some normals also had heightened senses when it came to things like that.

"Luke," he said, nodding to the rep as he took his place at the pub table. Then he acknowledged Neil.

"Owen," said Neil, raising his coke. "Nice to see you again."

"You too," he said finally. "I wish it were under better circumstances."

Neil frowned, still looking to Luke for an explanation but not getting nothing.

Owen caught the glance. "I thought you might have heard… at least about Jack?"

Now Neil was really confused. "What about him?"

"He's dead," said Owen matter of factly, but his eyes betrayed the pain of those words.

Luke leaned forward on his chair and Neil almost spilled his drink. "What? How?"

Owen looked down. "Week before last, in a hotel room in Edinburgh. He was on tour with his band, one of the roadies found him. He'd OD'ed on drugs." This wasn't too much of a shock, as Jack had always been fond of stronger vices than drink. If something was being passed around in a club, he'd usually be the one trying it. It also fitted with the kind of lifestyle he was used to these days, the gigs, the fans. Sex and drugs would be no stranger to Jack, not to mention the other… activities he was used to. But the fact he was dead? Jack was the strongest of them, always had been. "Thought there might have been more coverage of it by the media, but I guess they saw it as just another mid-list rocker paying the price for his own overindulgence."

"I… I just can't believe it," said Luke.

"Me either." Neil was still in a state of shock, gripping his glass so tightly he was in danger of shattering it.

"There's more," said Owen looking up again, eyebrows still stooping. He hadn't even asked for, or bought, a drink yet. They waited for him to continue, which he did eventually. "Adrian…"

He couldn't get the words out, but both Luke and Neil knew what was coming next wasn't good. "Middle of last week, Adrian... Well, the police in his area are calling it a mugging that went sour—for Adrian *really* sour. He was stabbed."

"Christ," breathed out Luke. Neil knew how he felt: first Jack, now Adrian?

"Is he...?" Neil began.

Owen nodded. "He was on his way back to his car after work. They got him in the car park, three times in the gut. His case and his wallet were missing when he was found."

"Hold on!" said Neil, then lowered his voice. "We're... I mean people like us, we're not that easy to... you know... kill, are we?" Maybe he was hoping Owen had got it wrong somehow, that neither Jack nor Adrian were gone. They couldn't be, there was so much he wanted—*needed*—to say to them.

"We are not," replied Owen. "Which is why when I heard about them I did a little digging. I called in a few favors to get the reports on both Jack and Adrian, and do you know what I found?"

Luke and Neil shook their heads.

"Someone went to a lot of trouble to make these look like random events, but they weren't. It didn't make any difference to the investigation, so it was overlooked—but both Jack and Adrian's deaths were connected."

"What are you talking about?" asked Luke.

"I'm talking about silver." He let that particular bombshell sink in before continuing. "It was found in Jack's system, trace particles of it that I think were probably in his drugs. And it was found in Adrian's stab wounds. Whoever it was killed him used a silver knife."

Neil shook his head again, this time in disbelief. "A coincidence, surely?" He had no idea how traces might have ended up in Jack's drugs, but a silver knife wasn't that uncommon, was it?

"Are you *fucking* listening to what I'm saying?" Owen was breathing hard through gritted teeth and his raised voice drew a few glances from the patrons of the *Oak*. "Silver. Don't you see the link here?"

"You're not suggesting that the same people killed them both, are you?" Luke said.

"Not only that, I'm saying they knew Jack and Aide used to be part of the same pack. *Our* pack. That's why I got in touch with everyone who's left, to warn them."

"But who…?" Luke was having as much trouble with all this as Neil, it seemed.

Owen swallowed before answering. "In my line of work you see… you hear about a lot of crazy things. Nobody in authority makes connections like these, because nobody knows about people like us. But some folk do—out there. And some hunt them."

Luke and Neil exchanged glances once more. "Hunt?" said Luke, looking pained. It was interesting the way the dynamic had changed between Luke and Owen. Once upon a time, Luke might have been the one to call the shots—his job demanding confidence, balls. He had the looks as well, which meant the meat always flocked to him and he'd get first choice. But after years in the police force, Owen was the one with the confidence now. He was also apparently the one with insider information, however paranoid it might sound.

"This is crazy," said Neil. "Hunters…"

Owen leaned across the table. "I'm telling you, they *exist*. And one or more are out there, trying to pick us off before the next full moon." That was in a couple of days' time. Neil had been feeling the urges more and more frequently during its approach.

"You're off your head," Neil said to him. He'd been looking forward to tonight, albeit anxious about what the other guys might say to him. But he'd just been told two of his oldest pals were dead, and another believed there was some kind of conspiracy to take down the rest. He wasn't going to sit around here listening to any more of it. Neil stood, making to leave. "It's been nice catching up," and he looked at Luke primarily when he said that, "but I'll be going now, I reckon."

Owen grabbed him by the wrist and this drew even more looks from customers. "If I'm so crazy, where's Ryan? He's half an hour or more late."

That wasn't anything unusual for Ryan, though. He'd always been known for his shit timekeeping, always the last to arrive at meetings. "That doesn't mean anything," Luke told Owen, echoing Neil's thoughts—and finding a little of the old courage that had once made him their unofficial leader.

Owen glared at him, then nodded. "You're right. Okay then, how about we all wait for him to show, see what he has to say about my theories."

Luke looked at Neil. "How about it? It has been a long time since we were all together like this."

And would be again now, thought Neil—his mind filling with memories of Jack and Aide, the former screaming out his lyrics at the mike, the latter with his cheeky chappie smirk. He still couldn't believe he would never see them again. Still, there was Luke here, there was Owen. He owed them something. Owed them his time at least. "Okay," Neil said, sitting. "But I can't be late back anyway."

Owen sneered at that. "Still with the…" Neil could see him thinking about what to call her. "…little lady then?"

Neil said nothing. Whatever he attempted in reply would be wrong, he knew that.

"I'll get you a drink," said Luke to Owen. "Still the usual? J.D. and coke?"

"Make it a double," said Owen. "I've got a feeling I'm going to need it."

They sat in silence until Luke returned, the buffer that would keep them from talking about her…

Julie.

…at least for the time being. The conversation was steered more towards what had happened to both Owen and Luke in the last fifteen years. Luke was still repping, but growing increasingly tired of the lifestyle. In a strange sort of way, when he talked about it Neil got the distinct impression Luke was envious of him. Of what Neil had. Somewhere to call home, someone to return to at night.

(If he only knew.)

"It's just getting a bit old, you know?" he said, and now Neil saw more lines on his face marring those good looks. Time didn't stand still for anyone.

Owen, as it turned out, was not just a policeman, but a plain clothes detective now. So the outfit he was wearing actually *was* his uniform. "See, it's my job. I *detect*," he told Neil. "That's why you should be listening to me about Jack and Aide."

Trying to avoid another argument, Luke said, "A werewolf cop, eh? I think I saw a movie like that once." Though his words were flippant, there was little humor to them. How could there be after what they'd been told that evening?

"And you Neil? Still working in the library?" said Owen.

"You bloody well know that's where I am, *detective*." He'd mailed him there, for Christ's sake.

"Still stacking shelves and doling out romantic fiction to middle-aged women who can't get any?"

Neil ignored the remark. "I'm senior librarian, if that's what you mean."

Owen smirked. "Senior, eh? I'm impressed. You get to stack the big books."

Neil was beginning to wonder if the main reason Owen had got in touch was to have a go at him. "Since when did you become such a dickhead? You used to be okay, Owen. Oh, right, I forgot—you joined the filth. We used to spend most of our time avoiding brushes with the law, remember that?"

Owen snorted. "Better to be on the inside, then, isn't it. Now, I *am* the law." It made him sound like fucking Judge Dredd or something, and it was all Neil could do to keep from bursting out laughing.

"Guys, guys…" said Luke, holding up his hands as if ready to keep them apart. He looked like a referee in a really bad boxing match.

Owen batted Luke's hand away. "It's no more than you deserve, being stuck here like this… after—"

"After what? After meeting someone and settling down with them, after falling in love?"

Another snort. "Love? Do me a favor. They were food, women like her. Always were, always will be."

"Owen, people have to go their own way, live their own lives," said Luke, which earned him a third snort.

"Bullshit. You reap what you sow."

"What did you just say?" asked Neil.

"If you can sit there," said the policeman, "and tell me you're better off now than you were then, I'll—"

"I don't have to listen to this crap," said Neil and this time when he got up nobody was going to stop him from leaving.

"Look at the time," said Luke. It was almost half nine; they'd been waiting here an hour and a half. Ryan was late. *Really* late. Maybe literally. Neil paused, not needing anyone to stop him now.

"We should go to Ryan's place," said Owen. "See if he's okay."

Luke nodded, his expression grim. "I think you might be right."

Owen rose now, and stood opposite Neil. "You coming?"

Neil thought about it, but shook his head. It wasn't so much the promise he'd made Julie, it was more a case of not wanting to know for sure about Ryan. If they found him at home slashed to bits, then that really would mean there was a hunter—or *hunters*—running around after their hides (how much would a werewolf skin go for out there, anyway… was there even a market?…probably, people would buy anything, and it would more than likely be a lot, even without the hair). No, they'd find Ryan safe and sound, probably drunk or asleep or—

"Doesn't have permission, y'see," said Owen. "That bitch won't let him play past his bedtime."

That was it. Neil lunged for Owen, growling. "Just like you did with Ryan all those years ago, eh? Remember?" snapped Owen, grabbing hold of Neil's jumper in return.

Luke tried to force them apart, but the pair barged into him and he ended up knocking over the table they'd been sitting at. The landlord of the *Oak*, a burly man Neil knew called Kev— who was ironically hairier than any of them at present, with his lamb chop sideburns and shirt open to reveal the rings of black curls on his chest—was on them in seconds.

"Gentlemen," he said, pulling them apart. "Fucking well pack it in!" He looked at Neil. "I'm surprised at you. Never pegged you for the trouble-causing sort."

"Oh, he's just full of surprises, aren't you?" Owen grunted. Then he pulled out his ID and the landlord shrank back. He must have been the only one in that place who hadn't realized Owen was Old Bill.

"I'm…. I'm sorry," said Kev, to Owen—but not Neil.

Owen nodded. "Don't worry about it. We were just going anyway." He helped Luke to his feet. "Come on."

Owen strode off towards the door, but Luke lingered. He gave Neil one of his cards, then asked for his number in return. Neil gave it, glancing over a few times to see Owen waiting impatiently by the door.

Then they were gone, leaving Neil with Kev. The landlord looked from the now empty doorway, to Neil, then said: "Someone's going to have to pay for the damage, you know."

Sighing, Neil took out his wallet.

* * *

By the time he arrived home, it was heading for eleven and Julie had gone to bed.

Eleven, on a Friday night? Neil cracked open another one of the tins of lager he'd bought from the off-license on his way back, slumping down in front of the TV, but keeping the sound

86

really low. He could hear still hear it, crystal clear.

He couldn't stop thinking about Jack, Adrian... Ryan. What Luke and Owen (the prick) might have found when they eventually got to his place. Who'd driven them there? Owen, after his J.D.s? Did that matter when he could just flash that ID of his? It would if he ended up wrapping them around a lamppost or something, doing the hunters' job for them.

Neil shook his head. No, there *were* no hunters. No such thing... Couldn't be.

But then there was Jack, Adrian and-

No; not Ryan. Out of all of them, Neil owed him the biggest apology for what he'd done, what he'd said in the back of that van. It was no worse than what he'd been willing to do tonight when he went for Owen, he reminded himself. And the trigger both times:

Julie. Always Julie.

As if having some kind of radar, she appeared at the living room door. "I *thought* I heard you."

Bullshit, he'd barely made a noise—in spite of the drink. Neil knew how to be silent when he wanted to. She must have been listening out for him, like she was his fucking mother or something. What did she think he was going to do, come back with a woman on each arm? (A woman he'd then—)

"You've been drinking," she said, pointing out the obvious. He was sitting there with a depleted six-pack on his lap, knocking back the strong lager.

"So," he said, looking at her properly now. She was wearing those hideous tartan pajamas she was so fond of, but he loathed. A far cry from some of the stuff she'd worn for him years back to make him happy: the satin, the lace, the... not much at all. Those red and blue creations were designed to hide a woman's figure, but he could still see hers beneath it. Could still see how her breasts—maybe not as pert as they'd once been, but still full—pushed against the buttons of the top. Could see the way the material clung between her legs.

Neil looked away, his heartbeat up.

"So: you've been drinking *a lot*, by the looks of things. Had a good time with your mates, then I take it."

Neil shrugged. *Not really,* he thought to himself, *couple of them have died horrendously and another might well be slashed to ribbons, but apart from that...*

"That all you've got to say for yourself? Jesus, Neil—"

"Jesus what?" he said, rising.

"Jesus *Christ*, you're a loser. I don't know what I ever saw in you."

Neil's pulse was quickening. He was staring at her, but wasn't fully seeing her. Whether it was the drink or what had happened back there in the pub, or just the closeness of that particular time of month, he didn't know but—

"Doesn't have permission, y'see. That bitch won't let him play past his bedtime."

"Love? Do me a favor. They were food, women like her. Always were, always will be."

They're meat... just meat.

"You don't know what you saw in me," repeated Neil, his words slurring slightly. "Here, let me remind you."

He'd crossed the room in seconds, much quicker than anyone should have done, and it startled Julie. She stepped back. "You keep away from me," she told him.

"Or what?" said Neil, his words more *strange* than slurred now.

"You touch her. Any of you fucking so much as look at her..."

"Or..." she said, but all the usual self-assuredness was gone. "Or I'll..." She was quivering, he could see it, hear the catch in her voice.

"I think... I think she's the one."

"There aren't any 'ones'. Only the next meal."

"You do know you can't have a normal life with this woman, don't you? How can you?"

He saw faces now, the faces of his friends—as they were back then, as the probably had been when death found them. Jack, Adrian and—

"Why don't you do yourself a favor and leave her to us, we'll take care of the problem."

Ryan's voice.

Maybe he should have listened.

"I-I'm going back to bed," said Julie, turning from him. But it was too late, she'd woken something up other than herself and Neil wasn't sure whether he could get it to go to sleep again.

Wasn't sure he *wanted* to.

He grabbed her arm, but she shrugged it off. Julie made a break for the bedroom, then she was inside and trying to slam the door on him. Neil put his foot in the gap, pushed hard with all of his bodyweight on the door itself.

It gave, sending her reeling back. Her legs caught the edge of the bed and she fell onto it, the springs protesting, squeaking— just like they had once with his weight on top of her.

"Neil," she moaned, crying, holding up her hand. "Neil, please… you're scaring me."

A grin broke its way free, and he pounced, covering the distance easily.

And now his weight was on her again, clawing at that stupid tartan, his mouth on her neck, feeling her pulse racing. As he tore his own clothes free, he recognized that look in her eye. He'd seen it once before when they'd first met, responding to his whims, his influence? No, something else; desiring the *animal* part of him. So she could feel as much of a creature as he was, abandon her humanity to him—to what they were doing. The beast with two backs.

"*This* is what you saw in me," he said, shredding her pajama bottoms and entering her, ramming into her so hard her breath was taken from her. Then her hands were at the base of his neck, urging him on. Faster, faster. Harder…

Until neither of them could fight it any more.

* * *

He was vaguely aware of a phone going off, a trill ring-tone that told him it wasn't the house phone, but his mobile—somewhere on the bedroom floor, after falling out of his trouser pocket last night.

Neil rubbed his face, rising and glancing across at the naked body lying next to him. There were claw marks down Julie's back, not that deep but still raw. At first he thought the body might be a corpse, but then he saw the steady rise and fall of her shoulders with each breath.

Things were a bit of a blur, just flashes, snatches of images of what they—what *he'd*—done. But he did remember that in the heat of it all, his wife had responded, as if on some primal level. Just like before, just like when they'd first met. Was it as simple as that, a vicious circle? As they'd lost that part of their relationship, as he'd sacrificed everything just to be with her, she'd started to lose interest in him that way?

The phone continued to ring, and he chased away the thoughts, swinging over the side of the bed to snatch it up. As he did so he couldn't help smirking when he saw Julie's tartan pajamas, not far away, completely ruined.

He checked the time on the phone before accepting the call. It was 1:15 in the afternoon. They'd slept the morning away, which was hardly surprising seeing as they'd been up most of the night. A good thing neither of them were working today. There was no caller ID, but he did recognize the number vaguely as the one Luke had given him back at the pub. He pressed the green button.

"Hello," he said, suddenly lowering his voice on the second syllable so as not to disturb Julie.

"Neil, thank Christ!" It was definitely Luke's voice, but even more panicked than it had been when they'd gone their separate ways.

"Is everything all right?" asked Neil, realizing that it was probably the most stupid thing he'd ever said. Of course it wasn't all right; he could tell that from Luke's tone, even if he didn't know why the man was ringing.

"No it bloody isn't. It's Ryan."

Neil pinched the skin between his eyes, head sagging. "You found him, then?"

"Yes, we found him." This was the bit where they described how messed up he'd been when they broke into his house and—

"He's been in an accident. At least that's what they're saying."

"What?"

"He's still alive, *barely*. It was a hit and run driver, a few days ago. When we got no answer from his place and figured out there was nobody home, Owen did some checking around. He is actually pretty good at all this detective stuff. Ryan's in *The General* hospital, banged up pretty bad."

"I'm really sorry to hear that," said Neil, though wasn't there another part of him which was relieved: that Ryan hadn't actually been murdered; that he was still alive. A hit and run was better than being murdered, surely... *if* that's what actually happened to Aide and Jack.

"You need to get down here," said Luke.

Neil looked over his shoulder at Julie, stirring. "Look, it's a bit difficult right now."

"Give me that," Neil heard another voice say, then suddenly it was Owen talking to him. "Neil, get your fucking arse down to the hospital—*right now!* We've got things to talk about."

"I..." He wasn't about to do that just because Owen was ordering him to. At the same time, he did want to see Ryan—and his old mate was hurt, not dead.

"Neil, fucking well get—"

He felt a hand on his back and he snapped off the phone, whirling to see Julie sitting up. "Neil?" she said softly, the bolshiness from when he'd got back last night gone. "Who was that?"

"A friend," he told her honestly.

"One of the ones you saw yesterday?"

He nodded. She dipped her green eyes momentarily, not sure whether to believe him or not. "Neil... look, I think we need to talk."

"We've got things to talk about."

"I can't right now. I've got to go, something's come up."

Julie's eyebrows knitted together. "Something's come up?' she repeated, the hard edge returning. "*This* is something too, isn't it?"

"My friend's in the hospital."

"What, the one who was ringing?"

"No, another one." He realized how ridiculous it sounded, like an excuse to get out of talking to Julie. Maybe it was. He didn't really want to sit here and chat about what had happened, his head was too full of other crap.

"I see," she said, drawing her knees up and folding her arms around them.

Neil went to the wardrobe, pulling out fresh clothes—that weren't torn—and began to dress. "We'll talk when I get back. I promise."

She just stared at him blankly, watching as he grabbed his wallet and keys, then left the bedroom. Neil shut the door behind him, leaning back on it and hanging his head.

Then he left the house without looking back.

* * *

When Neil arrived at the hospital, he hadn't been expecting Ryan to look like this.

The guy might as well have been cut to pieces, because he was hardly recognizable. 'Hit and Run' Luke had said, but Ryan looked like he'd been hit repeatedly, then backed over several times. In fact he looked like the car had been dropped on him from a great height.

Neil also knew that he'd recover. In fact, he should have been getting better already, so Neil was puzzled when Luke told him that their friend's condition was worsening.

"Owen," said Luke, nodding to the policeman sat outside in the corridor (only two being allowed to sit with Ryan at a time), "he thinks there might have been some silver involved again. You know, maybe on the bumper or something? Hard to ask without tipping off the staff."

"Again with the silver?" This was getting ridiculous. Not only was Owen saying that Jack's overdose and Adrian's mugging was by a fictional hunter or group of them, now they'd also run Ryan over? "Are you buying this shit?" Neil asked Luke.

He shrugged. "Kinda makes sense."

And would explain why he wasn't getting *any* better.

Neil looked back again at Owen. Despite having 'commanded' Neil to come, he'd pulled a face when he'd actually arrived. "She finally let you off the leash, then?" Owen had said.

"Fuck off," Neil replied. He hadn't come here for Owen, and definitely hadn't come to discuss his private life: he'd come to see Ryan.

Now Neil approached the bed, eyes like slits as he took in more of the injuries—Ryan's face so swelled it looked like it was about to pop. "I'm sorry, man," he whispered; for the state he was in, but also for what he'd done back in Jack's van. He thought once more that they'd spent the last several years so close by, but might as well have been on different continents. If only he'd picked up a phone or something. "So, what are his chances?" asked Neil finally.

Another shrug from Luke. "Owen's been waiting to talk to a doctor—not even flashing that badge of his has got him anywhere so far. He's off his patch, for one thing."

Neil was just about to say something else, when he spotted Owen rising. The policeman called to them from the door and they rushed over to an increasingly distracted Owen.

"There!" he shouted, pointing. They both looked, but saw nothing. "A bloke, he was standing watching from the end of that corridor," Owen told them.

"What the hell are you on about?" said Neil.

"When I looked up, he looked away—but I *saw* him."

"Probably just another visitor," Luke offered.

"I'm telling you, there was something dodgy about him."

"Owen, you can't-" began Neil, but Owen was off, up the corridor and sprinting past doctors and nurses.

Sighing, Luke ran after him—and Neil ran after them both, intending to give the copper another piece of his mind when he caught up. Him and his overactive imagination, that was the only dodgy thing around here. A wild goose chase, that's all this whole bloody thing was.

By the time they'd turned a couple of corners, Owen had vanished. Luke sniffed the air, but there were too many other scents here to pick him out. Too many people: patients, staff and visitors alike. "Maybe he got in the lift?" Neil suggested. It was entirely possible, but how would they know which floor he went to? After searching a couple of floors up in the maze-like building, Neil made another suggestion—for Luke to call Owen. But he couldn't do that inside the hospital itself.

When they got to the main entrance, Luke already had the number on speed-dial. He shook his head. "Can't reach him."

There was a group of people gathering outside, and figures in scrubs were pushing past Luke and Neil, obviously in a hurry to check out whatever the next emergency case was coming in.

Then they saw who it was.

Neil pulled a couple of bystanders aside to get a better view. Luke followed in his wake. And there, on the concrete in front of them—the medics working furiously on him—was Owen. His limbs were sticking out at odd angles, like some kind of weird insect tipped over on its back. And the base of his skull was leaking. Obviously cracked or even smashed, it was letting out blood and quite possibly other vital fluids meant to be contained.

"What happened?" Neil heard someone ask.

"Dunno, I think he threw himself off the roof," came the reply.

No. Not Owen. That's what this might *look* like: a random suicide. But it wasn't. He'd been thrown off the roof and both Neil and Luke knew it.

"He's crashing. We're losing him," said one of the women in scrubs kneeling in Owen's pooling blood. And it was only now, as she opened up the man's shirt, that they saw it. The chain around his neck. Easily mistaken for a necklace or charm, they didn't have to touch it to know what the thing was made from. A metal that Owen would never have worn in a million years, but would have ensured his fall from the building was fatal.

The woman pounded on his chest, trying to get his heart beating again, but it was a futile effort. Even if Neil or Luke had risked barging in, taking the chain off—without being branded thieves—the damage had already been done.

Open-mouthed, they looked from Owen's prone body to each other. Then they both swore at the same time.

Where Owen had gone nobody would be reaching him again, on a phone or otherwise.

* * *

There didn't seem much doubt anymore.

Owen had gone after the hunter (or hunters, they still hadn't established how many of them there were) and got himself killed. The old gang *were* being picked off, and the one member who knew the most—who had the skills that might help them get out of this mess—was now gone.

Luke and Neil searched the hospital again, but without knowing who they were looking for, it seemed pretty pointless. Owen was the only one who'd got a look at the guy that had done this (one of a team?). Besides which, what more chance would they stand than Owen?

Ironically, by bringing them together like this, Owen had actually made the task of killing them even easier. "Do you think that's what they had in mind?" asked Luke. "Maybe they counted on the fact Owen would put all the pieces together and get in touch with us."

"Maybe," said Neil. "Now there's only us left to deal with."

"Ryan," Luke reminded him.

"He's dying," Neil sighed. "We both know it's only a matter of time. Whoever's doing this is nothing if not thorough. They'd *make sure* he wasn't going to wake up again."

They had two choices now, get the hell out of town and hope they weren't being tracked (it was a slim chance) or try and stay alive till tomorrow and deal with the hunter(s) in their altered forms.

Neither option was very appealing.

"Well, I don't know about you," said Luke, "but I'm bailing." It was something the younger Luke would never have said, never have done, and Neil thought again how much he'd altered. Owen might have been a pain in the arse these days, but right now Neil would have swapped Luke for the arrogant detective any day of the week. At least Owen would have put up a fight. "If you've got any brains, you'll do the same."

But it wasn't as simple as that, was it? Luke had no ties, but Neil had:

Julie. Always Julie.

"Shit," said Neil, dialing the number for home as Luke waved goodbye—off back to the hotel to pack his stuff, then drive into the sunset. The phone was picked up on the third ring. "Julie... Julie, listen to me—"

"Neil? Where are you? You've been gone hours."

"That's not important. I need you to—"

"Not important? Not important!" she was practically screaming the last bit. "You do what you did last night, then leave after getting a phone call today telling me some stupid story about a hospital—"

"It wasn't a story, look—"

"I've had it with all of this. I'm going away for a bit, Neil."

"Good, that's good." He regretted the words as soon as they

were out of his mouth. He meant it was good because it was dangerous to be around him right now, but he couldn't explain that to *her*.

"Good? You think it's *good* I'm leaving you?" Now not even dogs... and people like Neil... could hear her, she was so shrill. And without being there, he had no way of talking to her (*influencing* her?), calming her down. "Fuck you, Neil." She hung up the phone with a click.

He tried ringing her back, but she'd left it off the hook—and her mobile was turned off. "Shit!" he repeated. In spite of how dangerous it was, he had to go back now. Neil crossed the road to flag down a taxi when his phone rang. He answered it quickly, not even looking at the ID.

"Julie?"

"Neil... Neil, you have to come, right now!" It was Luke, and he sounded terrified.

"Where are you?"

"At the hotel. There's someone. Neil... Neil you have to—" The connection fizzled out, and Neil had no more luck getting back in touch with Luke than he had with Julie.

When the taxi pulled up and he got inside, the driver asked: "Where to, mate?"

Neil thought for a moment, then said: "Wanderer's Lodge, Oakley Street."

* * *

Though Luke hadn't mentioned the room number he was staying in, and Neil knew that reception would never tell him, he was easily able to track his friend's scent. The corridors were relatively free of people, and those who were staying there had locked themselves away in their rooms, watching TV, screwing, or getting ready to head off for a Saturday night out. Again, that would have been Neil so long ago—not in a hotel room, but preparing to hit the clubs, on the prowl with his mates (who were all but dead now, and in the space of the last month). Plus which, with every hour that passed, Neil's senses were growing keener. By tomorrow night, they'd be at their sharpest.

Room 320, on the third floor. That's where Luke's scent led him. He was about to knock on the door, when he saw it was already open a crack. Neil contemplated running away, but after what he'd thought of Luke for doing the same, it seemed more than a little hypocritical. He toed open the door, then scanned the small room. There was nobody inside, but he could still smell Luke's scent. That stopped once he made it into the room itself.

The light was on in the bathroom, so Neil followed it, still poised to tackle anyone who might leap out at him. He could smell the coppery aroma of blood, but diluted somehow. Making his way inside the bathroom, he saw the tub there filled with red water. Luke was in that water, stripped to his boxers, staring up at Neil with glassy eyes. His veins had been opened, the razor used still on the side of the bath. Neil didn't need to examine it to know that this, too, was made from silver. Once more, whoever had done this had covered themselves—another 'suicide'. There was no way anyone, apart from him, would think otherwise.

Shaking his head, Neil backed out of the bathroom, knowing that the sight of Luke like this would follow him to the grave. How long he'd have until he faced that scenario was another matter.

He exited the room, left the hotel—looking over his shoulder the whole time. Luke had had the right idea: get out, run before the hunters could kill them. Only he'd been too late, the pursuers too clever.

Just as their enemy was being clever right now. A car waiting, crawling down the street. Lights coming on when the driver saw Neil, dazzling him. His only warning was the revving of a powerful engine, and then it was after him. Neil ran, very aware now of his belly and how much faster he would have been if he'd kept in Luke's shape (though it hadn't really helped Luke much, had it?). He needed to get to a more densely populated place, the nightlife

PAUL KANE

area for example. But the driver of the car had other ideas, blocking off the way Neil was going to go and more or less forcing him down a side street.

Was this how Ryan had felt when he was mown down? Neil wondered. Had he even had this much time before the car rammed into him? The car, Neil saw as he looked back, that did indeed have a silver bumper—with rough edges that, if they caught him, would definitely tear into his legs. Neil skidded round another corner, praying to see some signs of life: someone, *anyone* out on the streets. But they were all gravitating to the more exciting parts of town right now, which left the way clear for the hunters to run Neil to ground. The car was gaining on him again, but Neil did at least have one advantage. Though it had been a long time since he'd been out this far, the town hadn't changed that much, and there had been a time of day when he'd known these streets blindfolded. Better than whoever was chasing him, certainly, because there was a shortcut this way to the old canal.

Neil ran down one deserted street and up another, the car still behind but having to go slowly in unfamiliar territory.

Nearly there, nearly there, he was telling himself, puffing out breath as he went. What he would do when he actually got there, Neil hadn't really figured out. He just knew that cars couldn't drive on water, so that's where he should be heading. The car sped up when that water came into view, obviously realizing what Neil had in mind.

Neil was running towards the railing which stopped people from falling into the canal, maybe thinking he could leap that and climb down the side. But he didn't get a chance; the car pulled up alongside and clipped Neil. He was pitched over the railings, and suddenly was falling. It seemed to take a long time to finally hit the water, and when he did, it felt like it was hitting him back. He might have banged his head on something, but Neil definitely blacked out, letting both the darkness and the water take him.

* * *

99

When he woke, he ached all over.

He'd been pitched up on the bank some way down the canal, and it was light again. Neil blinked, coughed, and experimentally raised his head. That had been a bad idea. He looked at his watch, but it had stopped when he fell—was forced—into the dirty water.

It still said 8:30.

It had to be the next day, though. Sunday. *Damn*, he was lucky to still be alive. His head was sore, and when he touched the crown there was a lump where he must have knocked it on something before sinking.

Probably looked like he was a goner. Probably also why the people or person after him didn't come down to check, to finish the job properly. Neil lifted himself up, letting out a cry at the pain he was in. Luckily, that bumper hadn't caught him or this would have been so much worse. He'd be okay in a couple of hours, three or four at most. And later on was a full moon, which would see him growing stronger and stronger...

He was soaking, and he was hungry.

It probably wasn't the best idea, but Neil decided to head home.

* * *

He'd drawn some strange looks on the bus he'd caught, not least because of the smell, but Neil ignored them. It was late afternoon a church clock informed him, not long till evening. He'd made sure he wasn't being followed—as best he could, anyway—and had watched his own house for about half an hour before entering, just to make sure it wasn't being staked out.

It wasn't, he concluded, but entered through the back door anyway. At least Julie was away from all this. Had left hating him, but was safe.

Or so he'd thought.

The hunter(s) had been thorough as always, making it appear as if a burglar had broken in through the side window, that Julie had surprised the criminal and paid the price for it. Why hadn't she gone like she said she was going to? If only she'd—

Neil went to the body, face down on the living room rug amongst the books and DVDs thrown there to make it look like the place had been ransacked. He turned her over, but knew Julie was dead. Her neck had been snapped. Tears were welling in Neil's eyes, and as he sniffed them up, he smelt something else.

His wife hadn't been the only one to die that day. It probably would have been undetectable if he hadn't been who he was, probably wouldn't even have shown up on a test yet—but Neil knew. Not only that, he *smelt* what his son might have become had his life not been snuffed out before it really began: sensed all the triumphs and the losses he would have gone through; shared in the knowledge he would have learnt at school, then university; saw the job he would do, following his mother into teaching; saw the faces of all the girls he might have dated, before finally marrying one of them; saw the grandchildren Neil would now never have...

All lost, all gone.

He wouldn't have carried Neil's burden, either—having inherited more genes from Julie than him. His son would have led a normal life, free from being hunted like his father had been this weekend.

Neil bared his teeth, then he growled. Then he began to howl. He sniffed again; this time he smelt the interloper.

And now he had a trail to follow.

* * *

It ended in an alleyway, behind a row of nightclubs: the trail and that very long weekend.

The place was familiar to Neil, one of his old stomping grounds. It made him wonder whether he'd been lured here, whether following the scent was just another trap. If it was, he didn't care anymore. Didn't care about much at all as he crouched on a fire escape, stripped, observing the man standing with his back to Neil in the shadows cast by the full moon above.

The car—the one used to try and run Neil down—was at the head of the alley, abandoned, and the man who presumably owned it was just waiting out in the open. He looked to be alone, but might simply be the bait (others could have masked their scent somehow—they were sneaky bastards, he'd seen that). Neil might not care, but that didn't mean he was mental.

Now the man was crouching, too, just like Neil. He bent, the echo of his cracking knees reverberating throughout the alley, but was almost swallowed by the thumping techno beat from some of the clubs round the front.

What the hell was he doing? Neil squinted, then looked around again for any sign of companions. Nothing.

The man was rising again, preparing to walk back to his car. If Neil was going to strike, it had to be now.

"Fuck it," he whispered, then leapt down from the fire escape, transforming as he did so. (Getting back into shape.) He hadn't done this at will for a long time, and the quickness of it took him by surprise. His whole body tingled as the new hairs appeared, his eyes taking on that yellow and scarlet cast that gave them almost infra-red capabilities, tongue growing as his teeth lengthened and became much more pointed.

He landed awkwardly, not with the grace and skill he'd once been able to boast, and it alerted the man ahead of him, who opened his mouth in surprise. If he was shocked, then it was the first time since all this began that they—all right, Neil, because he was the only one left—had the upper hand. That didn't last long.

The man pulled something from his jacket and aimed it at Neil. There was no bang, as he might have expected, but Neil felt the impact of a projectile in his shoulder: hard and sharp. A bolt from a crossbow. A *silver* bolt that stung like someone had just rammed a red-hot poker into him.

Neil howled again, this time in pain—but he had the presence of mind to dodge the next two bolts fired, one flying over his head, the other whizzing past his thigh.

Clawing at the wound with nails that had matched his teeth in growth, Neil managed to rip out the bolt and tossed it aside. The wound still burned, but wouldn't prove fatal.

Neil lunged forwards, using his powerful back legs to propel himself. The man was trying to reload his handheld crossbow, but couldn't do it in time and so abandoned that idea. Backing off to retreat to his car.

Neil came bounding up behind, but if he thought it was going to be that easy, he was sadly mistaken. The man turned, suddenly, and lashed out with a chain. Slightly thicker than the one he must have used on Owen, this nevertheless had the same effect. It wound itself around Neil's neck, half-choking him when the man tugged hard. That same burning sensation struck Neil, and if the hunter had his crossbow to hand he might have been able to finish the wolf off while in this weakened condition.

But Neil gathered up enough strength to lash out with a claw, which only missed the hunter by millimeters. Closer now to the man, Neil was able to take in more of his features. He was older than Neil had expected. Older even than he was. The man's silver-grey hair was still hanging on to the remnants of a darker color, but the lines criss-crossing his face gave him away completely. Though he'd obviously looked after himself better than Neil, this man had to be pushing sixty.

The hunter let go of the chain and stumbled backwards again, breaking into a dash for the car. Neil dropped to his knees, tearing at the chain around his neck.

She finally let you off the leash, then?

Owen's harsh words made him think of Julie, and then he thought of her laying on the living room floor, thought about both her and the baby dying at this man's hands.

And that just made Neil go wild.

He shrugged off the chains and rose, roaring, into the night air. The thumping of the music from the clubs kept pace with the rhythm of his heart, accompanied the pumping of the blood around the hunter's body which Neil could hear. He bounded after him, faster and faster.

The hunter had made it to the vehicle, though, and was sliding inside, sliding the key into the ignition at the same time. He gunned the engine and began reversing at Neil.

The wolf hadn't been expecting that move, and when the car connected with him, it knocked him back into the alleyway. Luckily, the rear bumper wasn't silver—there was no fire when the car hit Neil—so he rose, quickly, shaking his head and snarling. The hunter had braked after hitting the wolf, but now floored the accelerator again, clouds of smoke pluming from the tires. He was planning to finish off the job, but Neil had other ideas.

Neil climbed onto the boot, claws digging into the metal so he could haul himself up. Then he was on the roof, ripping through it like paper, to get to the man inside—who braked again, attempting to throw Neil off. It only succeeded in swinging the wolf around, so that his legs hung over the front of the car and one knee cracked the windscreen.

Snarling, Neil continued to pull away pieces of the roof, like a child tearing wrapping off a Christmas present. The man was trying to open his driver's side door, but it was jammed, forcing him to go for the passenger side instead.

He just about got out as Neil ploughed his way in, the man crawling away back into the alley. Neil clambered out again through the roof and waited for the hunter to get to his feet. The man half-turned as Neil leaped on him, pinning him to the ground. He let out a cry but refused to show any fear.

"Go on!" he screamed into Neil's face. "Do it, you monster!" It wasn't the wisest thing to say when you had a werewolf towering over you. "Do it so I can be with Tammy again."

Neil was about to sink his teeth in when he paused...

Tammy? What was the guy talking about? He sniffed at the man, sucking up who he was, why he was here. Neil looked around, seeing the flowers the man had left on the ground not far away, and everything slotted into place.

That night, that last night he'd been out with the lads—the girls, the red-head, brunette and:

Tammy.

Tammy with her blonde hair, arms outstretched so Adrian and Owen could feast on her, then the rest could later. Tammy, who had lied about her age to get into those clubs in the first place. Tammy, who was only fifteen, but had always looked much older. And they'd taken her life away: she'd only led half of one anyway. Tammy, the (strawberry) blonde girl who'd had Julie's face in that alley.

Now Neil saw this man in front of him, *really* saw him. Her father, being given the news that she'd disappeared. He was the only parent she'd had, after her mother died of cancer when Tammy was just five. So he'd searched for her, all over the place––quitting his job and living on savings, picking up tracking skills as he went. They'd *created* this hunter (you reap what you sow, right? reap what you...), and he'd finally stumbled on the truth years later. An ageing rocker who couldn't keep his mouth shut, telling stories about wolves and killings to impress his druggie friends. They hadn't believed a word, but—on hearing those rumors—the hunter had. He'd put two and two together, gone back and worked out that Jack had been around the same time Tammy—

A bit more digging, and he had a few more names. He had Owen's, a policeman (so no point going back to them). But what he could do was use the man to get the whole pack before the next full moon. Get them, and anyone else mixed up with them. Anyone like:

Julie.

A single tear ran from the wolf's eye, and the father frowned. Neil morphed back into human form, his shoulder still a mess, neck still red-raw. "There was no need for any of... I ended all this a long time ago."

The man said nothing.

"I'm sorry," said Neil, letting the hunter drop and getting up. "But I didn't do it. It wasn't me who killed your daughter." Though God knows, he'd killed enough of other people's. Now this man had taken Neil's friends from him (if he could still call them that), had taken Julie too, and his son—who hadn't even been given half a chance at life.

But they'd taken Tammy first, they'd taken the one thing that really mattered in this man's life. In spite of everything, could Neil really kill him?

"Go on, get out of here," he snapped.

As with most things in his life, though, the decision was taken out of Neil's hands. Neil was ready to just let him go—regardless of the fact he might still come after him once this time of the month was over. Regardless of the hunger for blood this hunter had stirred up inside *him*.

But the father got up and rushed Neil, drawing the knife that had probably done for Adrian when he was 'mugged'. Neil acted instinctively as it arced down towards his back, twirling and transforming at the same time (it didn't take him by surprise this time; he *enjoyed* it).

Neil sliced through the man's wrist and both the hand and knife fell to the ground. Then he was on the older man, biting, clawing, sucking and eating. It was the first decent, fresh meal he'd had in years, and it invigorated him. Neil knew the wolf could leave no part of this man alive, couldn't pass this on to him because it was... well, it was a gift really (*not* an affliction, *not* a curse).

As Neil finished up on the father, he reflected how really he should be thanking the man. Not just for filling his belly, but also for reminding him of what he was at heart, freeing him—freeing him from Julie?—and giving him a fresh start. There was no need for him to feel old anymore, not if he didn't want to. He'd been living half a life himself, but he wasn't even halfway *through* his life. And there was so much time to catch up on.

When he was done, Neil shape-shifted again and went back to the car, climbing in. The engine was still running. It would make it to the outskirts of the city, where he'd dump it then steal another. It was time to move on, to get out of here. To live the life Luke had been living, or Jack.

As Neil sat behind the wheel, gunning that engine, he stared at the entrance of the alleyway.

And, for the first time in a long while, he thought about the future.

* * *

SIGNS OF LIFE

*Taken from the Astrological Handbook
Published by Beholder Press.*

*Welcome to the wonderful world of
Astrology and Star Signs!*

Much has been written about this fascinating subject in the past, and indeed we could fill a whole book with historical facts about it. From the way the famous seers of the Chaldean civilization in the ancient land of Ur gave future predictions and the Egyptians followed the passage of the stars and planets, up to the present day with various astrologers now becoming celebrities in their own right in newspapers and on television. The stars we read every day offer insights into possible events for our specific sign, attempting to answer questions we have or confront doubts we foster about particular situations as we travel life's journey. Because the future is such an uncertain thing this appeals to us greatly, and in many cases gives us comfort. We want to know if our day is going to be good or bad, so we can prepare for either.

But this publication isn't really concerned with the past or the future. The aim of this book is to present a simple, easy to understand guide to the twelve sun signs of the zodiac and their individual characteristics, including compatibility aspects, the best career choices, the way they handle and perceive money, plus health information to help each and every one of you lead a much longer, happier existence.

All of us, throughout our lives, are keen to learn more about ourselves, the reason why we do what we do, and the reason why things don't work out sometimes when we make these decisions. Hopefully, after reading this, you'll come away with a greater understanding of yourself.

And who knows, it might just change your life completely...

Taken from the Daily Record

Pisces: Today will definitely be a day to remember. Plans you have made have gone awry, but don't be too downhearted. Something you have always wanted is coming your way, and romance looks set to finally blossom for you. Red is your lucky color.

* * *

Tracy Simmons snapped the newspaper shut and put it down on the seat next to her. She didn't know why she even kept reading those stupid things. Every day, the same old drivel, the same agonizing false hope. Or even worse, it would tell her that she'd be going through a worrying time soon or that bad news was on its way. Well, of course she was going to go through a worrying time if she'd just been told bad news was on the way! It was a self-fulfilling prophecy.

But the days when it talked about romance and love, they were the hardest ones to take. Today love will come your way, this week will be a wonderful week for lovers. It never quite worked out that way. She wasn't the luckiest person when it came to matters of the heart. Maybe it was because she'd been a slow-starter. Slow? She'd practically been standing stock still most of her life. While other girls paired off and got into some serious lip-locks with the boys at school and college, Tracy had always shied away from this; more afraid than anything—afraid she'd do it wrong or that she'd mess things up somehow. Or had she been frightened that if she let anyone in and they walked away from her, she'd be devastated?

As it turned out she'd been right. The admittedly limited number of men she'd known in her twenty-seven years on this planet had been complete arseholes. Liars and slimeballs only after one thing. And when they'd got it…? She'd loved them—or thought she had. And they'd told her that they felt the same. The 'I think the world of you's and 'it feels like we've known each other forever's were just to get their end away, and she fell for it every time; even when she'd only known them so long. She was fed up with creeps who thought monogamy was some kind of wood. What she wanted, what she'd always longed for, was someone who would care about her for who she was. Who would hold her and tell her everything was going to be all right when she felt sad, stand by her through thick and thin, give to her what she'd give them in return.

It was a foolish delusion perhaps, an idealized version of love that didn't really exist. There were no knights in shining armor, no handsome princes that came along to whisk you off your feet. Only deadheads like the people she'd encountered on those internet dating sites. Oh brother, the stories she could tell about those. How could anybody be so wrong about themselves on their profiles? Caring, genuine, kind. They were just words on a screen, the products of desperation. A very different kind of desperation to hers.

"You expect too much from them," her flat-mate Joanne told her after the last flop.

"He spent all night looking at my chest," Tracy said.

"So? That's what men are like. They all do it."

"What, *all* night?"

"Well, maybe not all night. But you think I haven't had dates like that, Trace? It's a compliment in a way. Proves you're irresistible to the opposite sex."

Tracy knew all too well about Joanne and her dates. As much as she adored her, she wasn't going to follow her friend's example. Men came and went in Joanne's life. If things showed even the slightest hint of getting serious, that was it. She was in control, not them, and she liked it that way.

"All it proved to me was he didn't care much about my feelings. That he wasn't interested in getting to know me as a person."

Joanne laughed. "All that comes later, babe. First you check out whether you're... y'know, compatible."

But what was the use in that? So, the sex was mind-blowing but you found out later that all he wanted to talk about was football and sports cars. What kind of a basis for a lasting relationship would you have then? Surely it was better for there to be a mental connection first, for him to be your friend as well as your lover? That's all Tracy was after really; it wasn't too much to ask.

Of course, if he happened to look like George Clooney as well then she wouldn't complain.

The electronic screen in front of her flickered, throwing back a reflection of Tracy sitting below it on the row of seats: jeans, pink jumper—pink was almost red, wasn't it?—curly ochre hair. Then the new times came up. She scrolled her eyes down the list till she came to hers. There it was; ten minutes late. About as reliable as the men she'd known.

Again she cursed her luck about the car. Just one thing, one tiny thing wrong on the MOT and it had failed. The garage couldn't get hold of the shock absorbers for another couple of days, so now she was having to rely on public transport to make the bi-monthly trip to see her folks. One lousy little thing...

Tracy looked around the station, which had been revamped since the last time she'd traveled: automatic doors, a lift to take you to the other platform across the way—how did that work exactly?—a new café area and newsagents, which was where she'd bought her copy of *The Record* to pass the time, along with a women's magazine because it contained an article about what your dreams really meant. Sitting there, knowing she had at least another ten minutes to wait, Tracy wondered if the women's magazine had a stars section too. Probably did.

She opened it up and checked the contents page.

PISCES

(Represented by two fish swimming in opposite directions)

A romantic and idealist, your average Piscean is very open with their emotions. Extremely demonstrative and compassionate, they are sensitive souls who are hurt very easily by others. If you're in a Piscean's good books you'll soon know about it, as they will lavish you with affection from morning to night! This can sometimes be overwhelming, especially for the Piscean's partner. They look for the best in everyone, which on the face of it isn't a bad thing. But it can mean they don't pick up on deception until it is way too late. Being generous sorts they win friends easily and attract people, so they should be smart enough to choose the best alliances. Those which offer a way to advance themselves and fulfill some of those dreams they dream.

* * *

William Booth unloaded the case from his Nissan, then stuck the two-day ticket on the inside of the windscreen before locking it up. He crossed the zebra, looked towards the station, and smiled. It was good to be traveling again.

Even this short distance, even a piffling 150 miles. It didn't matter, he was on the move again. What was it Robert Louis Stevenson once said? 'To travel hopefully is a better thing than to arrive, and the true success is to labor.' Well, after three terms laboring, three terms of more or less solid English teaching he was grateful for the break. Not that he was leaving the career behind completely, oh no. If anything it was quite the reverse. This conference was supposed to be all about new teaching methods, student centered learning and exams. But Will knew there'd also be time to let his shoulder-length hair down a bit more.

He was flattered that they'd chosen him to represent the college, though not entirely surprised. Since he'd started lecturing there two years ago, he'd very quickly become a part of the fixtures and fittings. He got on well with his colleagues, who were, by and large, a great bunch of people; and he was pretty good at his job, all things considered. In lessons, students paid him respect and listened to what he had to say with something akin to reverence. In return he listened to their needs too, made time for them and always helped out where he could. This led to better results, which didn't do Will's reputation any harm either.

He was just as popular in the staffroom as he was in the classroom, his easy manner and calm confidence putting others at their ease. It didn't hurt that he could spin a yarn off the top of his head, usually about his travels here and there. The amount of times he'd been told he should write these down and sell them, maybe even put them in a book? But for now he had more than enough on his plate with the teaching thank you very much.

Will knew at the back of his mind that he had the potential to rise in the ranks at the college, perhaps even to head of department one day. The only thing stopping him would be his wanderlust. He'd been thinking about going back abroad and teaching over there again, perhaps in Japan this time or somewhere like that? He probably wouldn't have moved back here in the first place if it weren't for his little sister, and what she'd been through. Tess was the only family he had left since mum had died while they were both still at college themselves. Breast cancer.

And when Tess had found a lump…

Thankfully it had turned out to be benign and was quickly removed, but Will had stayed with her all through the tests and treatment, which was more than her shit of a fiancé had done. He was still stopping with her for the time being, but toying with the idea of moving out soon. Although Will loved Tess to bits, the situation wasn't exactly ideal, especially when it came to having a personal life. Whether he'd be moving further afield than just down the road was a decision he'd yet to make. A decision he was struggling with and would probably still be struggling with for a while to come. Fresh pastures were always greener, and he had a nice set-up here.

But still, it was good to be traveling again.

LEO

(Represented by the lion)

As their symbol suggests, Leos have something of a majestic status in the zodiac. Consequently, they can hold their heads up high, knowing they are valued and appreciated in all they do. This may lead to a serious case of big-headedness on their behalf, however, and some Leos will go to very great lengths to make sure you know just how fantastic they are—over and over again! The most negative types will be very impressed with themselves, though the vast majority will not have to boast: it's plain for all to see. The choice of career for a Leo is boundless because they'll put a lot of energy into whatever they do. They are well known for their creativity, and also take a special interest in children's welfare. Their organizational and people skills are superb, but they don't have much patience for simpletons. Perhaps this is why their close friends feel so privileged, because they know they've been chosen above everyone else to be the Leo's buddies. Family is also important to the Leo, and they will make quite a few sacrifices because of this. But they are adventurous as well and love to seek out people from new cultures. Leos like the limelight and are never happier than when they are taking centre stage. They are stable characters who find it very easy to make up their minds.

* * *

Tracy looked up from the magazine and noticed the man enter with his case. He was dressed in a blue polo shirt and trousers, and walked with a purpose she rarely saw in a lot of men. His hair was longish, just touching the tips of his broad shoulders. She looked away, conscious that she was staring, then risked another peek.

He walked past her, cast a glance in her direction. Tracy cast it back. Then he proceeded to the counter to get his tickets.

Please let him be going in my direction, she thought, and grinned as she realized the double meaning of her words. Waiting in the queue behind a family he turned and smiled at her. It was a winning smile, his. The kind of smile you could fall in love with easily.

Maybe it was her lucky day after all.

Compatibility Match
Pisces & Leo

As a couple this pair will have little in common. They would probably be better off as friends rather than lovers. The Piscean will be keen to be involved in every aspect of the Leo's life, particularly when it comes to them both living the high life, but the Leo will probably feel an overwhelming urge to straighten them out and order this dreamer around, leading to a rather one-sided relationship ultimately doomed to failure.

* * *

Katherine Pryce folded her arms and waited for her husband to deal with the man behind the glass.

"I'm sorry, sir, due to extensive repair-work at that particular station you are going to have to change trains and then take a coach to get to your destination."

"But when I booked it said it was straight through," said Ed Pryce.

"When was that?"

"A couple of weeks ago."

"Ah, well, you see the repair-work was a last minute thing. We gave customers a four-day warning that there might be delays and disruptions. It was posted on the website." The man feigned an apologetic expression, which contained more than a hint of 'I don't really give a crap, I'm off in half an hour anyway'.

"We don't use the internet very much. I mean, well, I don't."

"I'm sorry, sir, but there's not much we can do about it except apologize."

"I…" Ed sighed. "I understand. Thank you."

He turned to face his wife. "There's nothing they can do," he told her. "It was posted on the site."

Katherine rolled her eyes and took hold of her son's hand. Little Fraser Pryce's expression didn't change at the news. It never changed. It was a perpetual frown. She moved out of the way to let the man behind her get to the front of the queue. He nodded his thanks.

The Pryce family regrouped next to the timetable sheets, Katherine again waiting for her husband to catch up. She needed a cigarette. Badly. Like it wasn't enough that Ed had booked them on the same coastal holiday again, when he'd promised something different this year, maybe even abroad. Now it looked like they had a five or six hour journey ahead of them to actually get there as well. Katherine scrutinized the man she'd married fifteen years ago—no, that wasn't strictly true. She hadn't married this man; she'd married an entirely different one. Over time he'd become the person in front of her, stuck in his ways, unadventurous, happy to drift along and not upset any applecarts. The amount of promotions he'd missed out on at the solicitors, and all because his get up and go could neither get up nor go anymore. But one of these days, Katherine thought she just might show it how.

She remembered Ed when she'd first met him. Full of so many ideas, so many business schemes and plans. He was going to show them all, show the world in fact. He'd set up his own firm and make a mint, taking on only the high profile cases. Katherine had thought it wise to hitch herself to his star and be quick about it. But, as all the brightest tend to do, this star burnt itself out early. It hadn't helped that they'd had his mother interfering every step of the way. Telling him he should stick with the firm he was in, know his place. But more than that, respect it.

And then when the baby came along...

Safety, reliability, dependability. They became the unspoken buzzwords of the Pryce household. And yes, there was something to be said about this. At least they knew there was money coming in, that they had a roof over their heads. She couldn't fault Ed for taking on the cases that others wouldn't, for trying to help people with their claims of harassment. He was a good judge of character when it came to things like that, sorting out the genuine clients from those trying it on. It was just a pity he couldn't sense his own wife's unhappiness, couldn't see what was staring him right in the face.

Katherine's life before she met Ed had been dull, unadventurous and flat. She thought all that would change when she married him. She'd been wrong, oh-so wrong. If anything it was worse now than when she was young. And every moment that God sent she wished she was someone else, somewhere else, doing something else. It didn't matter what; all Katherine knew was that she was slowly losing her mind because of the monotony of her existence. Playing the dutiful wife and mother when she really wanted to jet off to another country and have a fling with a complete stranger experienced in the wilds of sexual experimentation. Ed must have thought it was called the 'missionary position' because you had to use it religiously.

Was it too late, she wondered? Could she make a fresh start, take Fraser away and make a new, more exciting like for herself somewhere? Could she really do that to Ed? These were selfish thoughts. But they plagued her all the time, so much so they found their way out through her mouth in the form of criticisms and sideswipes. If she wasn't careful she'd end up becoming the very model of a nagging old fishwife.

"So, I guess we're stuck with it," said Ed, putting down the luggage at the side of her. "We'll have to make the best of a bad situation. I might just ring the hotel though and let them know we'll be a bit late."

Katherine tutted. "Why don't you stand up for yourself a bit more, Ed? You spend all your time dealing with the unfair treatment of other people, and when your own family gets messed around…"

"That's different, Kath."

"No it's not. They should've let us know. Mind you, it wouldn't have happened in the first place if we'd been flying."

"No, there are never any disruptions when you fly, are there? I've been using trains all my life. They're much more… At least you know where you are with trains."

"And where are we, Ed?" Katherine asked, batting her brown eyes. "Where exactly *are* we?" There was a nasty tang to the words that her husband couldn't really miss.

"What do you mean?"

Katherine looked away to the side. "Nothing. Forget about it. Let's go and wait on the platform."

"No, hold on. I want to know what you meant."

"I didn't mean anything, Ed. Let's just forget about it." Behind her, Katherine could hear the man from the queue arguing with the ticket guy about something. She tuned in for a second and heard the words 'booking not registered'. The man with shoulder-length hair was threatening to speak to someone in charge unless they got the mess sorted out. Now that was how it should be done, that was the only way to make people listen. Kick up a fuss. It wasn't 'safe', but it got results, and no-one ever pushed you around.

Katherine pulled Fraser along by the hand. Her son looked how she felt. "For heaven's sake, Fraser, smile," she said. "We're supposed to be on holiday."

SAGITTARIUS
(Represented by the bowman or centaur)

The Sagittarian personality looks on the bright side of life nine times out of ten. Even if something is wrong in their world, they know that it won't be long before their life is back on track. Naturally they get upset sometimes, who doesn't? But this passes more quickly for the Sagittarian than for other signs. They are usually quite content with their lot. They are a lively bunch and love to be out and about with friends or companions—they hate to be repressed or restricted. The Sagittarian personality is also extremely intelligent and will enjoy reading or expanding their knowledge in some way. Their most distinctive trait is truthfulness. Again, as with other qualities we've discussed in this book, it can be a very good and a very bad thing. Obviously it means you can rely on a Sagittarian to give you an honest opinion. But watch out if they're riled because they're likely to tell you a few home truths about yourself that you might not like. They can be quite cutting with their observations, especially if they are upset or angry about something.

CANCER
(Represented by the crab)

Cancer people are amongst the kindest in the zodiac. They are considerate, and tend to put others first before themselves, which at times can lead to them losing the odd argument. Like their symbol, the crab, who scuttles along sideways, they tend to come at problems or situations from a sideways perspective. Extremely home loving, this can manifest itself in a need to feel safe and secure, and when challenged they will withdraw and hide. Cancer folk are highly attuned to the needs of others though (some even claim psychic abilities), which helps them when they are in relationships. They always see when something is wrong or needs attention and use their unique ways of tackling problems to fix whatever it is that needs fixing.

CAPRICORN
(Represented by the goat)

Capricorn people can often be misunderstood. They come across as serious, detached and sombre, full of pessimism and bleak warnings. Actually, they probably have the best sense of humor of all the signs, even if they are at pains to reveal this. So, what makes them so grave much of the time? Is it a sense of world-weariness, a 'seen it all before' mentality? Sort of. Capricorn people can tend to have a downer on the world, if they've had bad experiences or have been in a situation where they are picking up a lot of negative vibes.

* * *

The light in the toilets was blue, to stop the junkies from jacking up.

It didn't bother Zachary Tench. He didn't need to see his veins to take this particular drug. Just see the white powder, just find his nose. Fuck, that felt good. And he needed to feel good. He was in a bad, bad situation. If this stuff could make him feel better, then he was all for it.

He heard the main door go, but the coke was kicking in, tingling. He bent slightly in the cubicle; the footsteps passed by on their way to the urinals. It wasn't Terry or Pete, or any other of Wyatt's gorillas. Not that he thought it would be for one second. They wouldn't find out what he'd done for a while yet, and by that time he'd be long gone.

Zach sat down on the toilet, head resting against the cistern. A nondescript holdall was by his feet. But it wasn't filled with clothes or anything else he'd need for the trip. Zach reached down and opened it up. He just couldn't resist looking inside every now and again, making sure it was still there, making sure this gamble was all worth it. Life or death, win or lose: you play the odds and take your chance.

The contents of the casino's safe were still in there.

Calmer now, he took out one bundle of cash and thumbed the money. He fought the urge to whistle in case the man at the urinal heard him.

I'll say this much for you, Zachary Gavin Tench, you've got some nerve. A cool hundred grand.

The combination of the drugs and dosh took his mind off how he'd acquired this fortune for a moment. But it soon came back to him: stealing into Wyatt's office, then stealing the money right from under the man's nose like that. He could justify this by saying it was only what was owed. His retirement fund; payment for being Wyatt's hired hand these past few years. It made him want to puke when he thought about it. How Wyatt had deceived him; turned him into something he could no longer stomach, someone who stood by and did nothing to help that poor girl Colette. Zach gripped the money tighter when he remembered what that bastard had done to keep her quiet.

He knew the law was no protection against men like Wyatt; never had been. That's why he had to get away before the net tightened and he ran out of options. Go on the run, lay low for a while, and then maybe find a way to get out of the country. It wasn't going to be easy, he knew that as well. But anything was better than the life he'd been living as one of Wyatt's lackeys. Zach still had a few friends who might help him out, people he could probably trust—if they were paid just enough. There were no ties to keep him in this city anyway, no one he really cared about or who cared about him. There hadn't been since Sally walked out and the barriers had gone up again. He could hardly blame her after the way he'd acted, the things he'd said and done. It was better to keep your distance and not form attachments, especially in his line of 'work'.

The splintering of bone, the crack of broken arms and legs...

Zach heard the taps running outside now. The guy was finishing up. The hand-dryer coughed out its air and then the door went again. It was time for him to get out of here. He jammed the money back into the holdall, wiped his nose, and opened the cubicle door. Zach looked at himself in the mirrors opposite; he didn't like what he saw staring back at him. But he could live with it, just. He hoped.

SCORPIO
(Represented by the scorpion)

Scorpios have a bit of a reputation. They're seen by some as the bad boys and girls of the zodiac, and seen by others as just plain bad news. This is quite unfair really as the vast majority born under this sign are very nice people who are a delight to spend time with. All right, it may be true that they do blow their tops from time to time, and have a tendency to do things on the spur of the moment they might later regret, but it gives them character. They can be obsessive and even possessive, with fixed ideas about life, and can be a torrent of raging emotions beneath the skin. In their dealings with others they might distance themselves, possibly because they have been let down or hurt in the past when they have given more of themselves than they should.

In dealings with money, Scorpios come into their own. Everyone needs this to survive, but people born under this sign know that it can buy you influence, prestige, and is an important status symbol in today's society. They like to compete in the big money stakes even if they don't have that much of it themselves. They might bet the shirt off their back to raise some brass, or even get into debt to give the impression they are doing better than they actually are.

Whatever career a Scorpio chooses, it must have value. Their work life is very important and it must serve a purpose they feel comfortable with. They have to know that their efforts are leading to something worthwhile. It's also necessary for Scorpios to let off their pent up emotional energies somehow. And if this can't happen at work it must happen at play.

* * *

Mary Dowling was late. As always.

Careering along the platform, she bumped into a man coming out of the toilets, causing him to drop his holdall. He pulled back sharply but his reflexes seemed dulled. She stooped to pick up the bag, but his hand still got there first.

"I'm sorry," she said. "I'm... I'm sorry." Damn, she should just shut up now because she sounded such an idiot. She didn't know where her mind was half the time these days. "I'm late for the train." *You didn't have to tell him that, he doesn't want to listen to you waffling on. Shut up now, just shut up, Mary.* "That's why I'm in a hurry."

The man, who looked like he hadn't had a decent night's sleep in weeks, clutched the bag to his chest. "The train's been delayed," he told her.

"Has it? Has it?" *Of course it has, that's why there are people still on the platform. Now walk away, Mary.* "Oh, that's good. Thank you... I mean, I'm sorry. I... thank you."

The man walked off down the platform, looking back over his shoulder at her. Wanted to be away as soon as he could, probably. No big surprise; she was a walking disaster area, twenty million things buzzing around in her brain twenty-four seven. Worries about this, worries about that. Worries about work—the fact that they were laying off so many people at the mobile phone place—worries about how her ageing father was coping now that she'd finally moved away from home; and worrying about him worrying about her and how she was going to pay the mortgage. Worries about her friends and how they were dealing with various ups and downs in their lives—they always seemed to come to her with problems.

And worries about her voice.

That last one, the most important one at the moment, had kept her awake most of last night. Not that she slept much anyway, which was another thing to worry about. She'd spent all week trying to talk customers into buying the latest Nokia, Motorola or Siemens, sometimes going blue in the face explaining the different tariffs, contracts and the new gadgets that seemed to be coming out weekly to hook the punters. The latest was a big push about picture messaging, which as far as she could see was just a stupid gimmick so you could pull faces at your mates while you were on the phone... although it would cut down on the amount of infidelity that could go on, as husbands and partners would no longer be able to just ring in and say, "Sorry, darling, I'm working late again." But that was getting off the point, as Mary was often wont to do.

She'd been working—and talking—really hard in the hopes that she wouldn't get the sack, lose her new house, and end up with no money for food or anything else. There she was again. *Stick to the point, Mary, you muddlehead.* But as well as that she'd also been practicing for the talent show auditions taking place today, belting out numbers like 'I will Survive' and 'Dancing Queen' (the 70s were her favorite era for music) so loud that her neighbors came round to complain about the noise several times. Never mind, it would all be worth it if she could impress the judges. Although she wouldn't be impressing anyone if she couldn't get a note out. Mary quietly sang a verse of 'Brown Girl in the Ring', drawing a few funny looks from the family who'd just come onto the platform. She smiled at them and mouthed the word sorry. The little boy, clutching his mother's hand, frowned.

She tried not to worry about it. She'd been waiting too long for a chance like this one. Ever since she could remember, Mary had wanted to sing—properly, for a living. She used to perform at Christmas and birthday parties when the whole family was gathered, ignoring the aunties and uncles who called her dizzy whenever she forgot a word or line. Ignoring the put-downs from cousins who laughed whenever she fell over during her made-up dance routines. It was just nice to be up there, doing what she loved the most—in front of an audience, appreciative or otherwise.

Mary had fostered this love throughout her school years, even joining a choir so she could work her way up in the ranks to soloist. But dreams were all well and good in a dream world, and as soon as she was thrust into the real one with all its harsh practicalities, Mary's ambitions had taken a bit of a back seat. Only now, five years later, was she starting to think about maybe living her dreams again and trying for a shot at stardom. She'd seen the way others had got on in these kinds of shows: record deals, TV appearances, interviews, people clamoring to get their autographs. That was what she wanted for herself, what she'd always wanted. And some of them didn't have half as much talent as her, which wasn't a bigheaded or jealousy thing at all—just a fact. Mary had a lovely voice... that is she'd *had* a lovely voice until today. Now she wasn't so sure.

Now she was worried.

While she'd been busy worrying and singing, the train had pulled into the station: a long blue and yellow streak of metal that ground to a hissing halt a few meters away from her.

If you're not careful, you really will miss it, she said to herself and ran towards the opening doors. The auditions weren't that far away, a couple of stops down the line, but if she missed the train there was no way she'd get there by any other means.

Singing under her breath again, Mary boarded the nearest carriage.

TAURUS

(Represented by the bull)

Taurus people are the kind of people you can really count on in a crisis. They rarely lose their cool and allow themselves plenty of time to accomplish tasks. They are often scared to try new things or go in new directions because they are frightened of what they might lose in the process if they fail. However, those that do take the odd risk occasionally find it sometimes pays off. Your typical Taurean will work at things inch by inch, sometimes taking quite a while to get projects off the ground. They make loyal, loving and steadfast friends, but they have a small group of long standing buddies rather than a large group of casual acquaintances. They are dependable and practical and love to own their own place if they can, because of the sense of stability it gives them. One of the most good looking of all the signs, careers in the modeling or beauty industry are a good choice, or even some kind of performance work as Taureans tend to possess extremely nice voices.

* * *

The voice was talking to him again.

"Go on, get fucking moving then."

Jez Bingley climbed on board the train, looking to his left and his right.

"Now why don't you find a seat and sit down," it said to him. "We have to gather our thoughts."

Jez did as he was told. It was easier that way, he found. He pressed the button on the doors to his left. They hissed open and allowed him entrance to carriage C. There was a two-seater space just next to him, so he took off his coat and placed it on the window seat. Then he settled down in the red velvet of the outer seat. Jez stared at the plastic tray in front of him, held up by a little wheel on the back of the chair. He twisted the wheel and the tray dropped down on his lap.

"Fuck me, what are you doing now?" said the voice. "Just leave it alone. Go on, do as you're told."

Jez put the tray back and secured it with the wheel. His eyes caught the upright black armrest by the side of him, but he didn't bring it down.

"No, you can leave that alone as well," said the voice, reading his mind... which wasn't that difficult really because it was a product of that very same cerebellum. Some small part of Jez knew this, or thought he did. All those hours of talking to the people at the hospital as a boy, all the sessions explaining about the voice and the doctors who had told him it was just a case of misfiring neurons in his brain, just a figment of his imagination they could adjust. And the medication had worked; did its job and quietened the voice, his other half, his alter ego. They'd dulled, muffled and subdued it. But it hadn't stayed away forever. Eventually the voice had started talking to him again. Only softly at first, but persuasive, same as always. The first thing it told him to do was keep quiet this time, not let anybody know. Then they could have some real fun, the voice had promised. "You'll see."

It hadn't been Jez's idea of fun though. The voice had talked him and ultimately bullied him into things, terrible things. It hadn't been content anymore to see him hurt himself, to stick pins in his arms or stub lit cigarettes out on his stomach. No. It had forced him to go out in search of others to torment as well. To inflict this madness on.

Jez closed his eyes now and flashed back to the very first of them: a young girl, couldn't have been more than twenty-something, out walking her West Highland Terrier near the bank of a canal. The voice had made him spy on her first, looking, recording the information. Then the voice had started to whisper to him, how good it would feel, how if he hurt her it would save him even more pain. Jez tried to resist, fought against it so badly, but the voice had ranted and raved until he thought he would actually go deaf from the shouting. And so Jez had obeyed, dragging her into a nearby thicket, hand over her mouth; watching as the dog yapped a couple of times and then ran off. "Go on, do it, DO IT!"

Someone walked past him and brushed his shoulder. Jez flinched, his eyes snapping open.

"Excuse me," said the woman in the pink jumper and jeans. Jez attempted a smile but it came out all wrong. The woman carried on down the aisle a short way and found a seat, facing him at an angle. Jez caught himself staring and looked away. But his eyes kept flicking back to her every couple of seconds.

"She's nice," said the voice. "Very nice."

The woman opened up a magazine and started to read. Jez noticed that every so often she would peer over the top.

"Imagine what her insides would look like," the voice whispered.

* * *

Tracy Simmons took one last look over the top of her magazine.

He's nice, she thought to herself. Cute in an understated sort of way. He had that whole Tom Cruise thing going for him, but his smile could use a bit of working on. God, not again. First the guy with the cases, now an innocent passenger in her carriage. How desperate can you get? Chance meetings just never happened for her, unlike everybody else it seemed. The amount of times she'd heard the story of how her mum had met dad. She'd probably hear it again another dozen times this weekend.

"We just bumped into each other at the laundrette. It was love at first sight, over the spinning sheets and towels." If only something like that could happen to her. But you couldn't force it. You could no more control your destiny than those stupid horoscopes could predict it. Tracy flipped the pages and went back to reading her magazine.

GEMINI

(Represented by the twins)

Gemini folk are people of the moment. They are instinctive, restless and always on the look out for an opportunity. Gemini's are extremists. They swing from one extreme to the other—sometimes being generous and kind, and other times deceitful or even, in some cases, malicious. Because they are represented by the sign of the twin, this sort of 'dual personality' should come as no great surprise. Often Gemini's will act as if they are two people trapped in the same body. They need permanence, but at the same time always want to be on the move. They value friendships and are generally keen to meet new people. Yet at the same time they might let these friendships dwindle once the first waves of curiosity about a person have been sated. Equally, there are times when they just want to be alone and won't speak to anyone, then there are times when you just can't shut them up! They are certainly versatile, adapting to given situations readily with an almost chameleon-like knack. They do, however, find it hard to express their feelings. For them it is much easier to deal in the realm of thoughts and ideas.

Compatibility Match
Pisces & Gemini

There could be so many misunderstandings in this pairing it's untrue. The Piscean will long for the Gemini to show their feelings more and not be scared to tell them what they're thinking—but do they really want to know? The Gemini will be content to look upon this arrangement as little more than just plain business. They are likely to hurt the Piscean because they don't fully understand them.

Gemini: You'll feel the need to break out in new directions more than ever now. See new places and do new things. Let others criticize you if they like, you'll be having too much of a good time to care. Your individuality shines through at the moment, so don't be a sheep anymore. There's so much out there for the taking.

* * *

Belinda Gould held on to the back of a seat as the train started to move. It was time to take a little walk.

"Tickets, please," she said to some of the newest passengers on board. A middle-aged man with neatly cropped hair gave her an orange and green card. She clipped it and handed it back. "Thank you, sir," she said. "Hope you have a nice journey. Tickets please." Belinda moved on to the next set of seats.

Who'd have ever thought she'd wind up in this line of work? Not her, that was for sure. She'd long-since swallowed her pride though and accepted that the days when she'd be recognized by passers-by, or even passengers, were gone forever. They had been many moons ago. Her model looks and magnetism had got her far in the fledgling fashion industry, but that was over twenty years ago now. At nearly 50, she still retained some of her allure (her name, apparently, even meant beauty in Spanish), and her charm had never really deserted her—she could still sweet-talk her landlord into fixing the plumbing or heating when others in her block had to whistle. But she was a very different person to-day to the one who had posed for eager photographers back then. She'd learnt some very valuable life lessons, one of which was that nothing ever lasts.

Sometimes, when she was feeling particularly nostalgic, Belinda would take out those magazine covers and look them over; relive her glory days. But it usually upset her too much to do so; brought back memories. Some good, some very bad.

When she'd been plucked from obscurity after winning a sponsored beauty pageant to model for a well-known catalogue chain, Belinda never once thought she'd end up coming back full circle. The catalogue work had been good, and the money had allowed her to move out of home, but it had been well-known photographer Gerard Lewishon who'd really changed her life. He'd taken her under his wing and made her into a star, the pictures he'd produced accentuating every beautiful line of her face, and curve of her body. Today Belinda had more curves than ever before, just in all the wrong places.

Gerard wanted nothing in return, but after spending so much time with her he'd been helpless when *she* decided she wanted them to be more than just friends. That was before his much publicized battle against alcoholism. She'd been so eager to believe he was the one for her, understood her like no one ever had, that she'd overlooked these faults for so long. A mistake that led to a very nasty split and Gerard's eventual check in at a drying out clinic somewhere in Canada. They'd tried to patch things up several more times after that, but it hadn't been the same. She often thought how much better it might have been if they'd simply stayed friends instead of complicating things. Her fault. They hadn't spoken for so long now. But that was what life was all about: regrets and moving on.

Which Belinda did with style, making a fortune in the process. She'd also spent a fortune too. By the time the work began tailing off, it was too late to put anything aside for a potential deluge. Belinda soon found herself penniless and jobless. She'd listened to the advice of far too many people, including a new agent who swore he only had her best interests at heart, and had chosen badly in terms of her later commissions. It was surprising how many 'friends' she'd helped out in the past suddenly stopped calling her up, or crossed her off their invitation lists at parties. Add to that some pretty vicious rumors about her sexual habits since Gerard moved out—rumors that were completely unfounded—and Belinda Gould, the international model, was no more. That comedown had been a hell of a thing for her to get over; in fact she wasn't sure she *was* over it, even now. Unlike Belinda, people had short memories, and her face had been wiped from the history books by a succession of other gorgeous girls. When she thought about how much they earned today for doing exactly the same thing...

Times had been tough. There'd been days when she hadn't even ventured out of her house, which she lost anyway when it was repossessed. And she'd piled on the pounds, binge eating chocolate to get her through the day.

Then she met David, a charity worker from Essex: the kindest man in the whole world. He didn't know who she was; didn't care. All he cared about was her. If it hadn't been for him coming along, she might have pressed the self-destruct button once and for all. Had that been why she'd married him? Out of gratitude? And maybe it explained why she'd had an affair with a carpet-fitter called Jim a few years later. That had carried on for some time, with Belinda having absolutely no idea who to choose. In the end it had been taken out of her hands. David suspected something was wrong and confronted her. Belinda didn't even need to confirm it; just a downward turn of the eye and he knew. That look on his face, she'd never forget it as he walked out on her and the marriage. And when Jim declared all he'd ever wanted from her was a good time, Belinda had been left alone again. Her best friend and lover: gone.

To somehow try and make amends, she'd started working for one or two of the charities David was involved with. Belinda had always been interested in doing this, mainly because of the way David's eyes lit up when he spoke of helping others, so now she decided to actually get in there and try it herself. And it felt good. She did what she could: orphans, the disabled, third world. But there was so much more they needed. If Belinda could have her time back again, could have that money back that she'd wasted, she knew exactly what she'd do with it—no hesitation.

As for her post collecting tickets, it was something she'd fallen into by accident again. While waiting for a train herself, she'd spotted the position advertised. It was better than the cleaning jobs she'd been forced to accept to pay the bills, and at least people would be looking at her again—would be forced to turn in her direction as she said:

"Tickets please, thank you."

Finishing up in this particular carriage, she turned towards her admiring public. Then Belinda pressed the button on the doors and they hissed open.

LIBRA

(Represented by the scales)

Librans are people persons. They will go out of their way to make you feel comfortable, generally put others first and will do whatever they can to help out. As their symbol, the scales, suggests, they love balance and harmony. When things are out of kilter, they are at their most miserable. They can have a very relaxing influence on others, and can be eminently charming—thanks in no small part to their ruler, Venus. This also bestows upon them fantastic looks, so you might find they gravitate towards the beauty or fashion industries. And the more profitable the better, because they do love to blow their cash. But just because they like to see order in their surroundings, this doesn't mean Librans can find peace within themselves. Quite the contrary. Often they are so busy trying to sort out problems and calm others down that they end up being a big ball of anxiety themselves. It is perhaps a good thing they can mask this so well. Another recognized characteristic of the Libran is their famous indecision. They are just terrible at making up their minds and are likely to be swayed by what others have to say rather than thinking for themselves. They tend to put their loved ones on pedestals, and will work hard at relationships to stop them falling apart. Having said this, they tend to make the same mistakes over and over and never seem to learn from them.

* * *

Ed Pryce said nothing.

He'd said nothing while they deposited the luggage in one of the compartments at the side of the sliding door; he'd said nothing as they'd located a four-seater table space and sat down around it—Katherine on the other side, with Fraser; he'd said nothing as the train pulled away from the station. He might not have been very good at winning arguments, but he could sulk for Britain when it came down to it.

Everything he'd done in his life had been for his family. Okay, so he probably wasn't the most dynamic person in the world. But he always did what he thought was right and tried his best to make his wife and son happy. Ed looked at the expression on his son's face: the young boy appeared anything but happy. In fact, when was the last time he'd really seen him smile? Ed couldn't remember. *This atmosphere can't be any good for him.*

Katherine was staring vacantly up the aisle. Ed remembered how happy *he'd* been when she agreed to marry him. Without a doubt their wedding day had to be the most fantastic day of his whole life. And yes, he knew that in spite of her complaints sometimes she really did love him. He saw it in her eyes when she looked at him, when they shared those special moments together away from the world. Heard it in the responses to his touch, as they lay down together. She'd come around when they arrived at the coast; who needed trips abroad? This silly bickering was pointless.

Ed opened his mouth to say something, but Katherine got there first.

"I think I'm going to get a drink from the buffet car," she declared. "Do you want anything, Fraser?"

Fraser shook his head solemnly. Katherine got up, brandishing her purse.

"Could you bring me back a coffee, honey?" asked Ed.

He smiled at her hopefully. Katherine blinked a couple of

times and then headed up the aisle, towards the doors and beyond to carriage D.

She'll come around, Ed said to himself again. *She'll come around.*

Taken from The Daily Record

Cancer: A problem that's been plaguing you for some time will finally come to a conclusion. You can no longer ignore something that's right in front of you, Cancer. Wake up and smell the coffee. Once you've done this, things should smooth themselves out eventually. And in all probability your troubles will be over by the end of the day.

* * *

Zachary Tench instinctively looked up as the woman passed him by, purse in her hand.

Seeing it made him grasp the holdall more tightly. There were more than just a couple of notes and a handful of change inside there. And now she was gone, her skirt's swishing all he could hear. Zach let out a tired breath.

The effects of the high had now worn off, but he daren't chance going to the toilet again. He should try and keep a clear head now that he was finally on the move. And anyway everyone would be able to see exactly how long he was in there... with his holdall. Might raise suspicion. Zach couldn't afford for that to happen. Not now.

He should try and relax, maybe listen to some music. That always did the trick usually, although these were very unusual circumstances. Zach reached inside his pocket and pulled out a pair of earphones, only placing one in his ear so he could still tell if anyone crept up behind him. He switched on the small radio and tried tuning it in. He found a classics station first; not really his scene. Then there was some up-and-coming indie-band bashing away and singing about how terrible life was now they were famous, which was strange because all they'd ever sung about before was how terrible life was when you *weren't* famous. Zach thumbed the wheel again, and came across the news on a local station.

"... still looking for the murderer of five young women today, and are appealing for anyone with information to come forward. The first victim, Victoria Styles, was found last month dumped in woodland not far from her home. It's believed that she was out walking her dog when the attack occurred. Since then the bodies of Kaelene Marsh, Lindsey Thompson, Donna Gates and Sadie Noble have also been discovered in similar states. Chief Inspector Arthur Bellingham, who is leading the investigation, had this to say about the man they were looking for: 'We're dealing with a very sick and dangerous individual. If anyone out there knows any—'"

Zach thumbed on. Fucking police, there wasn't a chance in hell they'd catch the guy. They were worse than useless. Appealing for information because they didn't have a clue what they were doing. Was there any wonder people like Wyatt (people like him?) could get away with the things that they did.

He closed his eyes and saw the face of Colette. The bargirl hadn't deserved that, nobody deserved what Wyatt had done to her. And all because she'd seen a little too much and wanted to leave the Casino. There was only one way you left Wyatt's place once you were on the inside. Once you had information that could do him serious damage.

You should have done something to stop it. You knew what he was planning to do. But you didn't have the nerve, did you? Didn't have the balls. Had enough to pull a fast one when nobody was looking, though, didn't you? But you stood by when it was something important and you did nothing. Nothing at all. How does that make you feel, Zachary Tench? What exactly does that make you?

Zach didn't wish to answer that. He opened his eyes and spun the tuning wheel again, finally losing himself in a cavalcade of heavy metal music.

Taken from Lifestyle Magazine

Scorpio: We can all sit around brooding about past mistakes and about what might have been. The sky is now offering you a chance to put all that behind you if you can. I know what you're thinking, that's easier said than done. But if you're ever to find the lasting peace you're looking for you've got to give yourself a few breaks first, Scorpio.

* * *

The buffet cart wasn't particularly full, just a couple of people before her in the queue.

Katherine Pryce joined the line and waited for her turn. The figure in front looked around, and she recognized him as the man from the ticket queue back at the station. The man who had complained. Unlike Ed. His eyes caught hers for a fraction of a second longer than they should have done, and he smiled. Katherine did likewise.

The man turned back, but not fully this time. He was trying to see her out of the corner of his eye. Katherine looked him up and down, from his shoulder-length hair to his shiny shoes. He was about 5'11" or perhaps more—a good few inches taller than her—and broad at the shoulders. Very broad. Katherine's gaze lingered on him until he looked back at her again. She looked away, self-conscious.

When her eyes swiveled left, he was still facing her direction. He gave another smile. Katherine laughed, a little nervously.

"It can take ages to get served sometimes, can't it?" said the man, despite the fact the queue was now moving pretty rapidly. His voice was strong, confident, as if he was used to addressing people.

"Yes, it can."

"Are you traveling far?" he asked, then shook his head. "I'm sorry, it's really none of my—"

145

"To the coast... for a holiday," Katherine said.

The man nodded. "I see."

"How about you?" She couldn't believe she'd just asked that.

"I'm going to a conference."

"Oh, really? That sounds exciting."

He laughed now. "Well, probably not, but it'll make a change."

"A change from what?" Katherine probed further. "Listen to me. Look, you don't have to answer that."

"I teach English. In college." He added the last bit to show that he wasn't just any old teacher. "Used to travel quite a bit, but I don't get much chance these days. I'm sorry, talking away and forgetting my manners. My name's Will. William Booth." Will held out his hand and she shook it. Again, this lasted much longer than it should have, but neither of them seemed to mind.

"Katherine... Kathy. With a 'K'. Pleasure to meet you, Will."

"Pleasure's mine, Kathy with a 'K'." As he released her left hand Will felt the ring on the fourth finger. He looked down. "Ah," he said.

"Ah," mimicked Katherine.

"Sir? Sir?" said a voice. It was Will's turn to be served. He had trouble tearing his eyes away from Katherine to order, and even as he asked for the BLT sandwich and tea he kept glancing back at her. This time his eyes said something else; it was the same thing Katherine was thinking: What a shame.

Will picked up his food and drink, then paid. As he walked past Katherine, he said, "See you, Kathy," and smiled one last time.

Katherine watched him walk back out through the sliding doors, stop, and look round one final time. Then he disappeared.

It was a nice dream, she thought.

And now she really did need that cigarette.

Compatibility Match
Leo & Sagittarius

What a wonderful link-up! This couple has all the makings of a match made in heaven. This pair could have lots of wild and wonderful adventures together. For them, there are no limits. They have so much in common, especially when it comes to showing that they care, which these two would do at any given opportunity. And what's more, they have the same kind of outlook on life—in essence it's too short not to have a great time. Travel might be a particular pleasure for Leos and Sagittarians, in all its forms.

* * *

She opened up her mouth and tried to see her tonsils through her pocket mirror.

Ignoring the strange looks from the other passengers in her carriage, Mary Dowling gave a little "Arrgghhh" to see if the fleshy pendulums were inflamed at all. They weren't. The soreness was in her imagination, she knew that really. Just another thing to add to the worry, the pressure. There was nothing whatsoever wrong with her throat, her voice, or anything else come to that. She shut her mouth and checked her make-up. Was she wearing a little too much blusher?

No, no. You look fine, Mary. Better than fine. Think positive.

Mary wished she could believe that. More than anything she wanted it all to come together on that stage when she did her number, whichever one she finally chose: the voice, the look, everything. And she was so worried it wouldn't. She'd tried telling herself a million times that this wasn't the be all and end all anyway. That there'd be other talent competitions, other opportunities. That all good things come to those who wait. It was just that bad things came to those who waited, too. And for some reason this shot felt like the only one she'd ever have in her life.

Now how did the words to 'Dancing Queen' go again? Never mind the words, what was the tune?

From her handbag came a faint electronic ditty that didn't help in the slightest. Mary pulled out her mobile; it was a nice little black model hers, she'd done herself a really good discount on it at the store. The lime green display told her it was her dad calling.

Mary pressed the receive button. "Hi Dad… No, I'm just on the train…" *Never mind Dancing Queen, you're turning into a Cliché Queen now, Mary.* "I'm whispering because of my voice… That's right… Yes, yes. I've left myself enough time… Bit nervous, y'know… No, I'll be okay…" The miserable little boy sitting diagonally across from her with his father was peering down the aisle. Mary shrugged, as if to say 'you know what parents are like'. The code seemed to go unread by the boy. "Yes, I know you do, Dad... Thank you... Yes, I love you, too. Take care, bye." Mary pressed the button to hang up, then switched off the phone completely before she forgot about it. She didn't want it ringing in the middle of her performance, her dad calling to ask how she'd done while she was in the middle of actually doing it. Or even one of her friends texting her to ask 'u win?' One less thing to worry about.

Oh, but it was so sweet of her dad to care. His phone call had cheered her up a bit; there were times when all you really needed to do was talk to one of your parents. She just wished her mum could have been around to wish her luck as well. Maybe she was, somewhere.

Now Mary was aware that she needed to pee. She hadn't had time on the platform because she'd been zipping about, and had forgotten about it for a while, pushed to the back of her mind by all the other worries. But there really was an aching pressure pushing down on her bladder now. It wouldn't be the first time today and would most definitely not be the last. It'd only get worse as her nerves increased, as all the worries piled up. It was no good, she had to go.

The toilet behind her was in use, as was the one at the other end of the carriage: the red light signifying that people were inside, relieving themselves. The thought just made it worse for her and she wanted to go more badly than ever before. Mary crossed her legs, but that just heightened the problem.

Why do people have to take so long? she thought, knowing she'd never been quick herself in public loos—particularly ones on board moving trains. *What if I can't hold it?* Now *that* was something to worry about. Getting up in front of the judges after you've wet yourself. Not the best way to make a good impression.

Mary uncrossed her legs and crossed them again the other way.

Come on... hurry up, hurry up...

149

No, it was no use. Mary got up and decided to go for a walk in search of the nearest empty loo. Somewhere a bit further down perhaps.

She could also have another practice of her favorite songs, provided she could remember the lyrics, the tunes, and provided her voice was still all right. Maybe she'd check her tonsils again just to make doubly sure; there was bound to be a big mirror in the bathroom.

Taurus & Health

Taurus rules the neck and throat, so this can be their Achilles heel sometimes. If they are feeling particularly stressed out or run down, problems can occur with this part of the body. Perhaps they might lose their voice or even develop a stiff neck through tension. It is advisable, therefore, that Taureans keep a close eye on this in order to prevent difficulties arising in the first place. Prevention is, after all, better than the cure.

* * *

Oliver Collins finished cleaning his glasses with the cloth and put it back in his case, in the special compartment he'd fitted on the inside. A place for everything and everything in its place— that was his motto. Well, it wasn't actually *his*, someone else had come up with the dictum. But it was an exceptionally fine one and Oliver didn't think the originator would mind too much if he borrowed it from time to time.

Placing the glasses back on his nose, he looked out at the track; the scenery—trees, hedges, fields—passing by on either side. It gave him an incredible thrill to know that he pressed the buttons and turned the dials, monitored the readouts that propelled this great piece of machinery towards its destination. You could keep your cars, bikes and busses. This was the only way forward in Oliver's opinion.

He'd always loved trains. It probably stemmed from when his brother had been given that Hornby set for Christmas one year. George Collins hadn't permitted his younger sibling to touch the toys, hadn't even allowed him go near them for months, but Oliver had found ways to watch as his brother played. He spent many a good hour peering into his brother's bedroom through the crack in the door, wishing he could be the one to send those tiny trains around the track. Eventually, of course, George had grown out of it, but by that time Oliver too had 'come of age', and his parents had got rid of the set altogether. Oliver wanted to keep it so much, wanted to have just one go on it, to blow the whistle, to make the steam rise from those funnels. But he had been denied.

And now here he was, driving the real thing—the biggest train set money could buy. In more light-hearted moments Oliver imagined some great hand above the clouds tinkering with the control box to whizz his train along the tracks. That would make him titter to himself sometimes: God's own Hornby kit, he'd joke, with everything in *its* proper place.

Oliver couldn't believe he'd been so lucky to fulfill his child-hood ambition. When most lads in the playground had been im-aging themselves as spacemen or cowboys or detectives when they grew up, for Oliver it had always been a train driver. He'd applied for various positions as soon as he'd been old enough, anything at first just to get a foot in the door. And over the years he had worked his way up to this enviable position. He'd seen some changes in his time, that was true. New technology he'd had to keep up with—a far cry from one lever to go, one to stop. This had meant studying hard so he didn't get left behind by some of the upstarts snapping at his heels in the world of modern train-fare... that was one of his little puns. But he'd pushed himself, made sure he was up to speed. He'd seen the industry torn apart by privatization too; companies splitting up and doing their own thing instead of one big happy family. He really missed the old days when everything was under one umbrella. In its place. But you couldn't live in the past, no one could. You could only live in the present and the future.

And what exciting things that held for rail enterprises he could only guess. There was talk of monorails, of slanting trains like those in other countries that tipped on their sides to go faster. Now that would be quite something. Imagine driving one of those! Oliver scratched his head through thinning hair. Would he be around to see such changes? he wondered. He hoped so. He kept himself fit enough with a daily workout regimen, took vitamin and cod liver oil capsules. For the time being though, he'd content himself with driving this lovely lady, whom he'd christened Joyce. They'd all been called Joyce; every single train he'd ever driven. It was the name of the only woman he'd ever loved, now his brother's wife. A woman he'd worshipped from afar for so long but had never had the courage to approach.

Never mind. His Joyces had been adequate substitute wives, with this one his particular pride and joy. Oliver patted the panel in front of him, felt the vibration of the train.

He smiled and sat back in his seat. "Purring like a pussy cat, aren't you, my sweet?" She should be. He'd checked all the systems himself personally before they left the departure station that morning, just like always. It all ran like clockwork if he had anything to do with it, a place for everything; everything in its place.

VIRGO

(Represented by the virgin)

Virgo people are incredibly methodical and practical, being the second of the Earth signs. They gain great satisfaction in seeing a job done right, and will come down very hard on themselves if they feel they've let the side down. It's true they are sticklers, which is not necessarily a bad thing at work, but can drive close ones to distraction. They have a tendency to criticize others because of their impossibly high standards, and often these are extremely difficult to live up to. They can, however, be a tower of strength when trouble strikes. They do have difficulty dealing with their emotional sides, believing this might make them exposed. Consequently they will keep certain special people in the dark, and this can lead to all kinds of confusions and misapprehensions. Your typical Virgo can't help giving out these cold signals. They don't even realize they're doing it sometimes. It might just be that they're preoccupied with work and forget that those around them have feelings that can be hurt. They are more comfortable around, and will get on better with, people who they can understand and who can understand them.

* * *

Fraser Pryce was looking at his father across the table and frowning.

He was always getting told off for doing that, at home, at school. Why couldn't he lighten up, why did he have to look so miserable all the time?

"He's such a serious child," one of the teachers had told his mum and dad at parents' evening. Katherine and Edward Pryce had both agreed, "Yes, he is." At eight years of age, Fraser was supposed to be having the time of his life: causing mayhem, laughing and joking, out playing with the other children. Instead he read books in his room and watched the news and documentaries about global warming on TV. In his short stay on this planet Fraser Pryce had done a lot of observing, had come to a lot of conclusions about humanity as a 'civilization'.

He saw people buzzing around when he went out shopping with his mum. Hurrying to get somewhere, anywhere, and half of them had no idea where. Pushing and banging into each other, standing impatiently at check-outs and looking at their watches. Ignoring beggars and charity workers on the street, then spending their money on DVDs or compact discs they'd only watch or listen to once then forget about. Or filling their faces with junk food that they knew was slowly killing them.

Once he and his mum had passed two men arguing about a parking space. The first man had tried to back in while the second headed into the space forwards. The pair had collided. Fraser watched them getting redder and redder in the face, so red he thought he might see steam coming out of their ears. The men came to blows eventually and Katherine had dragged Fraser away from the scene, trying to shield him from the violence. Why do parents always try to do that? he thought as he was being pulled along by his arm. The sooner and younger kids came to terms with how the world was, facing up to the reality of life, the better. What was the use of sugar coating things, painting everything to be some candy toy-filled heaven, only to be hit smack bang with the truth later on?

Fraser knew all about wars, poverty, hunger. Knew about weapons of mass—and not-so mass—destruction, about the third world and about diseases that could wipe out the entire population of the world if they were ever to escape from the secret laboratories that housed them. One of his few friends at school, Marshall, was always boasting about the horror movies he'd seen at the weekend when he went to stay with his grandparents. They let him stop up and watch all the gorefests. But Fraser had never seen the attraction himself. There were more horrific things if you just looked around you, more things to scare you than a man with razorblades for fingers or an alien creature that could suck out your brains.

Even at home, there were things that frightened Fraser. *Especially* at home. The way his mum and dad were with each other sometimes. The way they'd argue about nothing, about who was supposed to have paid the poll tax or whose turn it was to feed the cat. His dad would always go quiet in the hopes of calming everything down, or maybe winning the argument by sulking. It never worked and inevitably he'd crack before Fraser's mum did. And the way she often looked at his dad, like there was something missing. For a long time he'd thought they loved each other, and though it was clear his dad did love his mum, Fraser knew that it wasn't mutual. If there was no room for love at home, if the two people who'd made him couldn't get on with each other, what chance did the rest of humanity stand? Fraser had come to the conclusion that they stood none.

Was there any wonder he was so depressed?

His dad forced a smile. "Come on, Fraser, cheer up. Won't be too long before we get there. Then you'll be able to see the sea."

Fraser looked across at his father and frowned. A man sitting at the other end of the carriage got up. He looked a bit like that famous actor who'd been in all the films—the one with the spiky hair all the girls went mad for in his class. Tom something or other. Fraser frowned at him as well.

The man frowned back, tried to smile, then frowned again. As if something inside had suddenly stopped him. As if something or some*one* was telling him what to do.

Taken from The Daily Record

Capricorn: Buck up your ideas and you might find you have a different perspective on life. It's all very well moping around but nobody will want to know you if you do. Lately it feels as if you've had the weight of the world on your shoulders, I know, and this situation won't improve immediately. In fact it might even get worse. One thing is for certain, though, if you don't change your outlook things never will. Reach out, Capricorn. Change has to come from within.

* * *

Belinda Gould was still working her way along the train when the young man bumped into her.

"Easy, babe. What's your rush?" she said.

He apologized politely, showing a thin line of teeth. The youth was quite handsome with his spiky hair, blue eyes. If she'd been a few years younger—ten… okay, maybe twenty—and still in her modeling heyday…

"That's all right. Do you have your ticket?" she said to him. Her nervously pulled it out and showed it to her.

"Thank you." Belinda handed the ticket back and he apologized again. He carried on up the carriage.

That's the effect you still have on men, Belinda, she said to herself, and giggled. She finished up and moved on through the sliding doors to carriage C. The first person she came to was a man facing away from her, listening to the radio, clinging on to a holdall. He jerked slightly when she came up behind him, pulling his earphone out.

"Yes? Oh, right, ticket." He fumbled in his pocket and brought out a crumpled orange and green card. Quite how it had got into this state since leaving the station Belinda had no idea. She stamped it and handed it back.

"Cheers."

"You know, you look a bit uncomfortable sat with that. There's space to put your luggage down here—"

"It's okay," he cut in, a bit too quickly. "I'll keep it with me. Thanks anyway."

Belinda noticed his fingers trembling as he held the bag. She was doing it again. *You know you really should stop intimidating innocent young men, Belinda.* She shrugged. "It's up to you, sugar."

Moving away from him and on to the next passenger, she turned back briefly. In those few seconds he'd gone, his seat empty. *Now you're driving them away completely*, she thought. Belinda shook her head and got on with punching some more tickets.

Compatibility Match
Libra & Gemini

This pairing could have some wild times ahead of them! The Libran will value the Gemini's freethinking attitude and active mind—and what a mind it is—plus encourage them to develop the more sensitive side to their personality. As potential mates they will work well on all levels, but in particular on an intellectual plane. Though if the Libran has anything to do with it there will be more than just mental stimulation to spare.

Compatibility Match
Libra & Scorpio

This couple just do not get on well together. An extremely thorny match, they will struggle to work each other out and in the end probably walk away. The Libran might quite like the Scorpio's ardor, but when they have to lose control completely that's when the problems ensue. Balance is everything to a Libran and they won't tolerate anything disrupting the equilibrium, whereas Scorpios tend to thrive on this and have a 'live for the moment' mentality. They mix as easily as oil and water.

* * *

Mary Dowling didn't have to trek too far to find the nearest empty toilet; it was a good thing. The next intersection after carriage E boasted a big, empty loo. One of those spacious modern ones with *Star Trek* style doors that you locked by pressing a red button.

She'd nipped inside and emptied her bladder quickly, moaning with relief. She didn't want to spend too much time in here because the next stop wouldn't be far away, but she still wanted to check her throat in the big mirror and maybe sing a note or two before taking her seat again. She'd probably even go to the toilet a second time, just to make sure she'd drained every last dreg out. It was silly, she knew, and only caused by nerves. But all the same...

Mary opened her mouth and said "arrrr." She couldn't see any inflammation. She'd risk a few lines from 'Heart of Glass'.

Stop it, Mary.

Mary started to sing, accompanied by the chuntering of the train as it sailed along.

There was a banging on the door.

Oh blast, somebody's heard me. No, probably just someone bursting for wee like you were before.

The banging came again.

"Just a minute. I won't be a sec," said Mary.

The banging came hard now. Mary quickly rose above her initial embarrassment and started to get angry. It took a lot for her to lose her rag, but this impatient person was really winding her up. It wasn't as if she'd been in the toilet very long anyway.

More banging.

Mary pressed the red button to unlock the door. It started to slide across. "I said I won't be a—"

A hand grabbed her and forced her back into the toilet, covering her mouth, shoving her against the sink. There was a sudden pain in her side and she realized it was the hard porcelain jabbing into her. Her eyes pinwheeled, taking in the features of this person: the piercing blue eyes, the spiky hair. Her breath came in short gasps through his fingers, muffled sounds emerging through her clamped lips.

Her attacker pressed the red button and the door closed again, sealing them both inside. Then he held up his other hand, fingers spread, palm outwards.

"Ssshh... Please, please be quiet," he said. "Please... *I* don't want to hurt you."

No, he just wants to rape you. Here, in a train toilet, on the way to an audition to sing 'Heart of Glass', or maybe 'Dancing Queen'? Things like that just didn't happen. In dark alleyways, maybe, on your own walking... walking your dog. But not here, not now!

Mary struggled against his body, wriggling beneath him. His free hand came down and held her by the shoulder.

"Stop. Stop it." The man cocked his head to one side, as if listening to something. "No. Please. I don't want to." He was bending her further back over the sink, then his forearm came up and he pressed it hard against her windpipe. It was so quick there wasn't time for a scream. Mary bucked, bringing up her nails to scratch his face, but he pulled back just in time.

"You said we could wait." The man was crying now. "You said not yet. Please..." He looked her in the eye. "I don't want to hurt you, but *He* says that I must. If I don't then something terrible will happen. Something really terrible."

Jesus, he's not going to rape you, is he? Not going to rape you at all. He's going to do something much worse unless—

Mary brought up her knee, driving it straight between the man's legs. She felt him crumple, the forearm dropping. She tried to yell, tried to call out, but nothing came. It still felt as if the pressure was there.

Look what he's done! There's no way you'll ever get a decent note out now. No way in—

Mary twisted around, falling over the toilet, reaching out for the red button. She got up, then felt hands on her again. They pulled her back. Her fingers stretched out, centimeters away from the button. So close, so close...

Then she was being twisted around again, and struck across the face. Her head rocked back and banged against the toilet roll holder. "I said, *don't!*" His face had changed now, it was contorted. Whatever—whoever—he'd been talking to was taking over.

And more than anything in the world, Mary needed pee again.

Compatibility Match
Taurus & Gemini

Oh dear, another mis-match. The Taurean, being an Earth sign, likes to lead with the heart and can be far too full on for the Gemini sometimes. Gemini's will feel smothered by the Taurean's emotional reactions to situations, and the Taurean will be hurt when all the Gemini wants to do is spend all their time on their own 'vital' needs. The Gemini will soon lose patience with the Taurean and there could be fights aplenty. It's difficult to see what attracted these people to each other in the first place, unless there was a third party matchmaker involved of course.

* * *

Zachary Tench threw a look over his shoulder.

He knew he shouldn't have let the encounter with the ticket woman spook him, but he couldn't help it. Whether it was an after effect of the coke, or he was just feeling on edge—and who could blame him?—he couldn't help being jittery. He'd had to get out of carriage C as soon as possible and kept walking. Maybe the ticket woman suspected something? Why couldn't he have been cooler about the holdall? She probably thought he had a bomb in there or something! Might even radio ahead to the stations and set up searches like they did when there was all that terrorism threat stuff.

"Excuse me, sir, but would you mind just opening your bag up. Now then, what's all this in here?"

A fucking truckload of cash, that's what. Wouldn't take Wyatt's men long to find him then. And he had long arms; jail was no safe place.

Why couldn't he have acted more relaxed? *"Oh, there are breakables in here, I'd rather not put them in the compartment if it's all the same with you."*

Because he'd fucking panicked, that's why. And the way she'd looked at him afterwards, like he was insane or something.

"Shit," whispered Zach. "Shit, shit, shit."

The door opened to take him through another space between compartments. He looked over his shoulder again, trying to see down through the carriages, to see the ticket woman. He stood on his toes. Still couldn't see anything. He backed up a couple of spaces...

And the toilet door behind him slid across. Zach whirled round, clenching his holdall, almost cradling it like a baby. A girl fell out of the toilet—couldn't have been more than twenty-two or three—holding a handbag. She was trying to say something but either he'd suddenly gone deaf or she couldn't get her words out. She looked terrified; her mascara had run where she'd been crying. Zach saw two hands grab her from inside the toilet, haul her back in. Her eyes pleaded with him for help.

Don't get involved, he said to himself. *The last thing you want to do is draw attention to yourself. It's just a domestic between boyfriend and girl-friend. He wants to do it in the bathroom and she's changed her mind. That's all. Leave it well enough alone.*

But a face, a name, suddenly entered Zachary's mind. Colette. He'd left that situation well enough alone and look what had happened. Swearing again under his breath, he approached the toilets. The door was just about to close again. He put his foot in it and the sensors reacted accordingly.

The door peeled back and he saw the girl again, held fast by a lad who wasn't that much older than her. Definitely her boyfriend. No, wait, hadn't he seen this girl before, on the platform, and she'd been on her own? Anyway, he'd tell them to stop pissing around and—

Zach saw the straight razor in the boy's hand. The kid with the spiky hair looked up and saw Zach. He was so shocked he let the girl go, and she stumbled out of the toilet into Zach's arms. He dropped the holdall.

The expression of surprise on the boy's face suddenly changed. He snarled… and brought up the razor.

Then the whole world turned upside down.

There are times, and they don't happen very often, when all signs face major upheaval in their lives. When the winds of change blow through and nothing is ever the same again. Take, for instance, when Mars passes through your sign. As can be expected from such a belligerent planet, you'll probably endure a time of turmoil, although whether this results in good or bad fortune is often left entirely to the individual. The only constant in life is change, so these minor shake-ups can be beneficial if seen in the right context. We all, no matter what sign, pass through pleasant and not so pleasant times. But these changes are what shape us and make us who we are. If we remember that, then whatever we are going through can't really be that bad. Can it?

* * *

At 9: 39 precisely a freight train traveling in a westerly direction came off the rails. A later report could find no reason for the buckling that had occurred in this section, though repairs had been made in the area the previous month. The train derailed traveling at 100 mph, skidded for a mile and then jack-knifed across the opposite track. At 9:42 and thirteen seconds, a mainline passenger train heading in an easterly direction was traveling along these tracks. Oliver Collins was the driver. He had very little time to realize what was happening, but he did note that something wasn't right. The freight train should definitely not be on his stretch of rail. It wasn't in its proper place. This annoyed him. However, what annoyed him more was the thought that someone, somewhere probably hadn't done their job properly, hadn't made the checks that he always made, hadn't made sure that everything was running like clockwork. And he hated that. If he could get things right, why couldn't everyone else?

Then his beloved Joyce hit the freight train, ramming it out of the way. Oliver didn't have time to flip any switches. Didn't have time to look at any of the read-outs, turn any dials, didn't have time for anything really except to console himself with the knowledge that this wasn't his fault. And that he and Joyce would at least die together.

The cabin was crushed instantly, and the passenger train started tilting to one side, just like those fancy trains from abroad. Sadly, Joyce wasn't designed to travel on her side. She was designed to travel straight ahead, on the tracks. And now, just like the freight train, she'd come off those tracks with terrible consequences.

The front part of the train broke off from the main section, which then tipped on its side and came to rest about 200 yards further down the line, sparks flying as metal ground against the gravel covered ground. The split occurred at the intersection between carriages B and C.

* * *

Scott Edmonds heard the sound of the crash immediately.

He'd taken a break to sit under one of his favorite trees, up on the hillside, and had fallen asleep there. The noise of the impact, the loudest bang he'd ever heard, abruptly followed by whining metal, stirred him from his slumber.

Scott could see the smoke now, twirling into the air in thick, black curls. He stood up, brushed down his cords, and grabbed his coat with the holes in the elbows. Scott stepped out of the shade of the tree. Putting his hand to his eyes he squinted down the hillside. He couldn't see anything from his angle—the hill was too rounded, and he was on the very top of it—but Scott knew full well there was a train track down there. He should do, he'd roamed these parts more times that he cared to remember. He liked it out here, it was usually so... so peaceful.

Scott couldn't stand the crowds, the commotion of city and town life. The headache of all those people surrounding him. He only ventured there when he needed any money. Then he grudgingly busked with his mouth organ in the underpasses and outside the large food-chain stores, ignoring the stares of folk who thought he was the lowest of the low. Some of the stares Scott could actually feel like a slap in the face. The judgments passed, the superior body language.

If he could avoid doing so, he did. It wasn't so much that Scott was a proud man, though he did still have some pride left, even living the life that he led. It was this contact with the outside world: a world that he'd never got along with and which had never got along with him.

Someone from the *Daily Record* had once done a piece on him. The local character, a thirty-five-year old hermit who shied away from people. They'd wanted to know the reason why. So he'd told them about how his parents had died in a car accident when he was just a kid and he'd ended up staying with one nasty relative after another until they got sick of playing pass the parcel with him and dumped him in a home. When that hadn't worked out, he'd run off and tried to make it on his own... which he'd been doing ever since. Nothing more complicated than that. Just pure bad luck.

But they'd paid him for the story and everyone had been happy. He could eat, they could all pat each other on the back for turning in a social conscience piece. Where had the state gone wrong? that kind of thing As if any of it mattered now. Scott was who he was, lived the life he lived. He wasn't looking for sympathy—in fact in some ways he knew he was better off than people who had so-called 'normal' lives. He liked his own company, he left the world alone and asked only that it did the same to him. On lazy days when the weather was nice he could escape out into the countryside and nothing and nobody would bother him. That's how it was mostly. But not today. Today the world had decided to bother him, had decided to give him a wake up call he'd never forget.

Scott scratched his stubbled chin and began to walk down the side of the hill. When he got so far, his walk turned into a run.

AQUARIUS
(Represented by the water carrier)

Aquarius people are not like any other sign. They are the oddballs of the zodiac, unique in every way. They don't seem to fit into society and any attempt they make to do so will fail miserably. It is important that they celebrate their individuality because that's what makes them who they are. They look at life from a different viewpoint to the rest of us, each one of them unique in different ways. Of course, they do share some common characteristics, and these include a fiercely independent nature (no one will ever tell them what to do or where to go) a stubbornness that sometimes causes them real harm, and a love of spontaneity. It's very hard to predict what an Aquarian will do or even when they will do it! Most of the innovators in history have been Aquarians. They like to go against the grain. And because they are an Air sign they tend to be incredibly intelligent people. They have a remarkable ability to disengage and look at things objectively. Because of this they've gained a reputation of being a bit detached and unemotional. That reputation is totally unfounded. Aquarians are the most caring people you could ever wish to meet, and they usually have a very wide circle of friends who are drawn instinctively to them. Aquarians are also great humanitarians.

* * *

The scene was like something out of a nightmare.

As Scott came down the hill, he saw the train wreck quite clearly. Actually, there were two trains involved, he could see now—one, looked like a passenger train, had hit the other then broken in two. Both were on their sides. And where the most damage had been caused, pieces of track were churned up and now clung to the main body of one of the trains like a metal spider's web. In addition to the smoke, sparks were flashing here and there along the length of the carriages. The smoke seemed to have infected the sky, which was now darkening considerably, clouds covering the sun, blocking out the daylight.

"My God," murmured Scott. He screwed up his eyes then opened them again, scanning the devastation. He saw bodies though cracked windows. Here and there doors had flown open and hung by their hinges. He needed to fetch help. But he saw that some of those bodies inside were moving. He broke into a sprint again, heading for the wreck. Those people needed help right now, and he was the only one around to provide it. Maybe the authorities already knew, perhaps they'd spotted it on one of their computer screens or whatever they used to keep track of… He'd worry about that later.

Scott skidded down the embankment, then got to his feet. He ran past the mangled yellow cabin that had probably been the driver's compartment. Nobody was getting out of there alive, that was for sure. A spark flew just meters away from him and he flinched, bringing up his arm instinctively to shield himself. If he was going to help anyone at all, he had to get inside that row of carriages on its side. Scott ripped his old tattered jacket in two down the spine, and started to wrap it around his hands. He quickly found a hand and foothold and started to climb up onto the train. Scott reached over the top and grabbed hold of the edge of the train. He pulled himself up onto its surface. The door was open here and he saw the carriage letter, upside down.

It was 'C'.

* * *

Taken from the Daily Record

Aquarius: Now is not a time for being selfish. You have lots of love and compassion to spare at the moment so show those special people in your life that you care. Perhaps organize a party or pick them up if they're feeling down. Only you will know what can work for the best today Aquarius, and it will pay dividends later on.

* * *

It was as though the universe had stood still for a few seconds.

Mary Dowling had fallen into the man's arms, trying to get away from that lunatic who was attacking her. And it felt so safe there. She'd held on to him tightly, never wanting to let go. Somehow she knew he'd protect her. Then something weird happened. She remembered a loud noise, and the floor seemed to slip away from under her. That's when the universe had stood still. Only for a little while, she thought. Or it might have been a lifetime; probably both. She'd looked up into the man's eyes, the man holding her, a man she'd bumped into once before that day. She saw those eyes dart from the toilet behind her, to the ceiling, and then he looked right back at her. Their gaze locked. Mary saw every single blood vessel in his eyes—saw herself reflected in those orbs. Oh, did she look a mess...

Then time gradually started to roll again. The man fell with her, toppling sideways. He tore his gaze away from her. She felt him fling her sideways, through the carriage door he'd come through only moments ago. As Mary fell she saw the whole train spin like one of those postcard competition tumblers on Saturday morning children's programs. Somebody, somewhere, was winding the handle and the whole train was tumbling around and around. Lights flashed on and off, and she was hurled to the ground—or what appeared to be the ground now. Mary held out a hand and grabbed hold of a luggage rack; saw the man who'd thrown her disappear from view. People were screaming from behind, she could hear them but blotted out their cries with 'I Will Survive'. Yes, she'd finally chosen her song. She played it over and over again in her head.

Everything seemed to speed up then, just briefly. Cases fell onto her, bags and coats. And as suddenly as the chaos had started, it stopped again. All was quiet and still. Mary remained there, under the luggage that had fallen on top of her, for some time. What had happened? Just what in the name of bloody hell had happened? Mary's own private world had been shaken up when that guy grabbed hold of her in the toilet. Then, as if mir-roring this somehow, the whole train had suddenly been shaken. It was too much information to take in at one time, too much to process.

She already knew what had happened. Something had gone wrong with the train and now it was on its side. She only had to look around to see that. Mary was trapped inside one of the lug-gage compartments, one of the spaces on the left or right as you entered a train carriage. And now *that* was the new floor.

But she couldn't stay there forever. Mary attempted to move, to push some of the luggage away. She found she was quaking. It seemed so dark now in the train. Mary wriggled up into a sitting position, her breathing slow, shallow. She made to push one of the bags away and realized it was hers, the handbag she'd used in the toilet to whack the guy—like some little old lady or some-thing. It'd worked though, allowed her to get away from him and press the red button, to open the doors and escape. Out of the frying pan…

Mary was suddenly aware that 'I Will Survive' had stopped looping in her head. She could hear the sound of crying and screaming from behind again. Not as loud as before, granted. Less like the screams of people going through some sort of major tragedy and more like the cries of people trapped and wanting help. Mary remembered her phone. Reaching inside her handbag she groped around. It wasn't there. *It has to be there, you can't have lost it. How would that look, you working for a mobile phone company and you've lost your phone just when you needed it the most? It has to be... Ah, there it is!* Mary's hand closed around the small object. Pulling it out she saw that the screen was blank.

Oh no. It's broken. You broke it when you hit the guy with your bag. What a stupid thing to do, Mary. What an idiot you are! But how was she to know she'd need to use it in a few minutes for this? All she could think about at the time was his hands all over her, the razor he'd held up.

No, you really are an idiot, aren't you, Mary? You turned it off, remember? So nobody would call you at the audition. God—the audition! They'd be lining up soon to get in, their numbers ready. But no number 35. "Where's number 35?" they'd call out and there'd be nobody there to answer because she was here, under all this luggage and—

Mary's mind was racing, not making any sense. *Dammit, concentrate.*

She switched on the phone and it lit up, a shining beacon in the darkness. Mary dialed a number and a woman asked which service she required. Mary opened her mouth and found she still couldn't speak. She was asked again: which service?

Mary found her voice this time, strong and sure. And she used it for a much more important purpose than singing.

"Hello... Hello... there's been an accident," she said.

Taureans are an Earth sign so being outside every now and again is fundamental to their happiness. They simply love getting back to nature and if they're enclosed in a man made environment for too long will soon start to feel the strain.

* * *

William Booth opened his eyes… and found he could only see through one of them.

He thought for a second he might be blind in the left, as he'd hit the side of the table quite hard. Perhaps it had taken out his eye? They weren't particularly sharp but given enough force even the bluntest of things could do considerable amounts of damage. Then he blinked and discovered that something was trickling into the socket, blurring his vision on the left hand side. He brought up a hand to wipe away the wetness. It felt sticky to the touch, and he knew it must be blood. His left temple was throbbing as well, where he'd connected with the table, slightly higher than he'd imagined. His eye was okay.

Will tried to get up. His body ached all over, a consequence of being thrown halfway across a train carriage probably. Nevertheless, he tensed his muscles and tried to raise himself. It was no good; his back was killing him. He couldn't stand. Looking around, he realized that he was now on top of that table… sort of. The aisle he'd been walking along was to his immediate left. Which meant that the train was on its side.

Brilliant observation, Will, he thought. *So long as that University education wasn't completely wasted.*

When had he been aware that something was wrong with the train? Only mere seconds before he did his Superman routine and flew up the centre of the aisle faster than a speeding bullet. Eat your heart out Brandon Routh. Hadn't even needed a red cape and Y-fronts to defy the laws of gravity, just a little push in the right direction and he was away. Will didn't know why he was thinking such things. It was no time for… for levity. This was a serious situation he was in. Even now his good eye was catching things all around him, a hand sticking out at an odd angle from behind a chair—it was snapped back so far it looked obscene. A couple of prone forms not too far away, one wearing trainers, the other high-heels; neither were moving. Smashed glass from a window lay all around, littering the carriage. Will strained his eye and thought he saw... He looked away, the sight of a shard of glass sticking out of someone's chest was too much. Will felt bile rising and swallowed it down.

That's why your mind is cracking Superman jokes, he thought. *It's a knee jerk reaction: protecting you from the reality of all this, trying to get you to focus on something else.* Will had once seen a documentary about survivors of plane, car and train crashes, about how they blocked out what was happening around them, and just focused on getting out of there. Would all this be a blur to him soon? Will doubted it; he had a photographic memory and right now it was recording every last detail. He'd relive the whole thing in glorious technicolor and surround sound every time he shut his—

Will blinked again, the blood clearing, but still it stung. He squeezed through the gap between the windows and the chairs, crawling along on all fours. He felt something squish under his knee.

Don't look down. For the love of sanity, don't look, Will.

But he had to. He had to know what he'd crawled into. Will looked down, lifted his knee up. It was covered in stickiness, but it wasn't like the blood from the gash in his head. He smelt at it——mayo. He'd knelt in his BLT sandwich. Will let out his held breath.

A hand grabbed his arm and made him start.

He was looking into the face of a young girl about seventeen, eighteen, couldn't have been much older than his students were. She had short-cropped hair and a stud in her nose. Next to her, holding her hand, was a youth with a leather jacket on.

"W-w-wha..." she began, but had trouble forming the words.

Will took her hand and patted it. "It's okay. Just stay where you are, both of you. Don't move. Help'll be here soon."

But would it? Will had no idea. Did anyone even know they'd been in a crash? Was anyone on their way? Christ Almighty, he hoped so. In the meantime he had to check as many of the people in the carriage as possible. He had some basic first aid training—it was a requirement of his job—so he'd do what he could for who he could. Will spent the next few minutes assessing those closest to him. Some were clearly beyond help, others he tried to make comfortable; made reassurances he couldn't personally keep—about getting out of here, about escaping from this nightmare. It jarred loose a quote from Keats: 'Is there another life? Shall I awake and find all this a dream? There must be, we cannot be created for this sort of suffering'.

Then above the crying and other sounds, Will thought he heard a distinctive call for help. The voice sounded familiar to him. He didn't know where from. Will started to crawl towards the end of the carriage as fast as he could. He passed other people in various states of distress and some, like the prone bodies back there, not moving at all. Unconscious or… worse. He tried not to think about it. Tried to block out everything but the sound of this one voice. Why was it so important? He didn't know. All he knew was he had to reach it as quickly as he could.

Leo & Health

The two areas of the body ruled by Leo are the back and the heart. A Leo should be careful to avoid straining their backs, so no heavy lifting or strenuous bending. They also like their food, but should try and steer clear of fried foodstuffs like bacon and have a nice salad instead as it's better for the heart. In matters both physical and emotional Leos are likely to be led by this muscle.

* * *

Belinda Gould couldn't move her arm. It was most definitely broken.

No more ticket collecting for a while, she said to herself, as if this was the sum of her problems. She stared ahead of her towards the smashed section, the crushed end of the carriage. She could so easily have been standing there when the split came. Luckily Belinda hadn't made it up as far as carriage B yet and the impact had thrown her backwards. She'd lost her balance and landed heavily on her arm. The weight she'd put on since her modeling days ensured it broke when she fell. She even heard the loud crack as it went. Belinda had once broken her leg falling down some stairs when she was eleven or twelve, but she didn't remember it hurting this much. The pain when her arm had broken was unlike anything she'd ever known. She'd almost blacked out a couple of times from it, except it was as if her body just couldn't decide whether or not to go the whole hog. In the end the pain had kept her in the land of the living.

The land of the living, and what a place to be alive in. The lights were off, electrics were sparking in the carriage. Belinda thought of the people who'd been in the front carriages: the alternative was much, much worse. She held her arm, which thankfully was now numb. *I look like I'm trying to flap my wings.*

Was she going into shock perhaps, her body shutting down bit by bit? She'd read somewhere that could happen in moments of trauma or crisis. This certainly fitted the bill. You couldn't get any more traumatic than... Of course, she'd also read that your life flashed before your eyes when you had a near death experience. Hers hadn't, and she was quite glad about that. She didn't want to relive her past again, where it had gone wrong with Gerard, the end of her career. Didn't want to relive cheating on David and the pain *she'd* caused *him*. Yes, there were good times in her life she'd celebrate gladly if she was shown the edited high-lights, but she always tended to dwell on the downsides. On the regrets.

There was a slight movement to her left, a mumbling. Belinda turned, wishing she hadn't almost immediately as the pain revisited her arm. There was a girl curled up between two of the seats. Belinda vaguely recalled taking her ticket just before all hell broke loose. The girl was young, pretty, wearing jeans and a pink jumper. At least it *had* been pink before the crash. Now it was stained with dark patches. Unlike Belinda, this girl's body had decided to switch off and she was just coming around again.

Belinda shuffled along the floor, reached out and touched the girl's leg. The girl shook her head a couple of times and then recoiled.

"Hey... hey, love, it's all right," said Belinda. She reminded her a little of how she'd looked at that age.

"Where... what's happened?" said the girl, her words slurring slightly.

"Something bad," Belinda told her. "How you doing?"

The girl grimaced. "I've been better."

"Tell me about it," said Belinda. "What's your name?"

"Tra... Tracy."

"I'm Belinda."

"My... My stomach hurts, Belinda."

"I know, sweetie. Just try and relax."

Tracy coughed. It sounded like she was gargling with mud. "Heh... And my stars were... were so good for... today," she said, eventually.

"Stars? You don't believe in all that, do you, honey?"

Tracy gave a shake of her head. "Not really."

"You make your own destiny, love. That's what I say. For better, or for worse. Nobody can see what's coming. We should know, right?"

"For better or for worse," Tracy repeated, and coughed again.

There was a noise from the far and of the carriage—the one

still attached to the length of the train. To begin with Belinda thought it was someone coming through from carriage D. Then she saw a man drop down from the 'ceiling' through the door now on its side.

"Is there anyone in there?" came his voice.

Oh thank the Lord, thought Belinda. *Thank the Lord.*

Taken from The Daily Record

Libra: So much for living the easy life! You'll find yourself in demand today, bumping into all sorts of people and generally chewing the fat. You might even meet a special person who could turn out to be a friend for life. Perhaps they'll remind you of the individual you once were and you'll decide to take them under your wing? One important factor to bear in mind today though, no matter how bad things look, where there's life there's hope. Remember that and you won't go far wrong. Oh, and you might find unexpected visitors dropping in on you, seeing as you're so popular. Lucky you!

* * *

Russell Prince and his partner Alice Swanson had only just emerged from the accident and emergency department of the local hospital when the call came through. The patient they'd dropped off had been an attempted suicide. Aspirin rather than paracetomal fortunately, which meant the guy might even stand a chance. Stomach pump, clean him out, get him some counseling. If it had been paracetomal, and he'd taken that many, there would be no chance. You might as well swallow a timebomb then sit back and wait for the explosion.

Climbing into the driver's seat of the ambulance, Russ picked up the radio and responded. "We'll be there as quickly as possi-ble," he told control.

"What was that?" asked Alice joining him inside.

"Been a train crash on the main line. Bad one by all accounts." He started up the engine and put the ambulance in gear. "That's the kind of thing that really narks me about this line of work and the things you see," Russ said, looking both ways as he came out of the hospital car park. "You get silly sods like that wanting to end it all, and then something like this happens."

"He had his reasons, Russ," said Alice.

"It's the coward's way out. Some people don't get a choice; he did. Doesn't seem to balance out."

"That's how it goes sometimes."

"It shouldn't."

Russ had known Alice about nine months now, ever since he'd moved to this area and taken the paramedics' job here. She was small, under five foot, but he'd seen her do things that would make so-called grown men mewl like kittens. Seen her cut into bodies and stick tubes in, slit open throats to provide airways... even stick her hand inside one biker's stomach to stem the internal bleeding until they could get him to surgery. Strength wasn't always apparent from looks alone.

It was something he'd already been taught serving in the army, that lesson. Russ had been a medic in Her Majesty's Infantry for seven years. And he'd seen action a couple of times during that period. Been in combat situations with youths who didn't look like they could blow up a paper bag, let along a munitions depot. They'd surprised him, though, just as Alice continued to do every day. Pity she didn't have as much courage when it came to standing up to that bastard husband of hers.

Russ had only met the guy once, at the Christmas do in the Lion round the corner, but he'd taken an immediate dislike to him. He'd also heard the rumors about their stormy relationship, though never said anything to Alice about it. Russ even kept his mouth shut when she arrived to work with that bruise on her arm—he'd seen it as she reached up to switch on the siren. A part of Russ felt like going round and doing the same to him. *Might be a reasonable explanation*, he'd said to himself, *wasn't forced to be her bloke*. It was best not to wade in with his size tens again, causing trouble. That's how he got into the majority of his scrapes. Anyway, he didn't think Alice would take too kindly to his interference; it was none of his business really what happened in her personal life, he didn't know her well enough to pass judgments. It was just that Alice was his friend, his oppo. And he'd learnt that lesson in the army too: you looked after your own, even if it meant you got a bollocking sometimes.

Alice had asked him once why he'd walked away from the forces.

"Because I knew that sooner or later I'd get booted out. Sooner like as much," Russ had told her. "It was starting to feel too... I don't know..."

"Restrictive?"

"I guess."

"Too many rules and regulations?"

"Maybe."

"So you thought you'd join the ambulance services where there are hardly any," laughed Alice.

"Something like that."

"Just don't let Sheridan hear you talking like that." Sheridan was their supervisor, their immediate superior.

"Sheridan's like a big girl's blouse compared to some of the bosses I've had." Russ winked.

But Alice had a point. There were just as many rules and regulations in this profession, more probably. It took a long while for Russ to make up his mind about the job, whether he was doing the right thing. But these kinds of rules were different; they were geared towards saving lives not following outdated codes and traditions. In the end Russ knew he had to do this, knew he couldn't live without the adrenaline rush of life on the go. It was the next 'best' thing to being out there in the field.

He felt it now as they sped towards the scene of the train crash, not knowing what was waiting for them at their destination. Spur of the moment decisions without anyone looking over your shoulder.

"Wouldn't it be quicker to take Nelson Street and then the one way system?" Alice said, breaking the silence.

"No, if we cut through Manor Grove we can get there in half the time."

"Traffic might be bad."

"We'll get there."

Alice stayed silent for a few minutes. At last, she said, "You think there are many people involved?"

Russ waited for a beige estate to pull in and let them pass. "Wanker," he griped. "Many involved? Enough, from what I could gather." He knew Alice was feeling the same way—that mixture of dread and excitement. Of wanting to get there, but at the same time wishing they never would.

Alice gazed grimly ahead.

Russ put his foot down on the accelerator.

ARIES
(Represented by the ram)

Some of you might have heard the phrase 'Hot-headed Aries'. Now although this description isn't wholly fair, it is justified occasionally. Aries people are leaders of the gang and tend to act on instinct a lot. They like to be in the middle of the action if they can, and they have tons of energy, vigor and tenacity. You'll very rarely see them stepping back, preferring instead to try and control their destinies and getting hot under the collar when they discover that things don't always work out the way you want them to. They're adventurous sorts, one of life's natural born thrill-seekers, vigorous and unstoppable once they get going. There's not much chance of them getting tied down and if this does happen they won't be best pleased. They hate being told what to do because they have natural born leadership abilities themselves—they are, after all, the first sign of the zodiac. They have a very fixed view about situations, and refuse to admit that there are grey areas. They can be unintentionally sharp when disagreeing with people, and always have to be right.

* * *

Jez Bingley was being punished.

He'd always known that 'his' actions would catch up with him one day. And that day had finally arrived. He hadn't wanted to follow that girl to the toilets; hadn't wanted to do the things he'd done to her… to any of them. It had all been down to the voice, it had told him that he had to or he would suffer. And now… and now…

"Where are you?" he asked it. "Gone, that's where."

This was Hell. His sins had caught up with him at last and he was in Hell. Jez could think of no other explanation. The screaming he could hear, the tortured souls. It was just like those pictures in the Bible his Gran had shown him when he used to stay with her for the holidays. The place where he'd end up if he ever… did things to himself, if he ever had *those* kinds of thoughts.

"Don't you listen to Lucifer or you'll end up there with all his demons, Jeremy, you mark my words."

Oh, he'd marked them. He could mark every last one of them. Turned out she'd been right. The voice had led him into temptation, and he'd listened to all it had to say. Obeyed—struggled sometimes, but still obeyed. Now he was paying the ultimate price for his actions. When the end had come, when that terrible something Jez had always feared finally arrived, he'd fallen back into the toilet, banging his knee on the metal of the bowl. Then the floor had been taken away from him. He'd hung on to the toilet as the whole room was pitched onto its side. Things fell out of the first aid box next to the door, striking him like miniature missiles. The lights flickered, then went out completely. And the door itself—which was now above him—had jammed halfway across.

A body slumped down though the gap.

It dripped spots of blood onto him, gazed down with lifeless eyes in the half-light. Jez knew it was the man who'd found him in the middle of... The man who'd held the girl and then pushed her out of the way, as he himself was slammed against the walls, tossed around until he came to rest there. Just above Jez, his body broken, neck shattered, tongue lolling out of his mouth like a fat, slimy slug. His face was a grotesquery, a patchwork of cuts and gashes. Jez didn't dare go near it, let alone try and move it out of his way. It was blocking his exit from this chamber.

But where would he go anyway? This was Hell, wasn't it? And it was his punishment.

Jez wondered where his razor might be.

Taken from The Daily Record

Gemini: Be sure your sins will find you out, Gemini. Whatever have you been up to? Nothing? I very much doubt it. Whatever it is now's the time to come clean, as confession could be good for the soul. Before you might have felt in two minds about the whole thing, but now you're thinking much more clearly. If you're feeling hemmed in, then you've really only got one person to blame, haven't you?

* * *

Scott Edmonds stepped into carriage C, responding to the voice.

It was a woman, calling out, asking for help. There were more—some coming from the next carriage—but these were the closest and Scott only had two pairs of hands. He'd work his way up through the train from this end, until the emergency services arrived at least. As he walked in, clambering over the debris of bags and luggage here, he saw two women. One was older than the other. Mother and daughter perhaps? No, the closer he came Scott could see that the middle-aged woman had a uniform on.

"Are we glad to see you," she said. The younger woman

didn't speak, she just offered a weak smile.

He crouched down at the side of them. It was a real effort for him to speak at first, he felt awkward, nervous. But the look of pure relief on their faces snapped him out of this. *Look at what they've been through, these poor people, and* you're *worried about feeling uncomfortable. Just get on with it and help them.*

"Are you badly hurt?" Scott asked them.

"I think my arm's broken, but I'm okay. Tracy's..." The woman pointed to the blood on Tracy's jumper and Scott rubbed his bristled chin.

"I'm going to try and get a few people together and help them out of the train. Maybe best not to move... Tracy for a while."

"I think you're right. Okay, you have a name, love? Otherwise I'm just going to have to call you my knight in shining armor."

"I've been called some things before, but never that. My name's Scott," he replied.

"I'm Belinda. You already know Tracy."

"Hi Tracy."

"I'll go and check out the rest of the carriage. Will you two be okay for a minute?"

They nodded and Scott got back up. He clambered over the seats and tables that now formed the uneven terrain of the carriage. As he was climbing over one set of double seats, he almost trod on someone cowering in the cubbyhole between the chairs and the table. It was a little boy, about seven or eight years old. As Scott bent over, he spotted a second person on the other side of the table. This man was about his age, but he wouldn't see another birthday. The table edge had somehow jammed him up against the seat, almost slicing him in two. He was slumped over, but lolling to the left now that the table was on its side. From his angle the little boy couldn't see the man, and for this Scott was particularly grateful.

"Hey there," said Scott softly, reaching down. "Give me your hand."

The boy was crying and shivering.

"Hey, my name's Scott. What's yours big man?"

In between sobs, the boy said, "F-Fr... Fraser... Fraser Pryce."

Scott smiled. "Hi there, Fraser Pryce. I'm going to try and get you out of there. Okay? Now, just reach up as high as you can. That's it." Scott grabbed hold of Fraser's hand and pulled him out of the hole. Seconds later and Fraser had his arms around Scott's neck. Scott cradled the back of the boy's head, twisting him away from the sight of the dead man before he had a chance to see.

Sniffing in Scott's ear, he heard Fraser ask: "Where's my Daddy?"

"Sshh. Let's get you out of here," said Scott, and carried him away.

An Aquarian will feel like a fish out of water if they're not surrounded by people. They're never uncomfortable in social gatherings of any kind, being able to use their in-built charm and personality to instantly put others at their ease. If an Aquarian can rise above their own needs and really give of them-selves to others—which most inherently do anyway—they will be a success in life and always be well loved.

Compatibility Match
Libra & Aquarius

This is a good match for both parties and the couple should get on famously. They will make great allies, and do even better in the business stakes. The Aquarian will warm to the Libran's compassionate nature and probably enjoy their flirting as well. While the Libran might even learn to be more assertive due to the Aquarian's knack for sorting out problems.

Compatibility Match
Pisces & Aquarius

These two will fall at the first hurdle because they come from two different solar systems! Any relationship that develops, even friendship, will struggle to get off the ground. In basic terms, it's better to forget about it.

* * *

By the time Russell Prince arrived at the scene of the crash, there were already a couple of fire crews, police cars and another ambulance on site. As he pulled his vehicle up, Alice Swanson turned to him and said: "Just look at that."

Russ *was* looking. Even in all his army years he'd never seen anything quite as shocking as this. You signed on for conflict, knew you might have to put yourself in a situation where there'd be bloodshed. This was something else entirely. These people had never signed on for anything.

The duo climbed out, collecting their kits from the back of the ambulance and jogging over to see who was in charge of the operation.

"So what's the situation?" Russell asked the fire chief when they found him.

"We think we've minimized the risk of electrical fires now," said the man, his face dotted with ginger freckles, tufts of red hair sticking out from beneath his helmet. "Some of your lot have already gone in to treat casualties, and we're trying to bring out a few of the least affected."

Least affected? Russ knew that this train crash would affect every single person here, whether they'd been injured or not. Whether they were on board or not. Russ looked over the train and saw one or two people climbing up through open doorways on the 'top' of the carriage nearest to him. Firemen were placing ladders up against the side so they could get to safety, and helping people down them. As he watched, he saw a band of survivors finally make it out of the train. Then a woman holding her arm was lifted out.

Russ and Alice went over after the fireman brought her down.

"Here, let's take a look at that for you," said Russ.

"Oh, thanks, sugar. It's started to hurt again now. There's a girl still inside though, could use your help. You'll probably need a stretcher."

"You look like you could've done with one yourself. Right, Alice, would you…?" Alice had a look at the woman's arm and declared that it was broken.

"He deserves a medal that man, you know. I don't mind telling anyone who'll listen. He's helped all those people inside…" Russ heard her telling Alice.

"Who's this? One of your staff?"

"No, Scott his name is."

Russ ascended the ladder, greeting the firemen present. He got to the doorway above and saw a little boy being lifted up and out of the train. A man dressed in an off white shirt and cords was next. His hair was tousled and he had about three days' worth of stubble on his chin.

"Let me guess, you must be Scott?" said Russ. "I've heard good things. Here-" Russ gripped Scott's hand and pulled him the last bit of the way.

"Thanks."

"I was told there's someone injured inside?"

"Tracy. Just inside the carriage there."

"I'm on it. Good work, Scott." Russ clapped him on the back as he went off to join the people he'd helped. Then Russ climbed down into the train.

Taken from The Daily Record

Aries: Watch your step today and look before you leap. As long as you do, all will be fine. You might even find a nice surprise waiting for you after a period of restlessness. Perhaps it's your reward for good deeds in the past. Whatever the case, enjoy it, because they don't come around that often, do they?

* * *

Mary Dowling wanted to sing as her rescuers pulled her out through one of the smashed train windows.

But she didn't. There'd be no singing today, she'd decided. Instead she told one of the paramedics treating her, a nice, kind woman called Alice, about the attack. She'd held Mary when the tears came again, then checked her over for any injuries—caused by the assault and the crash—and called for a police officer to come across. Mary repeated her story while Alice looked anxiously on, biting her thumbnail.

When Mary had finished, Alice asked: "Are you okay?"

"Considering everything that's happened today, and how much worse it could have been…" Mary stared at the train. "I'll say yes. They will find him, won't they?"

Alice brought her nail up to her mouth again, then lowered it. "Yes. Don't worry, Mary."

"People like that…"

"I know," said Alice quietly. "Look, I've got to go, but I'll be back. The police are right here so you'll be safe. 'Kay?"

Mary gave a nod. "Hey, do you know if they've brought the guy out yet? The one who stopped him from…"

"I'll ask around."

"It's just that… well, I want to thank him if I can."

"Yeah, I know," said Alice, and walked back to the train wreck. More ambulances were arriving, another fire engine and Mary could even see some TV crews up on the grass verge. The police had set up a cordon around the area and weren't letting them in, but one cameraman was still pointing his camera in her direction, focusing it on her.

Well, Mary, you wanted to be famous. Here it is, your fifteen minutes. Hope you enjoy it. Hope you enjoy it.

Taken from the Daily Record

Taurus: Be careful what you wish for, isn't that what they say? All the same, something you have sought for so long is now within your grasp. It has come about in a strange way, that's for sure, but it has come about all the same. The question you have to ask yourself now is do you really want the attention you once craved? Be careful what you wish for, because it just might come true today.

* * *

Katherine Pryce was placed on the stretcher and wheeled along, with William Booth still beside her.

Will had been brilliant. He'd stayed with her until the fire brigade and ambulance crews could get inside, holding her hand, letting her squeeze it whenever she felt the pain from her trapped leg. She'd called out for help, never expecting it to be him—again. Will. He'd talked to her to keep her awake, told her about himself, more about what he did, more about where he came from, told her stories about his travels… kept her awake. In turn she'd offered him a snapshot of her life: her husband, her son—who she was worried out of her head about. Will had been there as they cut away the twisted metal divide that had landed on her in the fall. And now, as the time came for them to part again, she found she couldn't let go of his hand. No matter how hard she tried. But more than that, she felt that Will didn't want to either.

"It's all right," one of the paramedics said, "you can ride with your wife to the hospital. We just have to stabilize that leg. And then we'll take a look at your head."

"Oh she's not…" Katherine heard Will begin to say. "I mean Kathy's not-"

"Sorry," said the paramedic. "I saw the ring and… My mistake."

The ring again, tying her to Ed. To a past she didn't want to be reminded about, a present she hated, and a future she wished she could change.

As she was being wheeled to an ambulance, Katherine made out a figure in the distance. "Fraser!" The effort was tremendous, but she called out again. The boy, who was with a fair-haired man, came running over as fast as he could.

"Mummy... Mummy," he shouted. He buried his head in her side and she held him with her free arm. Fraser looked up at his mother, and for the first time in as long as she could remember, her son wasn't frowning.

The man he'd been with walked over to them and said hello. "That's a very brave boy you've got there."

"Are you... did you get him out?"

The stubbled man confirmed that he did.

"Thank you, thank you!"

"This is thanks enough. I'm just glad to see... Nobody should be alone at his age."

Will turned to him and asked a question that Mary couldn't hear. She saw the man drop his eyes and shake his head. Will let go of her hand.

And she knew then that her husband was gone. Ed, the father of her child. The man she'd wished away so casually only moments ago. Jesus, she'd hardly spared him a thought.

The man bent down next to Fraser and said, "You go with your mum now, big man. Look after her."

The paramedics continued to wheel Mary away, Fraser by her side now. She risked one look back at Will, standing there watching them go. There were tears in her eyes as Katherine Pryce took her son's hand and held it tightly.

One of the greatest things about the Sagittarian personality is that they are eternally optimistic.

* * *

Whether it was the blood she'd lost, she didn't know, but Tracy Simmons felt woozy when the paramedic bent down next to her.

"Hello, Tracy," he said in his deep voice. It sounded like the most natural thing in the world for him to say. She didn't question the fact that he knew her name—Scott or maybe even Belinda had told him; that's what the rational part of her mind was telling her. The other part was insisting that he'd always known it, always been destined to say it. Her name seemed to trip off his tongue so easily.

"I'm Russ. Russell Prince. Here, let's just take a look at you."

Russ: his face hovered in front of her like something out of a dream, this handsome… prince.

She felt his latex-covered hands lifting her jumper, touching her; they were strong but gentle. She recoiled a little when he hit a sore spot and cursed herself for doing so.

"Sorry, did that hurt?"

"Ticklish," she said.

Russ grinned. "Live wire, eh? I like that. Don't worry, Tracy, it looks worse than it probably is. I'm going to just put some padding on your cuts, then we'll whisk you off to hospital to check out those bruises on your abdomen."

"So…" She coughed and he held her steady. It was almost worth enduring the pain for. "I'm… I'm going to live then?"

"You'd better," he told her, and winked.

Compatibility Match
Pisces & Aries

This couple will have a spark straight away, an instant attraction that may well develop given time. If this relationship is to work, however, the Arien needs to understand the Piscean's romantic wishy-washy ways and hold back on their lustful nature a little. If this can be achieved, and with give and take on both sides, a successful, lasting match might well be the result. They are first and last signs of the zodiac—the beginning and the end.

The end and the beginning.

Taken from the Daily Record

'... *authorities have described the train crash as one of the worst in recent years, ranking alongside Hatfield, Selby and Potters Bar. A report will begin on the cause of the accident as soon as possible. It left 15 people dead and dozens more injured, some severely.*

In an incredible twist, police have confirmed that the killer of five women, including Victoria Styles, was on board the passenger train when it collided with a de-railed freight train coming in the opposite direction. It is believed that the murderer, who can't be identified yet for legal reasons, was in the process of assaulting yet another woman—Miss Mary Dowling—when the crash occurred. Miss Dowling was on her way to audition for the regional heats of TV's "Quest for a Star". A police spokesman has neither confirmed nor denied rumors that the killer subsequently took his own life.

Even more bizarrely, perhaps, emergency services found a bag on board the doomed train containing considerable amounts of money. Nobody has come forward to claim this yet, so if you have any information regarding it please call the accident helpline on the number printed below. If the money goes unclaimed it will be added to the victim support fund set up by rail employee and charity worker Belinda Gould and Mr. Scott Edmonds, who has been hailed as a local hero for his brave actions on the scene.'

Taken from the Astrological Handbook
Published by Beholder Press.

We hope you've enjoyed reading this book and that it has given you some insight into the world of astrology and star signs. Remember, the signs of life are all around us. They are strangers, they are friends, our lovers, our enemies. They see us through the good times as well as the bad. And only by knowing more about them can we ever hope to discover what the future has in store for us.

From all at the Astrological Handbook, for now, happy horoscopes!

THE LAZARUS CONDITION

Prologue

'And he that was dead came forth, bound hand and foot with graveclothes: and his face was bound about with a napkin. Jesus saith unto them, Loose him, and let him go...'

John 11.44

No one paid any attention as the dead man walked down the street.

A familiar street to him, with children playing football on the grass verge, wives gossiping on the corner next to the shop. He took in all the streetlamps, never having noticed them, *really* noticed them before. Now he was scrutinizing everything, from the pebble-dashing of the council houses to the rickety nature of the peeling fences—which could so easily have been resurrected with a lick of paint.

Given new life.

He paused to look up at the sky, seeing the birds there catching the mild breeze, returned from their winter migration now that spring was here. They'd been drawn to sunnier climes, just as he was being drawn to this place, pulled as surely as if he was made of metal and someone was holding a gigantic magnet. He continued up the street, passing more people as he went: a man walking with a stick, newspaper jammed under his arm; a young woman pushing a buggy with a screaming kid in the seat; a postman making deliveries to each of the houses. None of them looked closely enough to *truly* see him. None of them ever looked too closely at anything, they just went about the business of their mundane lives, worrying about bills—the same ones the postman was shoving through letterboxes that very morning—about the weather, about their families.

He was almost there. The house he was looking for was just across the road. He stared at the overgrown hedge and front garden: once neat and trim with a pond in the middle and gnomes fishing with tiny rods. What had happened to those? He couldn't remember. In the great scheme of things did it really matter? Things came, things went. It was how it was.

He made to cross over the road, almost stepping into the path of an oncoming car. He pulled back just as the driver blared his horn, shouting through the open window: "What the hell's wrong with you? You tryin' to get yourself killed?"

The dead man watched him drive to the end of the road and follow the curve around. Those words went around and around in his mind: "Get yourself killed… Get yourself killed…" He closed his eyes, images flashing across his field of vision below the lids:

A flash of red, of light. Hands clutching at something, tight, white knuckles and a ring on the third finger of the left hand. A pair of eyes, dulled but open in shock. A—

He snapped *his* eyes open, flinching when he felt the hand on his arm. "Are… are you all right?" asked an Indian woman standing beside him. He searched her features but found nothing recognizable. Again he just stared, not saying a thing. In the end the woman let him be, not knowing what else to do. As she walked on up the street, she looked over her shoulder just once.

Turning, he checked for traffic this time, and crossed the road to the house.

He studied the small semi, the windows gaping back at him in disbelief. He put a hand out for the gate, which was hanging off by the hinges. It creaked heavily as he moved it aside, the latch long-since vanished. The path was overgrown too, each carefully laid slab now raised slightly at the side by the sheer amount of weeds pushing up from beneath, like a healthy tooth dislodged by its crooked neighbor. He trod the path slowly, dead flowers on either side, leading him to the front door, its mottled glass set inside a faded varnished frame.

Raising a hand he prepared to knock on the door. He hesitated. Why, he had no idea. This was what he was meant to do, he felt sure of it. And yet...

He shook his head and rapped twice on the wood. The wait was excruciating. He gave it a few minutes, then knocked again, cocking his ear at the same time. He heard movement from within, a voice calling, "All right, all right. I'm coming."

The door opened a crack and someone peered out. It was difficult to see clearly as it was dark inside the hall, but then the door opened more fully. It wasn't because the gray haired woman standing there was willingly allowing him entrance; it was more that she was in a state of severe shock.

She put a quivering hand to her mouth, eyes wide and filling with moisture. "Matt... Matthew?" The old woman made to take a step towards him, but her already unstable legs gave out. "No... no it can't be." He covered the distance between them in an instant, hands there to catch her as she fell back into the house. Her eyes rolled up into her head and she began gasping for air.

"It's okay, I've got you," he said, experimentally talking again. He half-carried her into the house, then closed the door on the outside world. He tapped her face gently with his fingers. "It's me, Mum," he told her. "It's really me."

But she fainted again—the result of seeing her dead son standing on the doorstep after seven long years.

One

Mrs. Irene Daley woke from her nightmare to find herself on the couch.

She'd had the most awful dream. In it she'd been watching the television, *The Breakfast Show* had just finished and she was about to turn off a report on the troubles abroad—the commentator stating that they were on the verge of yet another 'conflict.' Then there had been a knock at the door. She hadn't heard it at first due to the explosions on the TV, but when the knock came again she'd switched off the set with the remote then got up to answer it, her back aching as she lifted herself out of the high seat chair.

Whoever it was they were persistent. *Might be the postman?* she'd mused as she turned into the hallway. But why would he knock? No one ever sent her any packages, not even her own family. She was lucky if she got any mail at all that wasn't simply junk. She'd called out that she was coming, and she could see the shadowy shape through the misted glass at the door. Irene even considered putting on the chain, but it was the middle of the morning not ten o'clock at night. Nobody would be trying to break into her home this early on in the day, surely. She decided to meet the potential threat half way, only open the door a tiny bit. That way she could shut it again quickly if need be, but she could also see who was so eager to get her attention.

When she opened the door she thought her eyes were playing tricks. Through the gap she looked out at a face she hadn't seen in over half a decade. A face she'd adored more than anything in this world, last seen under a very different set of circumstances. Her boy; *her* Matthew…

But that couldn't be. It only happened in dreams, in nightmares. So when she'd collapsed in the hall and everything had gone black, it only lent more weight to the argument that it was all in her head. That she'd made it all up because yes, even after this length of time, she still missed him so, so much.

She'd heard him say something, but by that time darkness already had her. And now that she was rising from that deep pit of despair and pain she was even more convinced the events that put her there were a product of her imagination.

Irene resolved to open her eyes, get up, and pop the kettle on—to try and put this whole episode out of her mind. But that was going to be incredibly difficult, because as she turned her head and looked at the chair facing the couch, she saw him again. He was sitting there with his hands clasped, staring at her. No, that wasn't strictly true; his eyes weren't so much staring as burrowing into her. She turned away again, quickly, not able to meet his gaze, nor accept what must be the truth. That Matthew was in the room with her, right now. Unless she was still dreaming? Could that be it? Irene pinched the loose skin on the back of her hand, nipping it tightly and hoping the pain would deliver her back to the world she knew. Back to sanity.

She didn't fully turn, but caught him still sitting there in the periphery of her vision.

Seconds passed like hours, until finally she knew she had to speak. "Who... who are you?" Irene asked. "What do you want?"

"I..." he began, and she felt compelled to look at him now as he shook his head. "I'm your son." The man said it so certainly that for a moment she almost believed him. For one thing he was saying the words in her son's voice.

"No... no you're not. You can't be."

He nodded. "But I am."

Irene sat up against the cushions, where he'd placed her, and brought her legs around with a slight crack of the bones. "You look like him—"

"I *am* him," he interrupted.

"You have his face, but..."

Oh sweet Lord did he have her son's face. It was exactly the same, every line, the dimple in his chin, the crowsfeet that were beginning at the corners of his eyes even though he was barely into his thirties. Those hazel eyes were the same too, and the way his hair made him look like he'd just got out of bed in spite of trying to brush it flat. All the same, all the same. And those clothes… were the shirt and trousers part of the suit they'd buried him in, or just very, very similar?

"Why won't you believe me?" It was a simple enough question and yet staggeringly complex. "You know, deep down, that I'm telling the truth."

Irene could feel tears starting to form in her eyes. "You're…" she managed before she began to cry. The tiny beads of water crawled down her cheeks, running into the rivulets created by her wrinkles and breaking up. "You're… you're…" She couldn't get the word out, and when it did eventually slip free it came only as a whisper. "Dead."

He frowned, saying nothing. What could he say? If he was her son, as he so vehemently claimed, how could he deny that? Yet here he was, in the 'flesh,' in her living room—that was a good one, *living* room—sitting in the armchair he always used to occupy when he visited. "I can't explain it," he finally offered. "But I know who I am, and I know that I love you, Mu—"

Irene held up her hand. "Don't. Please don't."

He got up, putting his hands in his pockets. Walking over to the window, he pulled aside the net curtains and peered out. Then he looked down at the photo in the frame on the windowsill. He lifted it up.

"Put that down," said Irene.

He held it out instead to illustrate his point. It was a photo taken at least ten years ago, of Matthew with his arm around his mother. "Look," he said. "This is me… this is me here with you."

"No," said Irene again. She was crying freely now.

There was a noise at the back door and they both turned. A shadow appeared in the hallway, small and dark, followed by another: this one very much alive. The jet-black cat froze when it reached the doorway, the swinging and creaking of the cat-flap still carrying into the living room.

Irene was half standing, looking from the cat to the man holding the picture.

"Tolly?" he said.

The cat had something in its mouth. It looked like a toy at first, but when the animal dropped it onto the hall carpet they could both see it was a sparrow the cat had stalked and caught, just like it always loved to do. The feline—named after Tolstoy, because of its long tail—was now locked in a battle of gazes with him. He took a step towards the creature and its fur stood on end, hackles rising. On some level it could sense there was something wrong. Was this really the man it used to curl up to, making itself comfortable in his lap while pressing its feet into his thighs as if making a nest?

One more step and the cat hissed, spinning around and shooting off in the direction it had come, leaving its prey behind. The man stood and looked across at Irene. She knew exactly how the cat felt—didn't want him coming anywhere near her.

"Mum," he said.

"Don't call me that!"

"It's who you are," he insisted. "You're my mother."

"I was Matthew's mother. I… I don't even know *what* you are."

He looked wounded.

Perhaps she was losing her mind. Was that it? Were these the first signs of Alzheimer's? Or a brain aneurysm? Was she conjuring up this whole scene because she wanted to see Matthew so badly, at this time of year especially? Was this all her doing? Irene shook her head. No, this was real; the man in front of her was real. And she had to figure out some way of dealing with it before she really did go insane.

"I'm Matthew. I'm not an hallucination," he told her, seemingly reading her mind.

"I don't believe in ghosts," Irene said.

"I'm not a ghost either," was his reply. "I'm solid, as solid as I was in this photograph. See?" He reached over and grabbed her arm and she nearly fell back onto the couch in an effort to escape him. But there was no force in that grip; it was merely to illustrate

211

his point. "I carried you back in here, remember?"

Her eyes were wide and white as dinner plates. He let go of her, slowly, and Irene was profoundly aware that she was trembling.

"I'm sorry. I didn't mean to scare you. It's just, well, I don't know how else to convince you."

"T-Tea," said Irene, her mouth a straight line. "A cup of tea…"

The man smiled. "Of course, tea. The cup that cures." He said it like he knew that was her mantra. Like he knew that all the problems there had ever been in this house had been solved over a cup of hot, steaming tea. "I'll go and put the kettle on."

Irene almost laughed then, a nervous laugh. Her dead son, or at least someone who purported to be so, was now offering to go and brew up. She nodded and watched as he put the picture down on the coffee table and left the room. From the kitchen she heard cupboards being opened, the tinkling of china—he knew exactly where to look. Then the sound of the kettle being filled with water.

Irene snapped out of her daze. She picked up the cordless telephone she always kept down the side of the couch when it wasn't charging. And, with one last glance at the photo, she stabbed the buttons with her finger.

Two

"I remember there used to be a poster here when I was growing up, some band," the person claiming to be Matthew Daley said, examining the wall of what had once been 'his' bedroom.

The request had come after he'd brought back the tea on a tray, along with a plate of biscuits, taken from the jar Irene always kept on the counter next to the bread bin. He wanted to see his old room, asked her politely and with that same lilt Matthew once had in his voice. Irene simply agreed, not knowing what else to say. She led the way up the rickety stairs, checking behind her all the time to see if he was still there. He was, and he followed her to the room where her son had spent much of the first twenty-two years of his life.

"The TV was there, the stereo over... there." He pointed to a sideboard. "I bought it with my first month's wages from the plant. You used to keep telling me to turn down the racket, you remember?"

Another nod.

"It's not there anymore, is it?"

For a second she thought he was still talking about the stereo, but then she realized he meant the place where he'd worked since he was in his late teens. "They... they shut it down a few years ago," she managed.

He nodded and walked over to the wardrobe, a cheap flat-pack one that was still—remarkably—standing, after many years of service. He opened the door nearest to him, taking out a jumper on a hangar. It was navy with pink zigzag lines running across the middle. "I can't believe this is still here. You gave me this one Christmas when I was about fifteen. I didn't like it, but I wore it anyway because I knew you did."

Irene thought she had the tears under control, but now they came again. "How do you know all these things?" she asked him.

"I thought we'd been through that. I'm your son."

At the risk of repeating herself, she said it again; this time the last word was more emphatic. "My son is *dead*."

He thought for a second or two. "Then who am I?"

"I... I don't know."

He put the jumper back inside the wardrobe and his eye caught something on the floor inside. Stooping, he picked it up; it was a small red racing car. Irene stood in silence as he brought the toy up to his face, turning it over.

There was a knock on the door downstairs, much the same as the one she'd answered earlier that morning. The 'stranger' in her home didn't appear to notice; he was too transfixed by the car her son had once played with and which had been left, forgotten, in the bottom of the wardrobe. The knock came again and Irene made for the door of the bedroom. She thought at any moment he would try to stop her from answering it, but he didn't. There was no hand on her arm this time, no sharp words. He—whoever he was—seemed to be in a world of his own.

She ventured down the stairs, more quickly than she had ascended them. Another shadow was visible through the frosted glass, but this time she knew exactly who it was. And for a moment, when she opened the door, it was like déjà vu. Irene was back in time, seven years ago, the two policemen standing at the door waiting to tell her the news. Except this time it was the uniformed officers waiting for her to speak, not the other way around. She'd known instinctively that Matthew had passed on even before she saw the Police Constables, just as she still knew he was dead—*should* be dead. Now it was a case of how to explain it to the policemen without sounding like she was on some kind of medication.

"Mrs. Irene Daley? We've had a report of a disturbance," said the first copper, a young black man.

A disturbance? That was one way of putting it.

"That someone was in your house," chipped in the other officer, a much older man with a graying beard.

"Y-Yes," she said, not really knowing where to begin. "He's… upstairs."

"Right," said the younger man, entering the house. The older man put a hand on his shoulder and gestured up towards the top of the stairs. Irene followed their gaze and saw 'Matthew' standing there. It sent a shiver up her spine.

"Sir, would you mind coming down here?" said the bearded officer. "Hands where I can see them."

He started to descend, a disappointed but resigned expression on his face. He held his hands palm outwards, and there was nothing in them.

"Now," continued the older man, "perhaps you'd mind explaining to me what you're doing in Mrs. Daley's home."

The man said nothing.

"Mrs. Daley... have you been hurt at all?"

"No signs of forced entry at the doorway," the younger PC confirmed.

"I... I opened the door and..." Irene was still crying and they took this as a sign to proceed.

The young black officer turned the man around and hand-cuffed him, just to be on the safe side. Their prisoner stared at Irene, half in disbelief, half resentment.

"So, perhaps we can get a few things sorted out now," said the bearded PC. "Who exactly are you and what are you doing in Mrs. Daley's home?"

"I'm her son," he said at last.

"Her son, eh? Mrs. Daley, is this true?"

She hesitated for a second, then shook her head.

"My name is Matthew Daley," stated the handcuffed man as he was patted down. The young PC found nothing, no ID, no weapons—nothing, save for a small toy car in the man's pocket, which he handed to his colleague.

"So he's not your son?" pressed the bearded policeman.

"He... he looks like him, but..."

The police officers exchanged glances.

"I am him," insisted the man.

"You *can't* be!" screamed Irene, finally reaching the end of her tether. "My Matthew has been dead for seven years!"

The bearded man sighed. "There's obviously been some kind of misunderstanding here. I think the best thing we can probably do is take you down to the station for a little chat. Valentine, stay here and get a statement from Mrs. Daley." He tugged on the intruder's arm and tried to lead him out of the house. For a fraction of a second he held fast, refusing to move, and it looked like they were going to have a struggle on their hands to shift him.

Then he spoke again before allowing the bearded PC to take him. "Dad would have believed me."

Irene leapt forward, all her trepidation forgotten, her hands turning to claws ready to rake this intruder's flesh. Luckily the black officer saw this coming and was able to hold her back before she could do any injury. "Let PC Wilson take it from here," Valentine said.

"You'll see me again," 'Matthew' told her.

"All right, that's enough," said Wilson. The bearded copper led the man out the door and down the path. Irene watched with the other policeman standing alongside. A small crowd of people had gathered now, attracted by the police car at the front of the house. A man with ginger hair and a potbelly was leaning against his open doorway, scratching himself and eating a sandwich. The kids who'd been playing on the road had picked their football up; one held it under his arm like a headless ghost.

All paid attention now, all noticed. The handcuffed man was bundled into the back, PC Wilson slamming the door after him. Then the policeman climbed into the front and started the engine again.

The car drove off, away from the scene, and Valentine started to close the door. Something flew past them and out through the gap.

It was a small brown bird, a sparrow.

They watched it climb up into the air and join the others overhead, circling the house. Neither of them said anything. But as Valentine finally shut the door and took out his notepad, Irene couldn't help noticing the hallway was empty.

"So then, Mrs. Daley," Valentine said hopefully, breaking into her daze, "perhaps you could explain to me what all this is about."

Three

"Tell me again just why we're holding him?"

Detective Chief Inspector Robbins, a long thin streak of a

man with cropped hair and a chin that was so lantern shaped people expected to see a flame flickering in his mouth whenever he talked, was leafing through PC Wilson's notes on their new arrival. He'd been woken early that morning by a phone call from his third ex-wife asking him if he'd taken the hedge trimmer with him when he left the previous summer, and if so, could she please have it back as her new boyfriend would quite like to make a start in the garden that weekend. There were several cases waiting for him on his desk when he arrived, which looked in no rush to solve themselves. And his acid indigestion was playing up again, making it feel like someone was stirring his guts around with a red-hot poker. So he was not in the best of moods, and definitely not in the mood for his time being wasted.

"We're not exactly holding him as such, sir," replied the bearded man, "I just thought it best to place him in an interview room before coming to you with it… while we figured out exactly what had happened."

"So?"

"Looked like a simple case of forced entry, except he claims he was let in, and even made Mrs. Daley a cup of tea."

The DCI's eyebrows shot up. "Your average hardened criminal then. Why are you bothering me with this?"

"Also claims to be her long lost son."

"Long lost, as in Australian soap opera plot?" said Robbins with a sarcastic smirk.

"No. As in deceased, sir."

Robbin's smile faded. "All right, you've got my attention. Maybe we should bring up a few records on our…" He read from the notes. "… Mr. Matthew Daley. Where's the mother now?"

"Valentine's with her, going over what exactly happened." Wilson opened his mouth, then shut it again.

"Go on, you looked like you were about to say something."

Wilson nodded. "It's just that there's something funny about this whole thing, that's why I came to you with it. There's something about him that gives me the creeps."

"How do you mean?"

"I can't put my finger on it," Wilson scratched his beard. "He just doesn't seem right to me." The veteran policeman had come across many people in his time, from all walks of life, and Robbins knew this. You got a sense about them, whether they were lying, whether they were about to punch you. When he said something wasn't right about this business, Robbins would be a fool to just dismiss it.

"You think he might have a screw loose, that it?"

"I don't know."

Robbins shrugged. "All right, what the hell. Let's see what we can find out about him. Then we'll have a nice little talk with our deceased friend."

* * *

The chair was uncomfortable, nothing like those in the house earlier. In fact this one was *designed* to make people uncomfortable, ill at ease. But if *he* felt any discomfort at all he didn't show it.

Police Constable Frank Wilson stood by the wall as Robbins took a seat opposite the man. Wilson thought about the drive over to the station, how he'd kept looking in the rear view mirror, how the man had seemed to stare right back at him in the reflective surface. He hadn't said a word until they were halfway there, and then it was only to reiterate that he was Mrs. Daley's son, that he had made her a drink to calm her nerves, and he couldn't understand why he had been taken away. It was a thread that was picked up again when Robbins sat down, placing a manila file of papers on the table between them, and turning on the tape recorder to the left of him.

"Why have you brought me here? Am I being charged with something?" His words were even and considered.

Robbins turned it back on him. "Why do *you* think you're

here?"

The man sighed. "My mother rang you."

"And why do you think she did that?"

"She couldn't accept—"

"Accept who you are," Robbins finished for him.

There was no reply.

Robbins took off his jacket and hung it on the back of his chair. "And who exactly are you?"

"Her son."

Robbins shook his head. "According to her, and..." He tapped the files in front of him. "... according to this, Matthew Daley died seven years ago. With the best will in the world, you can't be him... trust me."

"How do you know?"

"It was before my time here, but I've read the medical reports, seen the photos," Robbins said, narrowing his eyes.

"Photos?" asked the man.

"From when they brought him in. You don't know, do you?" Robbins looked back over at Wilson.

"Know what?" asked the man, leaning forward.

"That's interesting." The DCI faced him again. "You don't know how Matthew Daley died. Why is that?"

The man said nothing for a moment, then, "I can remember some things, but... others are a bit hazy."

"Well, there is no way on Earth that you can be him, I assure you. There's a resemblance, I'll give you that, but Mr. Daley..." Robbins stopped himself, unable to continue. "You can't be him; simple as that. Which begs the question, who are you? Who are you *really*? And what did you want with Mrs. Daley? Money, was that it?"

"Money?" The man seemed confused by the accusation.

"Yes, were you hoping to get money from her?"

"Why would I want her money?"

"You're telling me her money wouldn't interest you?"

"Course not."

"Were you hoping she'd be so confused and upset that she'd just hand over whatever savings she had to you?"

The man shook his head violently, slamming his fist on the table. "I didn't want her money," he insisted. "I... I just needed to see her. She's my mother."

"I don't think we're getting through to him, Wilson," said Robbins. "As I said before, Mr. Daley is dead. He's been in Westmoor Cemetery, in the ground, for seven years. You, sir, on the other hand, appear to be remarkably spry." Robbins folded his arms and sat back in his marginally more comfortable chair. "Surely you can see how we—and Mrs. Daley—would have a problem with that?"

"I can't explain it, I just know that—"

"Listen to me!" shouted Robbins, "I don't know what your game is, but in this station we don't take very kindly to men who scare little old ladies out of their wits for kicks."

"I never meant to frighten her. I just—"

"You just needed to see her, yeah you said."

The man was wriggling about now, agitated. "Isn't there some kind of test you can do? You said you had medical reports there–—"

"The reports from the *autopsy*," clarified Robbins.

"Isn't there something you can—"

Robbins laughed. "Why should we, when we already know the answer? You're not Matthew Daley, sunshine. Live with it." He realized the significance of what he'd just said and a mocking grin creased his face again.

"But—"

The DCI took something out of his pocket and placed it on the desk. "Care to tell me why you had this about your person when you were picked up?"

The man went rigid. His eyes were glued to the little red car now on the table.

"Thought it might be worth something?"

"It's... It's mine. Or at least it was."

The man reached out to take it from the table and Robbins grabbed his wrist. "You'd better start giving us some answers, whoever you are or…" He let the threat tail off, letting go of the man's hand as he did so. Ignoring him, the man carried on reaching out for the car and picked it up.

"PC Wilson, would you escort our 'guest' to a cell. Maybe some time alone will help loosen his tongue."

Wilson walked over to the man, hesitating slightly before taking him by the arm as he'd done when he led him out of Irene Daley's house. The man didn't look at Robbins as he left.

When they'd departed and the door closed; Robbins let out a long, slow breath. He rubbed his chin and opened up the file again, flipping through the reports and statements, notes from his predecessor DCI Croft. The same bloody Croft whose shoes he'd had to fill when he moved to this district. Hadn't been able to solve this one last murder, though, had he? Robbins was drawn again to the pictures, the photographs of Matthew Daley. He screwed up his face at the sights before him: the blood, the deep gashes, the plump bruising of the skin that had turned the flesh a dull violet color.

He slammed the file shut again and leaned back in the chair once more, arms behind his head this time. "No way," he said to himself in a whisper. "No way in the world."

* * *

PC Wilson placed the man in cell number thirteen, the only one free. It could have been worse, he thought, could've been a Friday.

"Here you go," he told him. "Now I suggest you think about what DCI Robbins said and drop the act, mate."

The man ignored him. His shoes and socks had already been taken off him, and now Wilson thought about asking for the toy as well. Prisoners weren't meant to have any personal effects in the cells. But something stopped him from doing so, and he left the man be.

"If you come to your senses, shout," said Wilson.

Then he shut the 'dead man' away, all alone in the small, dark, confined space. And as Wilson locked up and walked down the corridor he had the strangest feeling.

The feeling that this wasn't the first time the guy been shut away. That the last time it had been an even smaller, and even darker space.

Four

It was dark.

A blackness so overpowering, so unbearable it was like being drowned in pure liquid night. It was hard to gather his thoughts, but he felt sure he was walking, placing one foot in front of the other, just trudging on towards something. And he was granted a sense of where he might be—the walls of this place closing in on him, but they were round rather than flat, a roundness that stretched out into the distance. A tiny speck of light appeared at the far end of this tunnel. He felt compelled to look in its direction, an urgency to head towards it for some reason.

The light was growing stronger; it changed from a tiny speck to a bright glaring ball, meaning he was getting nearer to the end, although he didn't feel like he was walking at all anymore. Yet the light was still growing nearer. Perhaps he was floating; he had no idea, but it was a strange sensation. The light was getting bigger and bigger. Soon it would all be over, soon he would find out what was at the end of this conduit, what the light meant.

He put up his hands to stop it from blinding him, but it shone right through—such was its intensity. Then, suddenly, the light was upon him. He was a part of the light and it was a part of him.

All the answers, the things out of reach would soon be revealed.

Just a few more seconds, just a few more—

* * *

The hand shook him awake and gave him a start.

"Dead to the world." Inspector Robbins' face hovered above him in the cell. The man sat bolt upright on the bunk. "Time to wake yourself Rip van Winkle," he said in a snide voice.

The man swung his bare feet onto the cold tiled floor.

"We have a visitor for you."

"Mum?"

Robbins shook his head, grinning. "Afraid not. No, I thought about what you said—about checking you over. You're right; we have to make sure you're not whacked out on something that might be making you delusional. Wilson?"

The PC stepped into his field of vision, bringing someone with him—a woman in her late thirties, early forties. Her hair was a light shade of bronze, with the merest hints of grey beginning at the temples. She wore a beige trouser suit with an off-white blouse beneath the jacket. And she was carrying with her a black leather case.

"This is Doctor Preston," Robbins informed him. "She's going to examine you. Now, PC Wilson is going to be just outside, so don't give her a hard time, okay?"

Dr. Preston came further into the chamber, looking around her as she did so. Then their eyes met, only severing contact when Robbins said something to her.

"I'm sorry?"

"I said: twenty minutes all right?"

"Fine," she told him.

Robbins gave a satisfied nod. "All right then, we'll leave you to it."

The DCI exited the cell, with Wilson hanging back a few moments longer before leaving the door open a crack and waiting outside.

"So," said Dr Preston to break the silence that had descended, "what's your story?"

The man stared at her blankly.

"Not one for idle chit chat, I understand. Okay, well if you wouldn't mind getting undressed, we'll make a start."

He did as he was told, unbuttoning the shirt and shrugging it down over his shoulders. Then he took off his trousers; there was no underwear beneath. Preston opened her bag and took out the tools of her trade, listening to his heartbeat—steady and strong—looking in his ears, taking his temperature, testing his reflexes. It was there that she caught a glimpse of the birthmark on the top of his leg. It was dark red and shaped like a map of some unknown land. But she got on with her job, not giving it another thought. Everything seemed in working order. "Now this won't hurt much," she told him, taking out a needle, "I just need to draw some blood."

He nodded vaguely, looking down as she shoved the needle into his upper arm, pulling back on one end and filling it with redness.

"There, all done. You're in pretty good nick, if you'll pardon the expression," she said.

"I'm alive," he said as he got dressed again, and the sound of his voice startled her. She wasn't quite sure whether it was a question or a statement.

"Er... yes, in my professional opinion. Why, don't you feel very well?"

He laughed softly and caught her eyes again. "They haven't told you yet, have they?"

Preston's eyebrows creased. "About?"

"It doesn't matter, you'll find out soon enough."

"I don't like mysteries Mister—?" She waited for him to give her his name. When he didn't she said, "My first name's Bethany, by the way. Beth for short."

"Matthew," he told her. "My name's Matthew."

"There now, see—that wasn't so difficult. Right, well, I think we're all done here Matth—"

He shot out his hand so fast she didn't have time to move away, and his fingers were around her wrist seconds later—not tight, just enough to draw her face in closer. "What're you..."

She was just about to call for Wilson when he said:

"Don't blame yourself. You did everything you could." His hazel eyes were intense, piercing, and she felt a shudder go through her entire body. "*She* doesn't blame you."

"What?"

"You have to let it go, all of it. All the guilt."

She wrestled her hand free, moving back sharply as if stung. Beth grabbed her bag and raced for the door.

"Sarah's happy," said the man plainly.

She closed her eyes and opened them again, looking back at him. "What... what did you just say?"

"You heard me."

The doctor was gazing at him in disbelief. "You... you can't..."

He turned away from her. "I'll see you again."

Beth yanked open the door and virtually walked into the PC who was standing guard there. She motioned for him to lock the cell again.

"Are you all right, Dr Preston?" he asked her.

But she didn't hear him. She was looking through the slit in the door, watching the man in there as he held up a toy car and stared at it.

"Dr Preston?" His fingertips brushed her arm and she jumped back. "I'm sorry."

"Take me to Robbins," she said. "Take me to your DCI right now."

* * *

For the third time that day there was a knock on the door.

This time it was PC Valentine who answered it, welcoming in the visitor Mrs. Daley had called at his suggestion.

"Is there anybody who could sit with you? Anybody you could ring?" said the black policeman once he'd finished taking her statement—a statement that made about as much sense as the rest of that morning's events.

Mrs. Daley had nodded, and he'd handed her the cordless phone.

Now he was here, standing at her door. And just as the dark uniform that Valentine wore betrayed his profession, so too did the dark shirt and suit that this man had on. But the most significant piece of attire was the dog collar at his neck.

"Father Lilley?" asked Valentine of the priest who was only marginally younger than Mrs. Daley herself.

He bowed his head in greeting. "Where's Irene... Mrs. Daley?"

"Through here." Valentine took him to the dining room; he hadn't been able to get her back into the living room at all. She was sitting at a small round table with her hands clasped together, bible to the right of them.

"Thank you, my son," said Lilley to the PC, noticing the woman flinch at those last two words. Then she got up and fell into the priest's arms.

"Oh father, I'm so pleased to see you."

"There, there," said Lilley, patting her back. "Whatever's the matter, Irene? I couldn't make head nor tail of your call." He looked to Valentine for an answer, but he was asking the wrong person.

"Some... something terrible. Matthew..."

The priest's expression changed and he cut short the embrace. "Matthew? I don't understand. I thought you'd had an intruder?"

"She did," Valentine reported, "of a kind."

"He... he looked just like Matthew, Father," Irene added.

It seemed like Lilley didn't know what to say, then he talked slowly as if to a child. "Irene, haven't we talked about this before? Matthew's gone. He is with Our Savior the Lord where he has found his peace. 'His kingdom *is* an everlasting kingdom, and his dominion *is* from generation to generation.' The Book of Daniel, Chapter Four, Verse Three. Matthew wouldn't want you upsetting yourself like this, now, would he?"

"He said he *was* Matthew."

"The man in your house?"

She nodded.

"Said Arnold would have listened, would have believed him."

"Irene, Matthew's no longer with us. I buried him myself."

He saw that she remembered all too well that day: the angry clouds had gathered as if in sympathy, looking down at the patch of grass behind the church. A group of mourners, dressed in black, standing around the hole in the ground as the perfectly polished coffin with the brass handles was lowered into it.

Ashes to ashes. Dust to dust.

Irene had broken down on that day too. At one point he thought she might even stagger forward and follow the coffin into the ground. But instead she had held back, tears pouring from her eyes for a son who had been taken prematurely.

"Officer, who was this man?" Lilley asked Valentine.

"That's what we're trying to find out, Father. But he's insistent that he's Matthew Daley."

"That's impossible."

"I know," said the PC, a little offended that he had to explain that to the priest.

"I'd like to see him," said Lilley.

"Perhaps, in time," Valentine told him. "But for now…" He nodded towards Irene. "I think Mrs. Daley needs you here."

The priest's eyes flashed momentarily, as if he didn't like being told his job. Then the kindness returned to them and he said, "Of course." He led his charge back to her seat, pulling out the chair nearest to her for himself. "Don't worry, Irene. I'm sure this will all be sorted out soon. Everything that happens is according to God's design and purpose, even if we can't see it at the time. 'Trust in the Lord with all your heart, and lean not on your own understanding; in all your ways acknowledge Him, and He shall direct your paths.' Proverbs Chapter Three, Verses Five to Six." He held her hand in his and patted it. "Trust in the Lord, Irene, and He will show you the way."

* * *

"I don't like being hung out to dry, Steve."

Dr. Bethany Preston paced up and down in DCI Robbins' office, arms folded. He was sitting back behind his desk, watching her, like a member of the audience at Wimbledon.

"I wasn't hanging anyone anywhere," he said, after telling her repeatedly to calm down. He'd never seen her so agitated.

"You deliberately withheld information from me about that prisoner, didn't you?" As she said this last bit she jabbed her finger in his direction.

"I didn't want you walking into there with any preconceptions. Besides, you never asked."

Becky threw her hands up in the air. "And what exactly was I supposed to ask... oh and excuse me, but by any chance was this guy picked up for impersonating a dead man?"

"I told you everything you needed to know at the time."

"Bullshit. You told me he was a weird one, that he might be on something, and to try and get him talking if I could."

"You've done it before. You have a good... bedside manner."

"People tell me things, Steve. They trust me. I don't abuse that trust. Unlike some." Now she was standing with her hands on her hips.

"Let's not make this personal again, Beth."

"If I recall rightly, it was you who made things... 'personal' the last time."

He winced at that remark. "No need to dig up the past. What exactly did he say to you in there? What's really got you like this?" Robbins rose from his chair and leant against his desk.

She avoided his eyes. "Nothing."

"I don't believe you."

Beth raised her head, but her eyes were far from warm. "Your prerogative. But you're right about one thing."

"What's that?"

"He is a weird one. In fact, in all my years as a Doctor, and the last few years working for you lot, I don't think I've ever come across anyone quite like him."

Robbins folded his arms now. "No, me either. But he isn't Matthew Daley."

"You sound very sure of that."

"Oh come on, Beth. You've seen the photos and the report now, what that fucker did to him. It's just not possible. He was dead by the time they loaded him into the ambulance. The paramedics called it on the way to Accident and Emergency. They buried him for Christ's sake."

Beth rubbed her forehead. "I should be going," she said.

"Wait."

"Look, you want me to test the blood, Steve, I'll test it." She picked up her bag and left, shutting the door behind her.

Leaving Robbins to stare at the space she'd occupied only moments before.

Five

He saw things as he waited in his cell. More quick flashes he wished he could slow down, more images—this time accompanied by smells and sounds too. A burning, acrid aroma, a scream that turned rapidly into a yelp. The stink of faeces, a thudding. And there was music, a rock band belting out their latest hit for all they were worth. All of this mish-mashed into a nonsense as he sat there.

He'd been given his meals by Wilson, but the man couldn't bear to be in his presence for more than a few minutes. Not that it really mattered, not that any of this really mattered. The important work was still yet to be done; he felt that, knew it somehow. He knew what some of it should be, too, while other parts were still hidden. Just like his ragged and torn memory, some bits perfect, others barely more than fuzzy blurs.

As day passed to night and dawn broke again, he explored the confines of his cell more fully, discovering a spider's web in the bottom corner. There was no sign of the spider itself, but there was the carcass of one of its victims caught there on the fine gossamer strands. He felt exactly like that fly, stranded here. Trapped with no means of escape.

When Wilson next came in to bring him breakfast, he asked if there was any word yet from Dr. Preston. He also asked when he would be released and whether they were intent on charging him with anything.

Wilson could answer neither.

So he had to be patient. Wait until it all started to fall into place.

* * *

"It still doesn't prove anything," Robbins said as he gripped the phone tighter, bringing his other hand up and almost wringing the plastic.

"No it doesn't. But the man in your cells and Matthew Daley definitely had the same blood type," Beth told him down the line.

"Along with how many other millions?"

"Granted. But here's the thing: I noticed yesterday that the man you're holding has a birthmark on the top of his left leg."

"So? The autopsy reports don't mention anything about a birthmark," Robbins snapped.

"That's because the thigh was a bloody mess, Steve. But according to Matthew Daley's local practice, he *did* have a birthmark on the upper part of his leg."

"All right, so they've both got birthmarks."

"Same blood type, same birthmarks, same height, hair color, eye color…" Beth continued.

"All right, all right," Robbins said. "But they can't be the same person. What're we talking here, twins?"

"I think Mr. and Mrs. Daley would have noticed if there was a baby missing at the birth," said Beth.

"A fluke, a look-alike?"

"I don't know what to tell you, Steve. None of this makes any sense to me. Not really."

Again he wondered just what had spooked her in the cell yesterday.

"But there were certain... anomalies in the blood itself," she said after a pause.

"How do you mean? Drugs?"

"No, he was clean, like I said. It's just that his white blood cell count is incredibly high... and his humor immunity is quite outstanding."

He swapped the phone to his other ear. "In English, Beth."

"There are an inordinate amount of antibodies in his system. Triggered by what, I don't know. Some exogenous antigen I can't identify."

"I do believe I said English."

"Simply put, it means he's extremely resistant to infection."

"Okay," Robbins said slowly.

"And there's something else."

Robbins sighed. "Do I have to ask, or were you planning on telling me eventually?"

"Matthew Daley had type two diabetes, but there's no sign of that now in this blood."

"Then it *can't* be him."

"You'd think so, and yet... Steve, we really need to do some more tests."

"Look, Beth, I'm not really interested if he's the scientific discovery of the century. The bottom line is, I have someone in custody and I don't know what to charge him with... if anything. Trespass, possibly. But there aren't any laws against looking like someone who's died. Give me something to go on."

He could almost hear her mind ticking over. "The case is still open, right?"

"Technically yes. They never caught who did this to Matthew Daley."

"Then get a decent DNA sample. The people who were handling all this back then weren't exactly CSI material. Exhume the body, Steven."

Robbins asked her to repeat what she'd just said in case he'd misheard it. He hadn't.

"Jesus... we can't do that, Beth. The mother would go ballistic, and as for the church... Valentine says that the local priest hasn't left Mrs. Daley's side since this happened."

"Get a court order."

"By tomorrow? You know how many strings I'd have to pull?"

Becky tutted. "You're telling me you can't? From what I hear Croft would've been able to manage it."

He ground his teeth. "It'd be professional suicide."

"And the career always comes first, doesn't it?" said Beth.

Robbins exhaled another deep breath. "The shit's really going to hit the fan."

"It's the only way to be sure."

"About what?"

She didn't answer that one, but he knew the answer anyway. He placed the 'phone in the crook of his neck, took a packet of indigestion tablets out of his pocket, and tapped a couple into his palm.

"I'll see what I can do," he said, tipping the tablets into his mouth.

"One more thing," said Beth before she hung up.

"Yeah?"

"I want to be there."

"What?"

"I want to be there when they open the coffin up."

"You?"

"Don't sound so shocked. You're the one that brought me

232

into this, Steve."

"Okay," Robbins promised her. Then he looked up at the ceiling, wondering just what he was about to set in motion.

Six

The morning was an overcast one.

As the group waited around the grave they resembled the mourners from the funeral that had been held there seven years ago. Except these people had only come to know about Matthew Daley's life in the last forty-eight hours or so. They hadn't watched him grow up, hadn't loved him or grieved over his passing. They were here for one reason only: the truth.

Bethany Preston had arrived early, as soon as she'd been given the call. Robbins told her that it hadn't been easy, but they'd been granted express permission to exhume—in spite of Father Lilley's protests. Lilley had been particularly vocal when the teams of police and forensics experts arrived at Westmoor. Said it would be a sacrilege in the eyes of the Lord. Valentine had to hold him back from the scene, while Robbins tried to explain their position.

"I'm really sorry, Father, but this has to be done."

"Heathens, all of you. 'Depart from me, all ye workers of iniquity; for the Lord hath heard the voice of my weeping!' Psalm Six, Verse Eight," shouted Lilley, shaking his fist. When that didn't work, he tried another tack. "My father was a Captain in the army. He died in the war. Died so that our freedoms should be upheld."

"We need to give Mrs. Daley peace of mind. There might be evidence in that grave which could help in the investigation—"

"Investigation!" Lilley spat. "You couldn't find the person who killed him the first time, what makes you think you will now? Leave the poor boy in peace, I'm begging you."

"And what about Mrs. Daley's peace of mind?" asked Robbins.

Lilley squinted with one eye. "This is about the man who came to her house, isn't it?"

"It might help to settle things," replied Robbins, deflecting the question.

"In the name of the Lord our God, man, she doesn't need things 'settling.' She knows already, knows that man *cannot* be her son. The peace of mind you're talking about will only be shattered by this."

"The case was never closed though, Father," said Robbins. "This is important."

"This is unheard of! You'll burn for it," Lilley warned them. "All of you. 'Upon the wicked he shall rain snares, fire and brimstone, and a horrible tempest; this shall be the portion of their cup.' Psalm One Verse Six."

Beth had heard the commotion but was crouching by the gravestone itself, reading the inscription there.

MATTHEW KEVIN DALEY
Devoted son, husband, and father.
Taken from us early.
Sleep well, Angel.

There were a couple of stems from long dead flowers that had been left there possibly weeks or even months ago. When Robbins returned from his encounter with Lilley, chewing more of his tablets, he gave the order for the exhumation to begin. Beth stepped back to allow the police to start digging. It took them the best part of two hours to reach the coffin, though even then it was only because of their numbers.

She watched as the men in white suits fed straps under the coffin, signaling for it to be lifted out slowly and carefully. Like a huge wooden baby, it was cradled back down again to the earth.

"Are you sure about this, about being here?" said Robbins, now at the side of her. "It's not going to be pleasant."

234

"Steve, I'm a Doctor for Christ's sake. And I'm a big girl."

Robbins gave the order for the coffin to be opened, which the men did, again with the utmost professionalism, care, and respect. Beth and Robbins drew closer as the final nail was removed and the lid heaved off.

* * *

Irene Daley lay in bed, unable to move.

She knew what they were doing that morning. Father Lilley had broken the news to her as gently as he could. They'd obtained an order to exhume Matthew, earthly laws obviously carrying more weight than religious ones. She'd run the gamut of emotions then: surprise, fear, anger, resentment. But hadn't there been something else at the back of her mind, a little voice telling her that at least they'd know for sure when it was done? At least she'd be able to get the picture of that person out of her head, the man who'd sat in Matthew's chair, who'd looked around his old bedroom and found the forgotten toy car in the wardrobe. The man who'd told her that his father—no, Matthew's father— would have believed him.

Irene's eyes were dry that morning. There were no more tears left. In the past two days she'd cried so much she thought her eyeballs would simply float out of her head. But now, on the morning they were digging up her son's coffin, and opening it, she found she couldn't cry at all. She felt numb; she might as well have been in that coffin herself.

Yet as the hands on the clock next to her bed reached midday, Irene did feel something. At that precise moment she knew the lid was being taken off... and she knew what they would find inside.

She knew more positively than she had ever known anything in her life.

That was when she started crying again.

* * *

"So what happens now?"

"I honestly wish I knew," Robbins, still clearly stunned, told Beth.

"We need to talk to him again."

"We?"

"We," she repeated.

Robbins rubbed the back of his neck. "Heavens knows what I'm going to tell my bosses. This is growing way beyond a simple cold case now."

"I think it was before." She tentatively placed a hand on his shoulder. "You did the right thing, Steve."

"I doubt the priest back there sees it that way. Did you know we're all going to burn in Hell for this, Beth?"

"Been there, bought the t-shirt."

"None of this makes any sense."

"No it doesn't."

They began walking away from the grave again, back towards the church. Robbins marched past Valentine and Lilley without meeting their gaze. Neither Robbins nor Beth spoke again until they reached the police cars parked on the road. Then one of the women police officers there—Adams, Beth had heard him call her—took Robbins to one side. Beth shifted her weight from one foot to the other and waited as the WPC whispered something to him.

"What?" she heard Robbins say, raising his voice. "He can't be… Well how did…?" Robbins listened some more, then shook his head violently.

Beth rushed over, but waited until Robbins had dismissed the junior officer before asking what had happened.

"He's gone," the detective told her bluntly.

"What do you mean?"

"What do you think I mean, Beth, *he's fucking gone!*"

She recoiled as if slapped.

"'I'm sorry," he said, but his voice was still hard.

"I don't understand... how can he just be gone?"

"One of the duty officers found Wilson in there, sitting in the corner of the cell. They can't get much sense out of him, he's talking nonsense."

"Didn't anyone see anything?"

"Apparently not. And there's nothing on the bloody CCTV cameras either." Robbins broke away from her and started towards his car.

"Wait a minute, where are you going?"

"Where do you think? Back to the station, I'm going to try and work out where our boy is... before anything else happens."

Seven

Jason loved dinner hour.

All morning long he'd been stuck in a fusty classroom working first on math problems, then looking at a book where the principal character traveled back in time to visit some of the most famous historical events, like the Roman era and the middle ages when knights battled it out with big swords. Jason didn't want to *read* about such things. He wanted to be in the sunshine, acting them out, just like he would be in the holidays.

So, after a dinner of what was supposed to be some sort of stew, followed by a dessert that was part sponge, part custard, and part something else he hadn't been able to distinguish, Jason had raced out onto the playground attached to the small school, swinging his imaginary sword and chopping away at an imaginary black knight. A surge of boys and girls came behind him, breaking off into smaller fragments: some going into corners to trade cards from the latest Japanese cartoon series; some kicking around a small tennis ball on the floor; some playing chase; others simply racing around and around, screaming at the top of their voices, as if trying to release all the energy that had been building for the last few hours.

Jason had now dispatched his evil opponent and was looking for any dragons to tackle—although, as his teacher Miss Bellamy had tried to drive home to them all that morning, dragons didn't strictly exist during that era. Didn't exist at all, in actual fact.

"What about St. George?" asked one little girl near the front, Mary Hodgkins.

"Ah, well, the tale of St. George and the dragon is what we call a fable, children. Like Sleeping Beauty. In this case the dragon just represents a form of evil."

"Did they have talking lions in the middle ages, Miss?" asked Leon Keogh.

She'd sighed wearily. "No Leon, it wasn't Narnia. This was real."

But Jason, like Leon, wasn't too fond of the real. Real was boring, and dragons breathed fire and had scales and were, when all was said and done, pretty damned cool. In his imagination, he found the dragon he'd been looking for: a bright red one that flapped its wings on approach and was guarding a cave full of treasure. He ran at the beast, swinging his sword left and right, dodging the fire that came his way. And running straight into the path of one of the school helpers, Mrs. Shaw, a woman who could, in her own way, also lay claim to the title of dragon.

She towered over Jason, holding the youngster by the arm. "Why don't you look where you're going?" said Mrs. Shaw in that rasping voice of hers. She was one of the old crowd, one of the small handful of helpers and teachers who still thought it had been a bad idea to get rid of corporal punishment, because a smack or several hadn't done them any harm when they were little—apart from giving them the impression it was okay to do that to others later on. Mrs. Shaw would never openly strike any of the kids there, but every now and again she liked to put the fear of God into one, just to keep the rest in line.

Jason hoped today wasn't his turn to be on the receiving end.

"I'm... I'm sorry," he said. He wondered about telling her

what he'd been doing, but thought better of it. Mrs. Shaw wasn't the kind of person you told about your imaginary fights with fantasy creatures. Mrs. Shaw wasn't the kind of person you told anything to really.

"Come here," she said, pulling Jason into a small corner of the playground, away from the windows of the school. Away from prying eyes.

"Please, I didn't mean to—"

"Don't give me any of that sniveling," she rasped again. "I get enough of it from my husband."

Mrs. Shaw bent, bringing Jason closer as she did so. "If I ever catch you running about like that, swinging your arms again, I'll—"

"You'll let him go," said a voice from behind them. It was even and soft, but had a harder edge to it underneath.

Mrs. Shaw rose slowly. Jason had never seen this look on her face before, a look you get only when you've been caught doing something you shouldn't be. She immediately let go of Jason's arm, turning round to see who had spoken.

Jason saw the man a few seconds after her, as she moved aside, allowing him a clearer view. He was about average height, with dark tousled hair, and he was wearing a shirt and trousers. As Jason looked down, though, he saw the man was barefoot.

When Mrs. Shaw realized he wasn't a member of staff, nor did he look like anyone in any kind of authority—more like a tramp who'd wandered in through the gate—she shouted, "And who the hell are you?"

"That doesn't matter," he told her.

"Some kind of pervert, eh? Come to spy on the kids at play-time?"

"No."

"Well, we'll just see what the headmaster has to say about that one, shall we? You do realize that you're trespassing?"

He said nothing, merely stared at her.

Mrs. Shaw took a step towards him. "What's the matter with

you anyway? You on drugs or something? And where are your shoes?" She took two more steps, then paused, and took another.

The man saved her the trouble of coming any closer and covered the remaining distance himself. He grabbed her arm, just as she had done with Jason in the playground. She didn't have time to get away. Mrs. Shaw was about to scream when he said, "Do you ever think about him anymore, Jean? Do you ever think about Oliver?"

"What... what are you talking about?"

"You can tell yourself that what happened to him was an accident, that you had nothing to do with it, but you made his life a misery. And for what? All because he was a bit overweight?"

"Who are you? How... how could you know...?"

"How did you feel when you heard the news, Jean? When you heard how he'd died? You can keep moving, but it follows you wherever you go, doesn't it?"

Mrs. Shaw wrestled herself out of his grip and backed away, pointing at him. "You... you stay away from me!" She gave him one last look, then turned tail and ran away in the opposite direction.

Which left Jason alone with the man.

"Hello, Jason," said the older of the two.

Jason didn't reply. He'd been told often enough not to speak to strangers. But wasn't there something about this man, something he recognized, however vaguely? And hadn't he just helped Jason escape from Mrs. Shaw's clutches?

"You've grown so much since the last time I saw you."

Jason wanted to run—should be running away, just like Mrs. Shaw had done. But something was keeping him here.

"You're not afraid of me, are you?" asked the man, coming nearer.

The nod Jason gave was barely a tremble of the head.

"Don't be, I've come such a long way to see you. Probably can't remember me, can you?"

Jason half shook his head, half nodded.

"I'm not surprised. It's been a while. You were still a toddler when I… when I left."

"W-Who are you?" asked Jason.

This time the man gave an answer. "I'm your Dad, Jason. I'm your Dad."

* * *

When a very shaken Mrs. Shaw returned, with the headmaster in tow (he'd already had some harsh words to say to her about abandoning one of their pupils to an intruder) the man had vanished.

Jason was standing in the same spot he had been when she'd run off, but now he had his back to them and was looking down at something.

"Jason?" said, the headmaster, reaching out a hand and pulling it back again.

Jason didn't look; he was concentrating on whatever he had in his hands.

"Jason, are you all right? Did… did that man do anything to you?"

Jason shook his head.

"What's that you've got there?" asked the headmaster, walking around to the front of the boy.

Jason finally looked up, then showed him the object that was in the palm of his hand. "It's a present."

The headmaster picked up the tiny red car and examined it.

"He gave it to me," Jason said. "Said to keep it safe. And he said he would see me again very soon…"

Eight

Constable Bernard Wilson was lying down on the cot in the cell when they arrived back. A policewoman was trying, unsuccessfully, to get him to take a sip of water. His face was the color of spilt milk.

Robbins indicated with a wrench of the neck that she should leave them alone, which she promptly did.

"Wilson?" asked the DCI. "Care to tell me what happened here?"

Beth pushed past him to check on the PC, feeling his pulse first, then his brow. "His heart's racing, and he's quite hot."

"My heart's racing as well," snapped the detective. "There's a man out there on the loose who's…" He let the sentence evaporate.

"What happened?" asked Beth this time. "Where did your… prisoner go?" She hated using that word, but couldn't think of anything else to call the man. They'd been keeping him here against his will, after all.

Wilson looked at her, his eyes large. "He… he told me things," was all he would say.

"I don't suppose he told you where he was going by any chance? *After* you let him out." Robbins' voice had lost none of its harshness.

Beth scowled at him. "Steve, can't you see he's still in a state of shock?"

"Aren't we all? But we need to find this man and we need to find him right now!"

"You think I don't know that? But this isn't help—"

"He… he told me my aunty and uncle were safe and well. Told me he'd seen them," Wilson interrupted.

"And you let him go because of that? Because he told you he knows your family? Jesus Christ!"

"My aunty died in 1985 of cancer, my uncle ten years later. T-They brought me up." Now it was Wilson's turn to snap. He sat up and his voice had a chilling edge. "T-Told me things only they could know."

Both Beth and Robbins were silent.

"What did you find in the coffin?" asked Wilson. "He wasn't

there, was he?"

Robbins ignored the question, and repeated his own. "Where is he now, Wilson? Do you have any idea?"

"I'm right, aren't I?" said the policeman, but Robbins still didn't answer him. Wilson turned again to Beth. "Who is he, doctor? *What* is he?"

"Right now, he's missing," she replied. "And we need to find him if we're to answer any of those questions."

"Sir?" came a voice from behind. It was the WPC again. "You're wanted on the phone."

"Can't it wait? I'm busy here." Robbins flapped at a fly that was buzzing around his head, making its bid for freedom through the open door.

"It's about the man from this cell," she told him. "There's been a sighting."

* * *

"I should have seen this coming. Why didn't I send a uniform to keep an eye on the place as soon as I knew he was free?" Robbins banged the steering wheel with the palm of his hand.

Beth, in the passenger seat, stared out the window at the small school they were approaching. The red brick of the building, and gray-slated roof, looked remarkably like her old primary school. "No wonder your stomach is always playing up. Which, by the way, I've told you to get looked at... Listen, you weren't to know this would happen."

"You read the gravestone same as I did: 'Devoted son, husband and *father*'. He'd already visited Mrs. Daley. There was a huge probability he'd try to get in touch with his... with *the* son again. Shit!"

Robbins was still reluctant to recognize the man as Matthew Daley, even after what he'd seen. She recalled the conversation they'd had on the way to the station when he'd asked her for theories. "How about this: Matthew Daley dies, is pronounced, then buried. But he's not really dead."

Robbins grimaced. "What do you mean, not really dead? How can he not be dead when he's had a fucking autopsy?"

"Happens more often than you think," she replied. "Patients even wake up in the middle of autopsies sometimes. Or when they've been buried prematurely. The medical term for it is Catalepsy, where the patient suffers from a form of temporary paralysis and appears dead." *Sleep well*, it had said on the gravestone—and perhaps that's all he had been doing, just sleeping. "The latest thing now is to put a web-cam in the coffin so you can keep checking on the deceased."

Robbins pulled a face. "Beth…"

"Ask Poe, it scared the crap out of him."

"I suppose you'll be saying next that *he's* alive and well and still churning out stories," Robbins said snidely.

"Now you're just being a dickhead."

"Can we just cut to the chase?"

"Okay, so say he does wake up for some reason. Starts banging on the coffin—"

"Nobody would hear him."

"Say that they did," Beth argued. "Say someone dug him up then just put everything back the way it was."

"Why? Why would they do that? And why would he wait until now to come back?"

"I've no idea. You're the detective."

"But the state of him, Beth… How could anyone recover?"

"I don't know. A freak of nature, recuperative powers, something to do with the blood…"

"None of which was picked up in the autopsy."

"Perhaps it was where he worked."

"What's that got to do with anything?"

"Steve, that place was closed down because of all the leaks. God knows what working there for so long might have done."

He waved his hand dismissively.

"At least we have some samples from the coffin. We can

work on a DNA match now." And they'd left it at that, not getting any further at all. Now here they were, looking for a man who should have been inside that coffin but wasn't. A man who had come to see his little boy.

They pulled up, the white and orange car following them doing the same. Valentine and Adams waited inside their car while Robbins and Beth got out and went through the school gates, pressing the buzzer at the main door. A secretary opened it and Robbins flashed his ID. They were taken through to an office where the headmaster of the school greeted them with a worried frown. "We've never had an incident like this before," he assured them, "we pride ourselves on keeping the pupils safe."

"I understand," said Robbins. It was difficult to tell from his voice whether he was being sarcastic or not.

"Mrs. Shaw, one of our helpers who drew this to our attention, was very distressed by the whole thing and had to be taken home."

"I'll bet. We'll need to talk to her later, get a statement. Now, if you wouldn't mind…"

The headmaster gave a nod of understanding, taking them through the school where lessons were carrying on as normal that afternoon. "We've put him in the quiet room," the headmaster told them. When Beth and Robbins looked puzzled, he explained, "Oh, it's where the children go if they want to read alone or have some time to themselves."

Inside this quiet room, which was much smaller than the other classrooms they'd seen, a little boy with tousled hair was sitting at a desk. He had a toy car in his hands, turning it over and over. The scene was like Robbins' first encounter with the man back at the station, only in miniature. The boy seemed to have the same mannerisms, even had a look of the man they were pursuing. Robbins crouched down beside him. "Hello…" He looked back over his shoulder at the headmaster.

"Jason," prompted the man.

"Hello there, Jason. I'm Chief Inspector Robbins."

The boy looked at him, then continued to study the toy car.

"Do you think you could answer a couple of questions?"

The boy shrugged.

"That's a nice car, who gave it to you?"

Jason shrugged again. Robbins looked over to Beth for help.

The doctor walked to the desk and pulled out a little chair, sitting down opposite. "Hi Jason, my name's Beth. It's very important that we talk to the man who gave you this. Do you know where he went?"

Jason shook his head. "He didn't say, but I'm going to see him again. He told me that."

Robbins gave Beth a worried look.

"Let me through. Where's my son!" A commotion at the door to the 'quiet' room drew their attention and they turned to see a woman with short black hair pushing her way in, past the headmaster.

"Mrs. Hill, you got the call—" he began, but she ran to Jason and hugged him tightly, checking every inch of him over with her eyes. It was only then that she seemed aware of the other people there. "Who are you two? What were you doing with my son?"

"Please calm down, madam," said Robbins.

"No, *you* calm down. I'll calm down when I find out just what in God's name is going on."

"That might take a bit of explaining," said Beth. "We're not really sure we understand it ourselves."

"I saw Dad today," said Jason before anyone else could speak.

This took the woman aback. "Your Dad? Sweetheart, your Dad's at work. You know that."

"No, he said he was my real dad. What did he mean?"

All the color drained from the woman's face. She brushed a hair out of her son's eyes. "Sweetheart, that's... that's just not possible. Remember, we talked about this before. Your real father... he's not with us anymore."

"But I saw him," Jason insisted.

The woman looked up at Robbins and then Beth, confusion in her eyes.

"I think we need to have a little chat," said Robbins. "Alone."

* * *

The dead man had watched from a distance. Watched as Robbins and the doctor arrived, accompanied by two uniforms—one of them the black man who'd come for him at the house.

Then he'd seen her arrive on foot. Caroline. Her hair was much shorter than he remembered, but still that raven black, still framing the pretty face he could recall cupping in his hands—so vividly they *had* to be his memories. He couldn't stop the recollections then; they came with a vengeance and he closed his eyes to savor them. The first time they'd met at that café one Saturday afternoon, and he'd looked up from his drink to see her walk in with one of her old girlfriends. They'd exchanged quick glances the whole way through their coffees—he'd actually made his last much longer than usual—until eventually the friend, Sally, noticed and came over to him because it looked like neither of them were going to do a thing about it.

"So, you single?" she'd said getting to the point right away.

"Er... yes."

"So is she. What are you waiting for? She's free tonight."

The inevitable first date complete with nerves, the 'getting to know you' conversations, the first time he'd walked her to her flat, and kissed her lips.

The first time they'd shared a bed, after a party when they'd drunk more than they should have, but not so much they couldn't do anything about it when they got back to her place.

He could feel the movement of her beneath him even now, her hips arching, legs hooking around him as she often did, urging him on with her moans.

Their wedding day, her standing there in that white dress, looking almost... almost like an angel. And when he'd danced

247

with her and looked into those deep blue eyes, he'd known he would love her forever.

Then suddenly he saw the other images again, felt the pain this time—heard the scream, cracking of bone, the blood... saw the light, saw the tunnel...

Snapping his eyes open he noticed Caroline emerge from the school, holding Jason's hand. He almost went to her then, just as he'd been compelled to do before. But for one thing she was crying, and for another she was getting into the back of the squad car, the police about to escort her home.

It wasn't the right time yet. He knew that.

But soon, as he'd told Jason, he'd see them again.

* * *

"So where do we go from here?" asked Beth as they stood by the car and watched Valentine drive off.

"My superiors will want to try and contain this," Robbins said, not really answering her question.

"That's going to be a bit difficult." Beth leaned on the top of the car. "For starters, we don't know where he is. We don't really know *what* he is."

"He's a problem," said Robbins. "They'll bring in... outsiders. I've seen it happen before."

Beth raised an eyebrow. "You've seen *this* happen before?"

"Not this exactly, but other situations just as serious. I once saw a whole crime squad get muscled out when there was all that terrorism stuff."

"With the best will in the world, Steve, this is not a terrorist threat situation."

"You're right. It's much, much worse. There isn't a handbook about what to do when a dead man comes back and wants to talk to his family."

"So you're accepting the possibility that this could be Matthew Daley now?"

Robbins rubbed his face with his hands. "Oh, I don't know what to think anymore. But I do know we need to find him." He thought for a few moments, then said. "When we get back to the station, I think the best thing you can do is head to the hospital. Do those DNA tests before they bring in a bunch of government scientists I don't know. Get me some answers."

"And what are you going to do?"

"My job," he told her. "I'm the detective, remember?"

Nine

Caroline Hills poured herself a brandy.

Jason was upstairs in his bedroom, TV blaring. Today hadn't really fazed him at all, but that was kids for you. He spent half his time in a fantasyland anyway. She, however, was still trying to get her head around what she'd been told. It wasn't everyday you found out someone was impersonating your dead husband. Although, hadn't there been something in the Chief Inspector's voice, something in the looks that doctor kept giving him? Like they were holding things back from her. Then she'd pushed for it; pushed for answers which they'd given, eventually. Told her what they knew, told her what had happened over the last couple of days. And it was then that she wished they'd simply kept lying to her. It was then that she felt as if she was losing her mind.

It was like that scene from *Dallas* when Bobby Ewing had turned up in the shower and the previous season had been a dream. Had her life for the last seven years been a dream too? Had the tears she'd cried for months been just a nightmare, had facing life as a single parent just been a hallucination? Had finding someone else, when she thought she'd never love again, been just—

Jesus, what was she going to say to Rob? What could she say when she didn't even understand herself? The words they'd spoken, she'd thought they were a joke at first—kept expecting them all to start laughing at any moment, for a presenter to come out and tell her where the hidden cameras were. In poor taste, but a joke all the same. Yet when she put it together with what Jason had said, that's when it really hit home.

"Why wasn't I told about this before?" she screamed through the tears (though would she have believed it—did she even now?). "I'm still his widow, aren't I?"

But was she? Was she still his widow now that he might be out there somewhere, back from the grave? Caroline gulped the brandy, the fiery liquid scorching her throat, and poured herself another.

She carried it to the window and looked out through the net curtains. The police car was still out front, down the street, in case the man should try to make contact with Jason again. Caroline's hand shook at the very thought of it. If he should come here, if she was to see him...

Forget the fact that he was meant to be at rest—how *would* she feel seeing someone she never thought she'd see again... at least not here on Earth? But even that, what faith she'd boasted had gone, along with her husband, while his mother had been exactly the opposite: her belief was strengthened by the loss of her boy. While Irene had taken comfort in the fact that Matthew would be with God now, Caroline had railed against a deity that would snatch away the man she loved (still loved?) so casually, so cruelly. She would have rung the woman, save for the fact that they'd parted on such bad terms. And as for the fact that Caroline had remarried...

Now, somehow, there was a chance that the man they'd both loved so much was back. (How? How was that possible?) She dropped into a chair and drank more of the alcohol.

And waited for her husband to return from work.

* * *

Robbins spread out the files on his desk, running his hands

through his short hair.

He looked at the notes DCI Croft had left behind him, all leading to dead ends. There had been an investigation into Matthew's death, of course there had—the media had demanded it— but it had turned up precisely nothing. In fact, reading this, Robbins couldn't help wondering if it was the pressure he'd been under that had led to Croft's retirement and his eventual heart attack, paving the way for Robbins' transfer and promotion.

But there had to be something here. Some clue, some pattern, some explanation as to what this was all about. As to why Matthew Daley was back.

He shook his head, and not for the first time. No, it couldn't be Daley—*how could* it be Daley?

He let out a tuneless whistle, picking up the photos again. Something Croft had missed and which he must find. Something that would be the key to this whole thing.

Something... something...

Robbins leaned back in his chair and tried not to think about how badly he needed a drink. He reached down and opened the drawer on his right, then took a bottle out.

* * *

It was growing dark by the time Beth returned to the hospital. There were a few messages waiting for her when she got back, some about the shifts she'd traded to take the day off, some about patients she was keeping tabs on, and one from an anesthetist she'd been out for a drink with the previous week and wouldn't leave her alone. Why she'd done it was beyond her now, the guy was a total sleazebag. But he'd asked, and she'd agreed, then spent the whole damned evening wishing she was somewhere else.

As she made her way down the corridor to her office, she said hello to the doctors and nurses she knew—and the porter, Gary. He was wheeling a patient back to his ward after going for a scan.

The lights were off in her office, so when she opened the door she reached around for the switch inside. Beth flicked it, but nothing happened.

"Blast," she said, considering going back out to look for Gary. Then she felt it. There was someone in the room with her. Beth scanned the dark office, the shapes of her filing cabinet, the desk, even the fish tank she kept on the side—the fish helped her to relax—but she could see nothing out of the ordinary. Yet...

She heard breathing, slow and shallow.

"Hello?" she ventured.

The lights came on suddenly and she jumped.

"Dr. Preston... Beth, you have to help me," said the man she'd examined yesterday. He was standing only inches away.

This wasn't like the first time. Now she knew what he was— or thought she did. Not just some oddball prisoner in a cell, but someone whose grave she'd been standing by that very morning. She tried to speak but couldn't get the words out.

"Please," he said. It was the one word she couldn't resist, and somehow he knew it.

"Matthew."

He clapped his hands together and smiled, albeit briefly. "Thank you, thank you."

"For what?"

"For calling me by my name," he said.

She slid sideways along the wall. "It's who you said you were."

"I *still* am," he replied. "That's what I keep trying to tell you people. You know, don't you? You've known from the start."

Beth found herself almost in the corner of her room, and re-membered how Wilson had been found. She stopped. "How did you get away this morning, what did you say to PC Wilson?"

"Nothing he wasn't meant to hear." His voice poured ice wa-ter over her. "Same as you. Sarah *is* happy, you know. She doesn't blame you."

"Stop it," said Beth, shaking her head. "I don't—"

"It wasn't your fault."

She rounded on him now. "I've heard that from the best counselors around, I don't need to hear it from you!"

"Hear it from someone, hear it from her maybe?"

Beth remembered what Wilson had said about his aunty and uncle. She'd heard enough. "Stop it, stop talking about this right now!"

"I'm sorry," he said.

"How dare you!" Beth's eyes were starting to well up. "How bloody well dare you? You come back here and expect people to just take it in their stride—your mother, you son, your widow— to deal with it like it's something that happens every day of the week. And now we're meant to think you're in touch with..." She couldn't finish her sentence. "I hate to break it to you, but that's not normal. None of this is normal."

"You're upset, I—"

"What do you expect?" She was having trouble staying on her feet now, and he made to help her. "Stay back where you are."

"I should go," he said, half turning.

"No, wait," she replied instinctively. "Let me call Robbins."

"And be locked away again?" He stared at her. "Or worse? I just thought you could help, that's all. I was wrong."

Was it her imagination or was there genuine hurt in his voice? She blinked away another tear, tasting the salt water as it trickled into her mouth. "What is it that you want?"

He hesitated before speaking, then examined a spot on the floor. "I'm seeing things. Things from when I died, I think. But it's all so muddled. I can feel the pain. I can remember bits and pieces and a tunnel of bright light."

She couldn't help laughing at that. "Pretty standard for NDE."

"For what?"

"Near death experience."

He nodded his understanding.

"White light, figures beckoning, then something stops the person from going any further and they come back. Not exactly what happened to you…"

"No," he agreed.

"If you're really who you say you are, then you've been where nobody has before."

"I don't know what to tell you. All of that, all the important stuff is a blank."

"But the fact is you've come back, Matthew. You've come back. The question remains why? And how exactly do we all deal with it?"

"Will you help me to remember?" he asked her.

She chewed on her lip a moment before answering him. "On one condition. You let me take you to Robbins, so he can call off the search."

"I'm not going back to that cell."

"He's not as bad as he seems, you know. And he might be able to help you get to the bottom of this too."

"All right, I believe you," he said finally. "So, where do we begin?"

"Tell me everything you can remember about the night you died," said Beth.

Ten

The dead man talked for the better part of an hour.

He told Beth what he could remember of the images, the sights, smells and sounds. She listened intently as she'd learned to do in her particular trade, pushing all thoughts about who or what he was to the back of her mind. For a little while at least he was simply another patient, one she wanted to find out more about. One she wanted to help if she possibly could. The talking was as much for her benefit as his, really. But it would take time for him to remember fully, she told him. Things would come back to him in small chunks, when they were good and ready. It was hardly surprising he'd blotted out so much of what was possibly the most traumatic thing that could ever happen to a person. Visual stimuli might help too, perhaps visiting familiar surroundings from that night. But for right now she wanted to get him back to the station, back to Robbins.

Beth led him out of the office and down the corridor. Past the doctors and nurses she'd seen on the way in—his bare feet drawing odd looks and whispers—past the wards of people in bed. The man she called Matthew glanced at them, with a certain amount of sadness. Especially at the ones with eyes closed, heads back on the pillow as if they had already given up the fight.

"You see it every day here, don't you?" he said.

"I'm sorry?"

"Death. People die all the time here."

Beth nodded. "Unfortunately, yes."

They took the stairs rather than the lift, bringing them out onto the floor of the Accident and Emergency department. There was a smattering of people waiting, seated on plastic chairs and looking up at a digital display that repeatedly informed them they would be there for some time.

Beth's charge held back as they entered. "I... something about this place. I remember something," he told her. Then he pointed. "I was here, but not here. I-I was sort of looking down on this."

"Like you were hovering over the scene?"

He nodded sharply. "I was here. This is where they brought me, isn't it?"

Before she could answer, the set of double doors at the far end of A&E burst open and two figures in green wheeled in a stretcher. All eyes turned in this direction, the most excitement they'd had all evening.

"Motorcyclist, got hit by someone pulling out of a junction," they heard the first paramedic state. "He's in a really bad way."

A doctor in a set of blue scrubs came to attend to the patient, then the gurney was wheeled out of sight, away from the people in the waiting room. The man who claimed he was the late Matthew Daley followed, breaking into a run.

"Matthew, no!" Beth wasn't far behind him, reaching out to grab his arm but missing by a mile. The crash team were working on the motorcyclist in a side room and hadn't had time to close the door—they were too preoccupied with trying to save his life. The nurses had cut away the leather of his jacket, and there was blood everywhere. The man's eyes were rolling over white into his head. Matthew was at the doorway looking inside when Beth caught up with him. She tugged at his arm to pull him away, but he didn't see her at all. He was in a trance.

"We're losing him," said the doctor, now holding the paddles of a defibrillator in his hands. The whining sound of the patient flatlining cut through the air. He told everyone to stand back and shocked the motorcyclist. His body jerked, and there was a weak pulse, then he crashed again. The doctor repeated this process three times but it was the same result. "I'm calling it at seven fifty. All in agreement? He'd suffered massive trauma; there was nothing any of us could have done. Have his family been contacted?"

"Come on, we shouldn't be back here," Beth told Matthew.

He shook his head. "No."

Pushing her to one side, he walked into the room. The doctor was so shocked he stood back. One of the male nurses came around the bed, in an effort to stop Matthew's approach, but it was too late. He was next to the motorcyclist and his hands were on the man's chest.

"Someone call security," shouted a female nurse.

The male nurse tried to pull Matthew away, but he shrugged him off. "No, I won't let this happen." He closed his eyes.

"Matthew!" shouted Beth, and the doctor recognized her.

"Dr. Preston? Who is that? What's the meaning of all this?"

There was confusion in the room, lots of voices and shouting. Then a sudden beep sent everyone quiet. It was followed by another... then another. The nurses all looked at each other, then the doctor looked at Beth. "Dr. Preston?"

The noise had drawn a crowd of people from the other rooms and cubicles in A&E, mostly relatives who were sitting with their sick loved ones, but a handful of patients too—their gowns flapping as they tried to get a better look.

"Did you see that?" said one person behind Beth. "He just brought that man back to life."

"You what?" said a late arrival.

"I swear to God. Just laid his hands on him. Doctors had given up."

"Bloody hell."

The beep of the heart monitor was strong and sure. The doctor who'd pronounced the motorcyclist walked slack-jawed towards Matthew and the bed. "What... what did you just do?" The nurse who'd called for security was crossing herself.

"Vitals are stable," said the male nurse, blinking at the monitor.

Matthew stepped back from the bed, retreating to the door. Someone out in the corridor held up a mobile phone and snapped a blurry picture with a mechanical *whir*. Matthew pushed past them all, pushed past a speechless Beth, and began to stagger back off up the corridor. There was a second's lapse, then she followed him again, back out of the department. He was running at a trot, but this time she did catch up with him, grabbing his arm and twisting him around.

"You can't just walk away like that. Hey!"

He faced her. "I-I think I know what happened to me," he told her. "I think I remember."

"Look, we can't stay here now. You're attracting too much attention." Beth looked over her shoulder at the group of people following them: relatives, doctors, patients.

"You're right. I have to go." He pulled away from her and ran out through the double doors into the ambulance bay. The doors flapped back on her as she tried to follow. Beth Preston pushed on them and stumbled out into the night air.

She looked left and right.

But Matthew was gone.

Eleven

Detective Chief Inspector Steven Robbins yawned.

It had been a long day, a long week, and he hadn't seen much of his bed. The statements, reports and notes on his desk were all merging into one. The photographs, though still disturbing, had now lost much of their power to shock since the first time he'd seen them. The Matthew Daley case would never really be solved until they found the man who claimed to *be* him. Robbins couldn't help smirking at that one; it wasn't every day that the deceased ended up helping the police to solve the mystery of their own murder.

He closed his aching eyes, then rubbed them.

The door to his office opened, the hinges squeaking just like they always did. "Never hear of knocking?" he said, attempting to open his eyes again. The figure before him was out of focus, like the letters on an optician's board when they put in the wrong lens. He screwed up his eyes, and the figure started to take shape. The man was older than Robbins, older than Wilson even. He took a seat opposite and smiled, the lines on his face stretching to accommodate it.

"Make yourself at home," said Robbins.

"Thanks," said the man, "don't mind if I do." He looked around the office, nodding contentedly. "It's changed a bit in here."

Robbins let out a tired breath. "Look, I don't know how you got in, but I'm a bit pushed right—"

The man reached out and picked up one of the reports from the desk. He flipped through it casually. "You're looking for connections where there aren't any," he said. "Frustrating, isn't it?"

"If I wanted the advice of a total stranger then I'd ring one of my ex-wives."

The older man laughed. "But I'm not a *total* stranger, Robbins. You know me."

Robbins studied his face, but couldn't place him. "If we've met before then I can't remember it."

"Ah, well, we haven't exactly met as such. But you know me all the same."

"It's getting late, and I haven't got time for riddles tonight," Robbins said impatiently.

"I've come to give you that one piece of information you're looking for."

A look of enlightenment suddenly dawned on Robbins' face. "You're here to take over, is that it? I'm being replaced? I wondered how long it would be. You're welcome to it, the whole fucking thing. I'm in over my head anyway."

The man chuckled again. "I've done my share and it was enough for me."

"I… I don't understand."

"I'm here to tell you how to solve the case. And to tell you where Matthew Daley is."

"Who are you?" asked Robbins.

The man stretched. "Nice to be able to do that again without the pains in my chest."

"Without the…" Robbins sat up straight in his chair. He shouldn't have been too shocked, though. It wasn't the first dead man he'd encountered this week. "Croft?"

"Bingo. How are you finding my old job? It's a killer, isn't it?" This last line was said in all seriousness.

"You… you're not really here."

"Then where am I? Feels like I'm here." He put his feet up on the desk, pulled a cigarette case out of his pocket, removed one and tapped it on the silver metal. "You got a light?"

"I don't smoke."

"Wise man," said Croft. He held up the cigarette between thumb and forefinger. "I smoked forty of these a day from being a kid. And I used to keep a bottle of scotch in that bottom drawer just there." Croft gestured towards Robbins' side of the desk. "Told myself it was for medicinal purposes. What a load of crap. You were just thinking you could use a belt yourself though, weren't you? Don't suppose there's any still in there?" He flapped his hand. "Naw, what am I thinking. I've been gone too long for that."

Robbins didn't know how to answer him, so he didn't bother; he just reached down and opened the drawer. Robbins produced the bottle of Milk of Magnesia he kept hidden away. Croft let out another long laugh as Robbins took a swig.

"Wasn't quite what I had in mind," said the erstwhile DCI finally. "You know, you should get that stomach sorted out. I left things till the last minute and look what happened."

"It's fine," stated Robbins.

"Ignorance is bliss, eh? We're not that dissimilar, you and I. You're a man after my own heart."

"With the greatest respect," Robbins told him, "I certainly hope not."

Croft took a drag on his cigarette. "I'd imagine it was quite a thing when you realized about Matthew."

"That's one way of putting it. Now, you said you had some information about the case."

Croft smiled again. "Getting straight to it, I like that in a DCI. Very good. Life's too short, if you'll pardon the expression."

"The information," Robbins pressed.

"It doesn't become clear you see... until *afterwards*. Then you know everything. There are no secrets."

"I'm not following you."

"Not yet, no. Matthew's returned to find his peace, Robbins. His was such a sudden passing."

"I know. I saw the pictures."

"I saw the *body*," Croft reminded him.

"You're telling me he's after revenge on the person who did this?" Robbins pointed to the files.

"He's being tested."

"And you know who that person is."

Croft smiled one last time and blew out a stream of smoke. "Things aren't always clear cut, you know. Good and evil are rarely as easy to spot as we think. It's all a matter of judgment."

"Get on with it," snapped Robbins.

"Something's coming, Steven. The world's not going to be the same soon."

"It isn't now," said Robbins. "Tell me."

The phone rang loudly in his ear. Robbins woke with a start on the desk. He looked over at the empty chair opposite.

The ringing persisted and he picked up the receiver. "Robbins."

"Steve, I need to talk to you. I've seen Matthew."

"What?"

"He gave me the slip again, but listen... I think I know where we can find him. I think he's going to return to the place where this all began. The place where he died."

"No, Beth," said Robbins, his nose twitching at the smell of smoke which lingered in the air. "He's going after the person who killed him."

Twelve

They sat in silence.

Robert Hills was tracing the pattern on the carpet with his eyes. Caroline was nursing her third brandy of the evening. She'd done her best to explain, but it was so difficult.

"There's a police car outside," he'd said as he returned from the bank, then he'd seen her red and puffy eyes. "What's happened? Are you all right?"

Are you all right? It was a good question. Would she ever be all right again after today? "Something happened at school."

"Jason?"

"He's in his room."

Rob began towards the stairs, but she stopped him. "What's happened?" he asked again, his voice cracking. So she took him into the living room and she told him. Just like that. As if she was telling him they'd had a burst water pipe or the microwave was on the fritz. He'd looked at her that same way she'd looked at the detective and the doctor, like she was mad.

"Caroline, Matthew is dead."

"Tell that to Jason," she'd replied, a little too harshly. "Tell that to my son."

"*Our* son," he corrected.

Caroline didn't miss a beat. "He saw him."

"Saw someone who said he was Matthew, you mean."

"He saw… The police have… Rob, they dug up his grave."

"What?" He walked over to the fireplace and leaned a hand on the mantle. "This is ridiculous."

"I know… I know."

"How many of those have you had?" he asked, pointing to the drink.

"What, you think I'm making this up? You think I'm drunk?"

Rob rubbed his eyes. "No, it's just… How can it possibly be your dead husband? It can't be him. People don't just—"

"Come back from the dead?" she finished for him. "No, they don't, do they."

He couldn't say anything to that; they both knew it was impossible. Only here was his wife, the woman he trusted more than anyone in the world, telling him these things. "There has to be some kind of terrible mistake."

"I don't know. I just don't know."

"What did they tell you exactly?"

So she went through what the policeman and doctor had said. How they'd exhumed the body gaining authority because the case was still open on Matthew. How they'd been called to the school after he'd made contact with Jason. Everything. She'd laid it all out for him, and as she spoke it felt like she was explaining the wild plot of some sci-fi film. Caroline wasn't sure how much of it Robert had taken in, or how much she had herself, but when she'd finished he said: "So why are the police still here?"

"In case he comes back," she explained.

"To see Jason, or to see you?"

Caroline's eyes dropped to the floor. He'd slumped down in the chair then, and not said a word since. Now someone needed to speak. If they didn't do it soon Caroline feared they might never speak again. That they might just go about their normal (and what was normal anymore anyway?) lives in total silence from that moment on. "Say something, Rob," she pleaded.

He looked up at her. "What do you want me to say?" His tone was hollow and weird.

She felt the tears welling again and couldn't stop them coming this time. "Say that you love me, and that everything's going to be okay."

Robert said nothing at first, and then her whole body began to shake with sobs. He got up and went to her. She dropped the brandy on the floor as she got up and fell into his embrace. He held her tightly and she continued to cry, both of them with wasted expressions on their faces.

Then he told her that he loved her. That everything was going to be okay.

He meant the first part. Robert Hills had never loved another person the way he loved his wife. But as for the second... he knew that this couldn't have a happy ending, that things would be far from okay from this moment on.

* * *

He watched them from the shadows on the stairway.

A frozen image for so long, neither of them speaking, neither of them talking. He knew he must have caused it, however indirectly. Beth's words haunted him, just as surely as he was haunting this family: *"You come back here and you expect people to just take it*

in their stride—your mother, your son, your widow—to deal with it like it's
something that happens every day of the week. I hate to break it to you, but
that's not normal. None of this is normal."

Then Caroline, *his* Caroline—but at the same time not—
begged the man to say something, to tell her he loved her. And
when she began crying all he wanted to do was burst in and take
her in his arms, tell her what she needed to hear, that *he* still loved
her—had never stopped loving her in all the time he'd been…
away. He even rose slightly. But then the man—Rob, her new
husband—had got up and he'd gone to her, taking her in his arms
and holding her so close.

That was when the realization finally hit him: although time
had barely moved on for him, it had been seven long years for
her. She'd had to struggle on without him, had to bring up their
child alone. And she'd finally met someone else that she could
love. Not the same, never the same, but it was blatantly obvious
that she did. He could never turn back the clock and have what
he had then.

So he cried too. Cried because this never should have happened, cried because all this had been taken away from him.
Cried because none of this had been his fault.

It had been someone else's. Someone who he now felt compelled to visit.

But first, he had something to do.

* * *

The TV was still blaring away from its position on the side
unit, even though the light was off and Jason was fast asleep on
the bed, covers half over him, half kicked off.

The black and white images on the screen projected themselves into the room—a man and a woman in a graveyard—and
he heard tinny voices coming from the speakers. "They're coming
to get you Barbara. They're coming…"

He flicked off the set and walked across to the sleeping boy.

For precious moments he looked down on the lad, taking in the features. He had his mother's eyes but definitely his father's nose. He bent down to kiss him on the forehead. "Sleep well, son," he said.

Then as he rose he saw the toy car on the bedside table. He stood stock still, staring at it.

Jason rolled over in the bed, and said something, his dream broken. The man withdrew from beside him, just as the boy opened one eye a crack.

Jason thought he saw movement in the corner of the room, thought he'd heard someone talking to him. Not his mum or his 'dad' (his other dad, not his real one). But must have been mistaken; there was nobody here now. Except... except hadn't the TV been on when he'd dropped to sleep?

With tired eyes, he rolled over to the bedside table and reached out for the car that had been given him that afternoon. It was gone. His hand searched the table, fingers like spider's legs on the surface. Jason turned on the bedside light, squinting at its brightness.

His room was empty. Nobody in sight.

With a puzzled frown he sat back against his pillow. And although he wondered where his new toy had gone, it wasn't too long before his eyelids felt heavy again.

Then he settled back down in the bed where he fell back into a long, deep sleep.

Thirteen

Douglas Knowles was nowhere near drunk enough yet.

But he'd run out of money some time ago, nursing his last short for at least twenty minutes. And the more kindly patrons of *The Bull's Head* would only stand you so many rounds without seeing any bought back in return. Sometimes Phyllis the barmaid would let him finish off the last dregs of drinks that had been left by punters, but not tonight. Tonight she was being watched very closely by the landlord after he'd found a fiver missing out of the till.

(It had actually dropped down the side when she'd been putting it in the register, but neither of them would find it until the following morning when the cleaner came in. That didn't help Phyllis right now. And it didn't help Douglas either.)

So he had no choice but to return home, or the dingy little one bedroom flat he called home. He kidded himself that maybe he'd find a bottle or two of unopened spirits in there somewhere, but he knew he'd finished off whatever he'd had in the flat when his benefits had first gone in.

He hadn't resorted to drinking that bottle of meths yet. The one he'd bought originally to clean his brushes when he'd thought about redecorating. That had been after the last time he'd gone to AA, turned over a new leaf—yet again—in an effort to encourage Jane to let him see his two daughters. It hadn't worked, neither coming off the booze, nor convincing his estranged spouse. Tonight might just be the night he tried that meths. It depended on how desperate he was when he got back in. He looked at his watch, a cheap digital one with fading numbers.

Christ, it was only just turned ten. He'd be home by ten thirty, and then what? A night of not being able to sleep ahead of him, a night of remembrance when all he wanted to do was get completely smashed and forget everything. Not have to deal with reality.

It hadn't always been like this. He could remember the better days, the great days—when he had a good job working for an insurance firm, when Jane had looked up to him and the kids weren't ashamed to be seen with Daddy. He'd had a career with flexible hours, a nice car—

But then the problem had slowly crept up on him. At first it was only social drinking when he met up with clients. It was okay, he told himself, he'd gone out and got hammered most nights when he was younger, before Jane had come along, so he could handle a few every so often now. The only thing was that 'every so often' became more and more frequent. Slowly but surely the drinking started to take over his life. He began to crave that fix, the warm tingling you got whenever you were getting nicely merry. Some of his friends in the trade even slipped him soft drugs now and again; nothing hard, he insisted on that, just some coke or cannabis. What could it hurt? What harm could it do?

Plenty.

Especially that one night, the night he'd been at a late dinner with a couple of colleagues. Jane was at her folks with the kids that week for the holidays so he was in no rush to get back, not that it would have bothered him anyway. So it ended up being gone twelve when he'd climbed into the car, more than a little the worse for wear after two bottles of wine between them, some cocktails, and a few trips to the bathroom. One of the men had suggested taxis, but the other insisted that taxis were for suckers and why should he pay twenty quid to get back home when he had a perfectly good Audi sitting in the all night multi-storey across the road.

Sadly, Douglas had sided with him.

They'd said goodnight and gone their separate ways, Douglas climbing into the front seat of his souped-up maroon Sierra. Once out of the city, he'd taken the dark and lonely back roads to avoid any police traps that might be waiting for him—he wasn't that stupid! He'd enjoyed the drive, slipping in one of his favorite CDs and just cruising along the country roads that would skirt the town where he lived and take him into the suburbs. Take him home. He'd opened her up a little then, singing along to the rock tracks and pretending he was in one of those adverts where he had the whole road to himself.

Then it had happened. He'd just about negotiated a hard bend and skidded inside, skidding almost into the wall of the tunnel he'd entered. Douglas fought hard to control the steering, but his reactions were terrible. And then...

Douglas shook his head as he'd done so often in the intervening years. It never did any good; the memories always came back to him. He remembered making it back home, putting the car away in his garage. He locked up and staggered around the side of the house, then just about made it inside to the bathroom to throw up, before carrying a bottle of vodka to bed with him for comfort. It had taken most of the bottle to put him out and when he woke the next morning, he'd thrown up again on the floor. Not all of it down to the drink. It was as he'd been straining that the events of the previous night came back to him. Afterwards he realized he had a decision to make; there wasn't the luxury of time on his side. Now he was sober Douglas considered doing the right thing, but then he'd lose everything he'd spent so long building up over the years. The fact that he was on the verge of losing it anyway didn't really register. Then he thought about the people he knew in the trade, some less law-abiding than others. People he'd done favors for, fixed claim forms for. They owed him, and if ever he needed to cash in those favors it was now.

He'd picked up the phone and made a few calls.

By the time everything was splashed over the papers he was in the clear. The car was put to rights quickly and sold on through some disreputable dealer using fake documents. It wasn't unusual for him to swap his car as often as his underpants, not in his line of work, so no one blinked twice when he acquired a new one.

But when Jane returned with the kids nothing was the same. She'd started nagging him even more about the booze, the restless nights.

"What's got into you these days?" she shouted at him that final evening when the girls were in bed.

"Leave me alone," he said as he turned his attention back to the drinks cabinet. "Just leave me alone."

"Not until you answer my question," she'd persisted, grabbing his arm.

He'd only meant to shrug her off, but she'd tumbled backwards and almost banged her head on the coffee table.

Douglas made a move towards her, to help her up. "Jane, I'm—"

She slapped his hand away, eyes filled with hatred. Jane rose and stormed off to the bedroom, calling back, "I'll leave you alone all right!" Then he heard the door slam and knew that she'd locked it from the inside.

The next day she left and took the kids with her. Her solicitor demanded that the house be sold and that she get most of the profits. He hadn't argued. Most—if not all—of the fight had gone out of him. Problem was, that meant he'd lost his edge at work as well. Within nine months he went from virtually running the place to losing his job completely.

The government forced him to look for jobs, but he always screwed something up and was sacked. In the end they stopped hassling him, realizing that he was, over time, building up a re-sumé that made him virtually unemployable. Now he just went down, signed on, did the courses they sent him to—the last one was something about spreadsheets—and he drew his money, most of which went to Jane and the kids, the rest on the essentials of life. Or *his* life at any rate.

Which was how he came to be there, climbing the steps of the block of flats because the lift wasn't working (and someone had taken a shit inside it anyway). How he came to open the door and find someone waiting for him. Someone he recognized, but his brain told him that the man couldn't—*shouldn't*—be sitting in his torn second-hand chair with the wooden arms, so when Douglas turned on the light the man almost frightened him senseless.

"You... you..." said Douglas, his hand outstretched and quivering.

"Yes," said the man. "Me."

"I-I'm imagining this. It's the drink."

"Always the drink," said the man in the chair.

Douglas rubbed his eyes, scrubbed at them, in fact. The appa-rition was still there. He looked slightly different, that was true—

hair a bit longer and more unkempt—but there was no mistaking that face. It was the one Douglas saw every night when he woke up in a cold sweat; the face his mind had recorded that night as he'd swerved to avoid hitting the wall of the tunnel, only to hit something, some*one* instead.

It was the face of the man he'd killed seven years ago.

* * *

"I still don't understand. How do you know where to go?" Beth asked again. Robbins had answered the first time with a "You wouldn't believe me if I told you."

"I got a tip-off," said the DCI at last, letting the wheel slip through his fingers as he turned into a side road.

"From who?"

"That's not important, but... I believe what he said." Robbins had considered telling her about the conversation he'd had with his dead predecessor, but decided against it. If he began to go through it, he might just start to believe it wasn't just some bizarre dream. You could sleepwalk, why not sleep-smoke? The fact that he hadn't had any cigarettes on his person didn't come into it. "Just go through it again, what happened back at the hospital," he urged her.

She patiently explained about how 'Matthew' had been waiting for her when she got back, how they'd talked about the night of his accident and his hazy recollections. Then she related the incident in the Casualty Department. "I think something about the biker must have jolted his memory. They were in similar states."

"But you say he brought the man back to life?"

"That's what it looked like, at least. Davison, the doctor in charge, had called it. They'd given up the ghost."

Robbins pressed his foot down on the accelerator and they shot forward over a roundabout. "They might just have made a mistake."

"It's possible," Beth admitted. "But you had to have been there."

"I would have been if you'd called me."

"I was bringing him *to* you. He would have bolted if I'd rung you first."

"As opposed to what he did anyway?"

Beth hugged herself. "I did what I thought was right, Steve."

He looked over at her briefly, then returned his eyes to the road.

Beth waited for the apology she knew would never come. Instead he said, "So what's the conclusion about him then? Any more theories?"

"Plenty, but all crazy. Right now I'm thinking, what if Matthew's got some kind of virus."

"What, you mean he's sick? I thought you said he had a high immunity."

"What if that's part of the disease? Something that makes you well. Better than well, in fact. What if it can bring you back from the dead?" Robbins gave a half laugh and before he could dismiss what she was saying, she continued: "It would explain the weird results from his blood test. Think about it, a disease that can regenerate dead tissue. That can restart a dead person's heart, make the blood flow again in their veins."

Robbins' eyes narrowed. "That's just—"

"Ludicrous? More ludicrous than a man who's been dead for seven years turning up on his own mother's doorstep? More ludicrous than opening his coffin and—"

"All right, all right. I get the picture," said Robbins. "If what you're saying turns out to be true—"

"And we won't know that until more tests are done," she broke in.

"Right, but if it is… it really will be the discovery of the century, the millennium."

"Ah, so now you *do* care." She smirked. "Steve, it'll be the discovery of the last two millennia," said Beth, looking over at him. "Not that I'm going to get into the whole science versus religion thing, but you do realize what time of year it is, don't you?" He caught her eye for a moment, then they broke it off. They drove the rest of the way in silence, the inference hanging heavy in the air. And with the question still unanswered: who had passed this condition on to Matthew in the first place?

* * *

"Why don't you come inside and shut the door?" said the dead man. "We have things to talk about, you and me."

Douglas Knowles was freeze-framed in the entranceway. The words broke whatever spell was holding him there and for a second he found himself doing as he was bid, walking slowly inside. Then he stopped again.

Douglas was still staring at the man, unable to properly take in what was happening—or to grasp that it might be real. The last time he'd seen that face it had been through his windscreen, cracking the glass, panicked and bloody. (A scene his mind had recorded especially for him to play back the highlights.) Then as a dark lump in his rearview mirror after he'd finally screeched to a halt. Douglas had been breathing heavily, eyes flicking up to his mirror, then back down at the white knuckles clenching the wheel, his wedding ring digging into the third finger on his left hand. Rock music was belting out from the speakers, the soundtrack of this particular nightmare… and many more to come. Part of him had wanted to get out of the car and go back to see if the man was all right, but a larger part told him he didn't need to see that—if he drove away he might just get away with it. So before he knew what he was doing, he'd put the engine, still idling, into gear. He was bringing his foot off the clutch, finding the biting point; moving off, away from the scene.

There were no other cars around, no houses, just a road that led up to the chemical plant where the man must have been walking from, facing oncoming traffic just like you were supposed to do. But Jesus, how was Douglas supposed to see him in a pitch black tunnel like that? Even if he hadn't been trying to swerve to avoid the wall he might still have hit him. It had been an accident, that's all. An—

"Accident?" said the man, now rising. "An accident!"

"Y-Y-Yes," said Douglas, although there was hardly any conviction in his voice.

"You didn't even bother to report your 'accident.'" His tone was unforgiving. "I had to wait to be found. There might have been a chance if—"

"Get out of my head," said Douglas, closing his eyes and backing away.

"You still don't understand, do you?"

When Douglas opened his eyes again the dead man was standing inches away, grabbing him by the wrists.

"I'm real, Doug. This isn't one of your guilt dreams. I'm not the Ghost of Christmas Past. I'm here, in the flesh."

Douglas shook his head. "No, no!"

"I lost everything that night. Missed seeing my son grow up. And now my wife, she's…" He let the sentence tail off. "All because of you and your *accident*."

Douglas tried to wrestle out of his grip but couldn't manage it. "I-I didn't mean to—"

"You had a choice that night; I had none," said the dead man. "See… *feel* what I felt!" The dead man shoved something into Douglas's hand, a toy. A small child's car.

Suddenly Douglas experienced that night in a way he never had before. He was the one who'd set out to walk home after his shift, who'd been in that tunnel when he'd seen the light. Who'd felt the force of the car, doing almost 50 miles an hour on that bend, ploughing into him. His legs no match for the metal of the bonnet. He felt the agonizing pain as the bones broke in several places, as his hip cracked and he went tumbling over that same bonnet. Heard the music coming from inside, the loud thumping of the stereo. Saw the knuckles on the steering wheel, looking up to gaze into his own shocked face behind the wheel—the pair of them becoming intertwined in that moment. Then the rest of the 'accident' was filled in for him, spinning over the roof, his shoulder coming out of its socket, then back down onto the boot and finally colliding with the rough concrete of the road, raking his skin, shredding his thighs, blood pouring from him freely, nose breaking and splintering with the fall. He blinked once, his vision blurred, then again. Everything was black but he couldn't tell whether it was the darkness of the tunnel or that he was losing consciousness. And it hurt so much. He couldn't move a muscle. It hurt so much he actually prayed for death to come because then it would end. But he still managed to mutter one thing: "You'll... you'll see me again."

"Do you understand?" shouted the dead man, pressing him up against the balcony wall.

Douglas was crying now, and spit ran from his mouth. "Please... please... stop."

"You took my life away from me. Now—"

"Now," he blurted through the tears. "Now what? Now you're here to do the same, to take it away from me?" Douglas found hidden reserves from somewhere, his voice becoming stronger. "So do it. What do I have to live for now anyway?"

The dead man looked him squarely in the eyes, those tired eyes desperate for sleep. A sleep denied him by the drink. He looked back over his shoulder at the place where Douglas now lived. Was it enough, this punishment? How could he weigh it against what he had been through?

It was a decision, a choice only he could make.

And so he made it.

Fourteen

On approach it looked like a bird.

Robbins pulled up outside the block of flats just as the body fell. It seemed to drop forever, coat flailing behind like a pair of wings. Then right at the last minute it speeded up, like one of those slick shots in a TV show. It hit the ground with all the grace of a safe landing on a cartoon character's head. That is to say, it would have hit the ground had there not been something there to break its fall.

The body slammed into the roof of the middle car of three, parked just opposite and further down from them. The battered old Metro—nobody had decent wheels around there—crumpled up as if it had been placed in a decompression chamber, metal and glass folding itself around the shape that had fallen from the balcony above. They gaped at the wreckage, not one of them knowing quite what to do next. Then Robbins said, "Shit! We're too late."

They got out of the car, but still stood staring at the crushed roof of the vehicle. It was Beth who moved first, her instinct being to try and save whoever this was who'd plummeted the seven floors from above. Except as she got there, Robbins radioing for an ambulance as she did, she realized what a waste of time that would be. The man's face, white apart from the occasional dash of red, was pretty much intact: it was only his eyes that gave away his state, rolling back into his head like two boiled eggs. As for the rest of him, it was difficult to tell where the flesh stopped and the metal began. Both were twisted and intertwined, his limbs—for she could see it was a man now—were bent into the most awkward of positions. His legs were shooting out at bizarre angles, the bottom halves, below the knee, bending back like a contortionist's. His arm had split wide open at the elbow joint and there was bone protruding through, while his left hand, having been severed by the glass of the Metro's window, was dangling—almost off—by the tendons. Something dropped out of that hand onto the ground: a red toy car.

Beth reached into the hulk, scratching her hand on a piece of sharp metal as she did so. Robbins' face soured when she pressed her fingers to the man's neck. She turned to him and shook her

275

head. The DCI followed the diver's descent again, looking up to see another figure on the balcony where he'd fallen. Beth saw it too. This time Robbins called for backup.

"Matthew," she said out loud, "what have you done?"

They wasted valuable moments trying the lift in the block of flats, then were forced to race up the stairs.

Turning on to the floor that contained the flat they were looking for, they fully expected the figure to be gone by now. But he wasn't; he stood there looking down on the scene below, both hands on the balcony rail. The door to the flat was open behind him.

They approached him slowly, cautiously. Robbins spoke first, telling him to keep his hands where he could see them.

"You think I did this," said the man. It wasn't a question.

"I don't see anyone else around here," said Robbins.

"Matthew," said Becky, "why?"

He turned then to answer her. "It wasn't up to me to judge him, he knew that."

"What the hell's that supposed to mean?" asked Robbins.

The man didn't say any more, and he offered no resistance when Robbins took him by the arm, cuffed him, and started to lead him away. "We'll take him back to the station," he said to Beth, "but I've no idea what will happen after that."

Beth leaned over the balcony and looked down at the fall. She shut her eyes when she thought what that man had just been through. Then she followed Robbins and Matthew back down the stairs again. By the time they reached the street an ambulance had arrived, and the police. Robbins pushed his prisoner's head down as he deposited him in the back of a squad car. The residents of the flats, all used to minding their own business, came out through their doors to look when they heard the sirens. The owner of the car was screaming about insurance and asking who was to blame. (Ironically, in his heyday Douglas Knowles would have been able to point her in the right direction.)

More white and orange vehicles were arriving now and Robbins knew that this could go on well into the early hours of the morning. Statements would need to be taken, the body disentangled and taken away.

Beth joined him again. "What about Matthew? What about who, *what* he is?"

"Tomorrow," the DCI said softly, chewing on an antacid tablet. "We'll talk about all that tomorrow."

Fifteen

He'd sat with Irene Daley that night until she'd finally dropped to sleep.

They'd prayed and read from the Bible together, but Father Lilley was extremely concerned about her. It wasn't so much the stress of the last few days, although it was clear that had taken its toll. She was a shadow of herself, having barely eaten in all that time. But no, it was more the way her mind was working now. She was having dangerous thoughts about the person who had shown up at her doorstep and couldn't possibly be Matthew.

"But father, what if—"

"Irene, he is not your son. He *can't* be. You said yourself."

"And the grave?"

He shook his head. "I don't know, I can't explain it. But I do know that Matthew is with Our Savior right now, not walking this earth."

He firmly believed it. That *thing* might look and sound like Matthew, but it certainly wasn't the boy he confirmed, the man he'd listened to as he confessed. The man he'd put in the ground while his family stood around the graveside: a grave now thoughtlessly desecrated because of the *creature* pretending to be him. The more Lilley himself pondered on it, the more convinced he became that this person—if indeed he was a person at all—was here for the most wicked of purposes.

Already it was infecting Irene Daley's mind, and was in the

process of convincing others that it *was* Matthew. He looked to the good book—as always—for help and guidance, references to the Devil, how he might send his minions back to wreak havoc.

'And as ye have heard that the antichrist shall come, even now are there many antichrists' John 2:18.

Had Matthew's body been invaded by a demon or ungodly spirit? Lilley hadn't ever performed an exorcism and wasn't about to start now.

As he sat downstairs in Irene's house, the dawn about to break on this another day, he looked at the photograph of mother and son together. Lilley wondered how his own father, the staunch Catholic who had instilled in him all that was right and good, might have dealt with such a challenge of faith. He thought he could almost hear the man's voice telling him what to do then. Lilley nodded. It was time for him to become a soldier of God himself, to become the Lord's right hand.

He *had* to stop this evil from spreading. And there was only one way he could think of to do it.

* * *

The phone in Robbins' office hadn't stopped ringing all morning, and by midday he had his orders. The case was being taken out of his hands and the man they were holding with relation to the death of one Douglas Knowles was to be transferred to a secure facility for questioning. The further tests Beth had wanted to perform would also be handled by 'more experienced' government doctors, Robbins was told. Arrangements would also be made at some point to move Knowles' body from the local hospital.

"See," he told her when he finally emerged. "Just as I thought."

"They can't do that. What's going to happen to him?"

He looked her in the eye and said seriously, "I don't know, but you can't charge a dead man with murder, Beth."

Wilson, now back at work but refusing to go anywhere near the cells, drew their attention to the television in the corner. Several officers were gathered around it, listening to the report. Becky recognized a pixilated picture of Matthew from the hospital, the newscaster telling the world about the miracle recovery of motorcyclist Phil Barnes. There was also some confusion as to who exactly the man in the photo was, although the likeness to a 'hit and run' accident victim from seven years ago was definitely uncanny.

"It'll only be a matter of time before they link it with the exhumation and what happened last night," Robbins said.

By two o'clock that afternoon the police station was besieged with reporters and TV crews, and the internet was awash with rumors about Matthew.

Becky observed the crowds gathering outside. "It's going to be hard for anyone to keep all this quiet now."

An unmarked van arrived for their guest at four. Robbins was to give it an escort of squad cars until it reached the motorway, then the whole thing would be out of their hands. When Robbins and Beth went down to the cells, where he was under constant surveillance by three police officers, the man was still not speaking. He hadn't said a thing since the balcony.

"Time to go," Robbins told him.

As Valentine and WPC Adams led the man out of the cell, he paused when he caught Beth's eye. "Don't worry, you'll see her again," he told her.

Robbins watched him go. "What did he say? See who?"

Beth fought back a tear. "Doesn't matter."

They walked with him to the back door of the station, opening it up to see the van there in the car park, waiting. But even before they'd reached the second step at the entranceway a deluge of people started piling in behind the van. Someone had tipped them off and the news people weren't about to miss the biggest scoop of the year, if not the decade.

They all took notice of him now: the dead man. The people

there saw him walking. Soon the whole world would see it too.

Robbins barked at the uniforms on either side of him, telling them to get more men out for crowd control. The plainclothes officers driving the van backed up when they saw what was rapidly turning into a mob. There was total and utter confusion. Cameras flashed, Dictaphones were pushed through.

And there, at the back, Robbins saw her—short dark hair, craning her neck along with the other people to see who had gathered here today: Caroline Hills. He turned to see that the man they had in cuffs had noticed her, too. A look passed between Caroline and the person who so resembled the husband she had lost, and Robbins almost felt sorry for him. But then the DCI was being jostled to one side and more policemen were emerging from the station to deal with the numbers.

"Can we just ask—"

"Where are you taking—"

"What connection he has to—"

"What you found at Westmoor Cemetery—"

The gaggle of voices was terrific, so much so that they wove themselves into one loud hum.

Then it happened.

Beth spotted it first and grabbed Robbins' shoulder. There, in the crowd, was a hand clutching a gun. It was an old-fashioned type of pistol, nothing that might be used on the streets today—more like a relic from a museum. Robbins doubted whether it would even fire.

But it did. Three loud bangs.

He saw the man in cuffs go down, two bullets hitting him hard. Then Robbins felt a pain in his own arm, as he dove across to try and shield Beth. If there was confusion before, then there was mass panic now that the shots had rung out. Robbins tried to shout out to his men: apprehend the shooter; secure the area. But the plainclothes officers from the van had already pulled their own guns, which caused even more hysteria.

Robbins clutched at his arm and his hand came away red.

Then Beth was there, examining the wound.

She told him to keep the hand on it and apply pressure. "You silly sod," Beth whispered, and kissed his forehead, before checking on the other injured party. She scrambled along the floor to where he'd fell.

But when she got there she found nothing. No body, no Matthew.

Nothing except a patch of blood where he'd lay, spreading out like wings on the concrete floor.

Sixteen

The next few days were just as confused as that afternoon.

For a while the news had concentrated fully on what had happened: about Matthew, about who he might be, about where he might have gone after the assassination attempt, about his revenge on the man who had 'killed' him. It was discussed on every message board and talk show, theologians offered their opinions and scientists expounded on what Beth had already suggested. But there was no proof, no concrete evidence of anything. So rationality soon began to reign. If nothing else it was a diversion, a curiosity along the lines of raining fish and the Yeti. Certainly nowhere near as exciting as reading about which politician was having an affair or which celebrity had suddenly been diagnosed with bulimia.

Then, just as Croft had predicted, the world began to change.

The first thing that happened was that Phil Barnes, the motorcyclist Matthew had apparently brought back from the brink of death, got up from his hospital bed and went for a walk himself. The nurses thought he was going to the toilet, a good sign that he was recovering even more. But he wasn't. Phil was going down into the morgue.

He walked past the attendant in charge, who was listening to *Nessun Dorma* on his ipod at the time, as if he hadn't even seen him. The man asked him exactly what he thought he was doing and Phil simply replied:

"They're asleep, that's all. Just asleep."

Then he pulled open the freezer drawers and woke them up, one by one: men, women and children. In no time at all, the morgue was filled with reanimated corpses and the attendant had collapsed on the floor in a dead faint. He was used to cadavers making noises—groaning and farting as he moved them—but not used to them climbing out of their drawers. The last person to be woken was in quite a bad condition. His limbs were broken and he was still scarred, bruised and cut from the fall.

However, when he looked down on himself, Douglas Knowles found that he was entirely healed, that his body was as good as... no, *better* than new. Life surged through him, the blood pumping in his veins full of vitality. The last thing he could remember was being on that balcony. When the man he'd killed refused to put him out of his own misery, he'd suddenly been overcome with a sense that there was no point in going on. And he owed the person standing there some kind of justice. That was when he decided to throw himself off.

He smiled. It was a miracle.

"Come on," said Phil, showing the others a way out of their resting place, up into the light.

In his hospital bed, recovering from being shot and being treated for the 'full house' of ulcers they'd now found in his gut, DCI Robbins saw the strange procession go past. And saw Knowles tagging on at the end. But he put it down the strong medication he was on, just as he had the return visit from Croft.

"I can't stand these places," he'd told him, eating Robbins' grapes, "they remind me of the time I had my heart attack."

He'd mention it to Beth the next time he saw her.

But Beth would have other things on her mind entirely by then.

* * *

That night, Dr. Beth Preston was down in the lab—going through blood samples she'd squirreled away while she was still able to—when she was interrupted in her work by a child calling out her name.

She rose from the microscope slowly, then nearly lost her balance, clutching onto the desk for support and knocking over the vials.

"Hiya Bethany," said the little girl in front of her. She was the only one who'd ever called her by her full name.

"S-Sarah?" She shook her head, not trusting the evidence of her own eyes. "Sarah, is it really you?"

The girl with long golden locks ran over and hugged her. "Course it is, silly. Who else?"

Beth's hand wavered, then it found the child's back and she hugged her tight. The girl felt as real as anyone she'd ever met, as solid as... well, as solid as Matthew had been. Tears were tracking down the doctor's cheeks, and she could taste saltwater on her lips.

"It's... it's so good to see you," Beth told her.

"It's good to see you, too. I was getting bored of waiting."

In spite of herself, Beth laughed. She held Sarah by the shoulders and bent down. "I don't understand any of this."

"You're not meant to," Sarah said. "Not yet. But you will." She took Beth's hand and began to tug it.

"Where are we going?"

"You'll see."

Beth hung back. "Hold on, Sarah. I have to say something."

Sarah looked puzzled. "Can't it wait?"

"No," said Beth, shaking her head. "Not really."

Sarah looked up and nodded.

"I'm sorry," said the doctor.

"What for?"

"You know, for what happened."

The penny dropped and Sarah suddenly grinned. "Oh *that.*

It's okay, it wasn't your fault."

"But if I'd picked it up earlier then maybe—"

"It was *meant* to happen, Bethany," Sarah told her. "There was no way you could have known about the clot." She tittered. "Sounds like cream, doesn't it?" When Becky didn't join in, Sarah said, "Could've happened anytime."

"But I'm a doctor, I should've seen the signs—"

Sarah put a finger to her lips. "It made you a better one. Think about all the good you've done. Now," she said seriously, "we've really got to go, there are things to do."

It was Beth's turn to be puzzled. "What things?"

"You'll see."

"Wait." Beth pulled her back again. "I need to tell you one last thing."

Sarah sighed. "Kay."

"I love you."

Sarah beamed. "I love you too, sis. Now let's go." She pulled on Beth's hand and led her out of the lab.

* * *

These weren't the only occurrences.

All around the country, all over the globe, people were seeing the dead. Not ghosts, but living, breathing human beings—of a kind. Mrs. Shaw, the school helper, woke up from yet another troubled sleep only to see the figure of young Oliver at the foot of her bed, burn marks from the rope still around his neck. Terrified, and thinking she'd brought the images from her nightmare into the real world, she tried to wake her husband. But he just kept on snoring beside her.

Oliver held out his hand for her to take it, and she felt compelled to do so...

Across town Thomas Valentine was shocked to see that his best friend from college, Martin Raines, who had drowned during the Tsunami disaster in Sri Lanka, was playing computer games on the X-Box in his living room. Meanwhile WPC Trisha Adams' discovered that her Granddad, who'd passed away from a stroke when she was only a little girl, had come to visit offering her a bag of those sticky toffees he always used to bring.

And as PC Frank Wilson was sitting down to eat breakfast, he found that his Uncle Ted and Auntie Rita, the couple who had taken him in as a child and brought him up as their own, were suddenly in the room with him. Ted was making himself a cup of coffee and Auntie Rita was asking him if there was any toast left. He was scared and happy at the same time, but he wasn't really surprised. After all, the dead man in the cell had told him he would see them again soon.

* * *

In the cold, damp cellar he waited.

It wasn't comfortable: he was hungry and he couldn't feel his hands now, but he had to wait it out. What he'd done had been right, of that he had no doubt. But the authorities wouldn't see it that way. They'd probably been to search for him already, though he doubted whether they'd find this hiding place—used to protect the faithful during the blitz when the bombing had been fierce. Why, they'd even held services down here.

Smiling, he patted the instrument he'd used to rid the earth of that monstrous creation. His father's trusty old service revolver, given to his mother after the great man's death. It had been used back then in the name of good, fighting the forces of evil, and he'd put it to use in much the same way.

Father Lilley struck a match and lit the altar candle he'd brought down with him. He wished to consult the good book once again. But in the half-light he saw something stirring there. A shadow at the back of the cellar.

"Who's there?" he asked, snatching up the revolver.

The shadow drifted closer and, in spite of himself, Lilley let off another bullet.

"Put that thing down, right now," said the voice, stern but with genuine feeling. "Put it down before you hurt anyone else."

Lilley recognized the voice, but it couldn't be who he thought it was. "Father?"

The Captain, still in uniform, walked over towards him shaking his head. "Gerald, what did you think you were doing?"

"This isn't real," gibbered Lilley. "It's a trick, the Devil's work."

"He has been at work, yes, but not here. Not today. It was not me who told you to shoot that man." His father, the moustache he sported twitching, reached forward and took the gun from him.

"Our father who art in Heaven—" began Lilley.

"Not anymore," said his own father, seriously.

"Begone demon. I smite thee from the Earth!"

The army man picked up the bible and leafed through it. "You're so fond of quoting these passages, Gerald. Here's one for you: 'And I saw the dead, small and great, stand before God; and the books were opened: and another book was opened, which is the book of life, and the dead were judged out of those things which were written in the books, according to their works. And the sea gave up the dead which were in it, and death and hell delivered up the dead which were in them: and they were judged, every man according to his works.'"

Lilley's face froze. "The Book of Revelation."

His father nodded. "The immortal body is real, Gerald. And yet that same body can pass through an object, or pick up the object." He looked down at his old gun. "They also have none of the defects they had in life."

Lilley was shaking. His father grabbed him by the hand and started to drag him up the stairs to the hidden door beneath the altar itself. "No!" screamed Lilley. "It can't be."

The soldier dragged Lilley out into the church and forced him to look through the window. There, in the graveyard, were the dead. Each one standing next to the grave they had risen from, the soil on top untouched (in fact the only hole there was at Matthew Daley's plot). Their clothes ranged from the quite recent, to centuries old. All were looking at him, all were pointing.

"Now do you understand, Gerald? Around the world, those who have died in conflicts like mine—those who are *still* dying—they are coming back, too."

Lilley grabbed the gun off his father and placed it against his head. Before the Captain could do anything, the trigger had been pulled and the last bullet punched a hole in Lilley's skull. To the priest's own amazement, though, he didn't fall down. He dropped the weapon and touched the wound in the side of his head, looking at the disgusting mess on his fingers.

His father went to the font and dipped a cup into the water, bowing his head at the stained glass image of Christ above him. The he returned to his son and washed away the blood on his scalp. The hole was gone.

"'And immediately there fell from his eyes as it had been scales: and he received sight forthwith, and arose, and was baptized.' That's Acts Nine, Eighteen, Gerald," said the man.

Lilley started to cry. "I'm so sorry. I didn't know."

The Captain held him for a moment, then pulled away. "It's time to go, boy."

He placed a hand on his son's back and led him out of the church. Lilley turned and looked up at his much younger father. "Will I be spared for my foolish actions?" he asked.

The Captain didn't reply. He just carried on walking, the dead from the graveyard following them both on their way up the road.

Epilogue

Irene Daley woke from the deepest sleep she'd had in years. She could remember the priest being here, them praying and discussing Matthew. And then she must have fallen asleep, except she had the vaguest recollection of trying to wake up and not being able to. She looked at the clock by the side of her; it was just gone nine. But the date must have been wrong on it, because according to that she'd been in bed the past few days.

There was a knocking at the door downstairs. It was probably Father Lilley back again to tell her what was happening. She got up, feeling none of the usual aches and pains that came with age. No cracks of the knees, no arthritis, which was always wicked first thing in the morning. In fact she felt better than she ever had in her life.

Pulling on her dressing gown she went downstairs. There was a shadow waiting there and she hesitated, flashing back to that morning almost a week ago. But something told her not to be afraid this time, something told her to open the door.

So she did.

And it was like a replay of before: There was the man who'd looked so much like Matthew, who she now knew *was* Matthew, only he'd been changed, just like she herself had been changed. And it was time to go somewhere, she knew that as well, although she had no idea how.

"Hello Mum," said Matthew.

Instead of passing out this time, instead of being afraid, lashing out, she put her arms around him and kissed him on the cheek. "Welcome home, son," she whispered, her eyes watering. "I'm sorry. I'm really sorry."

"It's okay," he assured her. "None of that matters now anyway."

"We have to go, don't we?"

He nodded. "I was allowed to come and get you. But yes, they're waiting."

"Right," she said. Irene shut the door behind them and was about to lock up when she realized how daft that would be. She took her son's arm and he walked her down the path. Birds were flying overhead—huge birds, almost humanlike—and it was a beautiful day. The flowers were blooming on her front lawn. He opened the freshly painted gate and the new hinges didn't make a sound.

The streets beyond were full of people. Some she recognized from round and about, like the pot-bellied man from across the road, others she'd never seen before. Relatives: long lost sons, daughters, mothers, fathers, grandfathers, grandmothers, and back further still. It would be the same the world over; she knew that as well.

"Will he be there, too? Arnold?" she asked Matthew as they went through the gate.

"Dad?" he said. "Of course. He's waiting for us."

Irene smiled at that and patted her son's hand. "You're a good boy."

They joined the throng, fitting into place alongside them. The living, the dead—all were here. All were heading off over the horizon. As finally, it had come: a time to be judged rather than to judge.

The day that lasted a thousand years had finally begun.

'Marvel not at this: for the hour is coming, in the which all that are in the graves shall hear his voice, and shall come forth; they that have done good, unto the resurrection of life; and they that have done evil, unto the resurrection of damnation.'

John 5:28-29

PAIN CAGES

ABOUT THE AUTHOR

Paul Kane began his professional writing career in 1996, providing articles and reviews for news-stand publications (most recently he has worked for *The Dark Side*, *DeathRay*, *Fangoria*, *SFX*, *Dreamwatch* and *Rue Morgue*), and started producing dark fantasy and science fiction stories in 1998. His work has been widely published in many magazines and anthologies on both sides of the Atlantic, in all kinds of formats. He has written the collections *Alone (In the Dark)* (the fastest-selling BJM title of that time), *Touching the Flame* (which has been translated into German), *FunnyBones* (which went into a second printing), *Peripheral Visions*, *Shadow Writer* and *The Adventures of Dalton Quayle*, as well as the novellas *Signs of Life* (this reached the short list for the British Fantasy Awards 2006), *Dalton Quayle Rides Out* (introduced by Tom Holt) and *RED* (featuring art from Dave McKean – **MirrorMask**, *Sandman*, **The Graveyard Book**). He has appeared in the documentary **Assembly of Rogues** talking about his work, and his stories have been read on BBC Radio 2, recommended and nominated for other British Fantasy Awards, in addition to receiving honourable mentions in *The Year's Best Fantasy and Horror* and *The Best Horror of the Year* edited by Ellen Datlow. He was also the recipient of *Estronomicon* magazine's 2008 Dead of Night Award (Editor's Choice) for his short story 'A Chaos Demon Is For Life'.

He has a B.A. and M.A. from Sheffield Hallam University and in the past has worked as a photographer, an artist, an illustrator/cartoonist and a professional proofreader; he is currently working part-time as a Creative Writing tutor in the UK. Paul served as Special Publications Editor for the British Fantasy Society for five years, where he worked on projects with Clive Barker, Neil Gaiman, Brian Aldiss, Robert Silverberg, China Miéville, Muriel Gray, Graham Masterton and many others. He was on the organising committee of FantasyCon for two years (as Co-Chair in 2008) and is co-chairing 2011's event again with Guests of Honour including World Fantasy Award-winner Gwyneth Jones and John Ajvide Lindqvist, bestselling author of *Let the Right One In* (filmed as **Let Me In** for the US). Paul was also on the organising committee of the 20th World Horror Convention in Brighton, which headlined guests such as James Herbert, Tanith Lee, Les Edwards and Ingrid Pitt. He has himself been a Guest four times at Derby's Alt.Fiction Festival and was one of the Guests at the inaugural 'SFX Weekender' in February 2010. He is co-editor of the *Terror Tales* series of anthology books and editor of the *Shadow Writers* line. His story 'Dead Time' was developed by Lionsgate/NBC for the US network show **Fear Itself**, adapted by Steve Niles – creator of *30 Days of Night* – under the title **New Year's Day**, directed by Darren Lynn Bousman (**SAW II-IV**), with effects from Oscar-winners KNB (**Chronicles of Narnia**). Paul himself scripted **The Opportunity** based on his own short story – which features the vocal talents of Stephen Coates from the band The Real Tuesday Weld, and premiered at the Cannes film festival 2009 – plus **The Weeping Woman** filmed by award-winning director Mark Steensland, starring Tony award-nominee Stephen Geoffreys (**Fright Night**), with music from legendary Lucio Fulci collaborator Fabio Frizzi (**The Beyond, House by the Cemetery**).

His non-fiction books are *The Hellraiser Films and Their Legacy*, introduced by Doug 'Pinhead' Bradley (which reached the nominations stage of the BFS Awards 2007) and a book of interviews with horror writers, directors and actors called *Voices in the Dark* (featuring the likes of James Herbert, Graham Masterton, Mike Carey, John Carpenter, Stuart Gordon, Rob Zombie, Ron Perlman, Betsy Campbell and Zach Galligan). He is co-editor of the mass market anthology *Hellbound Hearts* (published by Pocket Books/Simon and Schuster), which gathers together stories inspired by Clive Barker's mythology from the likes of Christopher Golden and Mike Mignola (*Baltimore* and *Hellboy*), Kelley Armstrong (*Personal Demon*), Yvonne Navarro (*Species* & *Ultraviolet*),

292

Nicholas Vince (Chatterer Cenobite), Barbie Wilde (Female Cenobite from **Hellbound: Hellraiser II**) and Richard Christian Matheson (*Dystopia* & **Stephen King's Nightmares and Dreamscapes**), with a brand new cover Cenobite and introduction from Clive Barker.

His mass market novel *Arrowhead* for Abaddon/Rebellion, publishers of *2000 AD* (a post-apocalyptic reworking of the Robin Hood legend), came out in 2008 in the UK & US, its sequel *Broken Arrow* was released a year later, and the third instalment of this bestselling trilogy, *Arrowland*, is the latest to be released (see www.arrowheadtrilogy.com for more details). In addition he has two more unrelated novels out at the moment, *Of Darkness and Light* in hardback and paperback from Thunderstorm (with cover art from the award-winning Vincent Chong) and horror/crime thriller *The Gemini Factor* in trade paperback from Screaming Dreams (with an introduction from Peter Atkins, screenwriter of **Hellraisers II-IV** and **Wishmaster**). Forthcoming from him are a Sherlock Holmes story called 'The Greatest Mystery' in *Gaslight Arcanum* from Edge Publishing, and a hardback collection by the multi-award-winning PS Publishing. Paul's *Shadow Writer* site, launched on Hallowe'en 2001, which receives thousands of visitors each month and has featured Stephen King, James Herbert, Guillermo del Toro & Chuck Hogan, Douglas Preston, Joe Hill, Neil Gaiman, David Morrell, Brian Lumley, Kevin J. Anderson, Charles de Lint, Joe R. Lansdale and Thomas Harris as Guest Writers, can be found at www.shadow-writer.co.uk

Great titles from
BOOKS OF THE DEAD

BEST NEW VAMPIRE TALES (Vol. 1)
BEST NEW ZOMBIE TALES (Vol. 1)
BEST NEW ZOMBIE TALES (Vol. 2)
BEST NEW ZOMBIE TALES (Vol. 3)
CLASSIC VAMPIRE TALES
GARY BRANDNER - THE HOWLING
GARY BRANDNER - THE HOWLING II
GARY BRANDNER - THE HOWLING III
JAMES ROY DALEY'S - INTO HELL
JAMES ROY DALEY'S - TERROR TOWN
JAMES ROY DALEY - 13 DROPS OF BLOOD
JAMES ROY DALEY - THE DEAD PARADE
MATT HULTS - ANYTHING CAN BE DANGEROUS
MATT HULTS - HUSK
PAUL KANE - PAIN CAGES

CPSIA information can be obtained at www.ICGtesting.com
Printed in the USA
LVOW090827251111

256305LV00017B/1/P